BEWARE OF JOHNNY WASHINGTON

'THE DETECTIVE STORY CLUB is a clearing house for the best detective and mystery stories chosen for you by a select committee of experts. Only the most ingenious crime stories will be published under the THE DETECTIVE STORY CLUB imprint. A special distinguishing stamp appears on the wrapper and title page of every THE DETECTIVE STORY CLUB book—the Man with the Gun. Always look for the Man with the Gun when buying a Crime book.'

Wm. Collins Sons & Co. Ltd., 1929

Now the Man with the Gun is back in this series of COLLINS CRIME CLUB reprints, and with him the chance to experience the classic books that influenced the Golden Age of crime fiction.

THE DETECTIVE STORY CLUB

FURTHER TITLES IN PREPARATION

BEWARE OF JOHNNY WASHINGTON

A STORY OF CRIME

BY

FRANCIS DURBRIDGE

WITH AN INTRODUCTION BY
MELVYN BARNES

COLLINS
CRIME
CLUB

COLLINS CRIME CLUB
An imprint of HarperCollins*Publishers*
1 London Bridge Street
London SE1 9GF
www.harpercollins.co.uk

This Detective Story Club edition 2017

First published in Great Britain by John Long Ltd 1951
'A Present for Paul' first published by the *Yorkshire Evening Post* 1946

Copyright © Estate of Francis Durbridge 1946, 1951
Introduction © Melvyn Barnes 2017

A catalogue record for this book is available from the British Library

ISBN 978-0-00-824205-3

Typeset in Bulmer MT Std by
Palimpsest Book Production Ltd, Falkirk, Stirlingshire
Printed and bound in Great Britain by CPI Group (UK) Ltd,
Croydon CR0 4YY

MIX
Paper from
responsible sources
FSC™ C007454

INTRODUCTION

FRANCIS Henry Durbridge (1912–1998) was arguably the most popular writer of mystery thrillers for BBC radio and television from the 1930s to the 1970s, after which he enjoyed a successful career as a stage dramatist. His radio serials are regularly repeated today, while his stage plays remain among the staple fare of amateur and professional theatre companies.

He was born in Kingston upon Hull and educated at Bradford Grammar School, Wylde Green College and Birmingham University, and as an undergraduate he began to pursue his schoolboy ambition to become a writer. Although he later worked briefly in a stockbroker's office, his career as a full-time writer was assured by the BBC in the early 1930s when he responded to the broadcaster's voracious appetite by providing comedy plays, children's stories, musical libretti and numerous short sketches.

It was nevertheless his first two serious radio dramas, *Promotion* and *Murder in the Midlands*, that showed the sort of scriptwriting he particularly favoured. In 1938, at the age of twenty-five, he established himself in the crime fiction field when the BBC broadcast his serial *Send for Paul Temple*. Listeners ecstatically submitted over 7,000 requests for more, no doubt finding his light touch and characteristic 'cliff-hangers' a welcome distraction from worries about the gathering storm in Europe. Almost immediately Durbridge became one of the foremost writers of radio thrillers, with a prolific output that he further expanded by sometimes using the pseudonyms Frank Cromwell, Nicholas Vane and Lewis Middleton Harvey. To place him in context, in the mid-twentieth century his closest comparators were Edward J. Mason and Lester Powell (both coincidentally born the same year as Durbridge), together with Ernest Dudley, Alan Stranks and Philip Levene.

Send for Paul Temple was broadcast in eight episodes from 8 April to 27 May 1938. In this first case for the novelist-detective he meets newspaper reporter Steve Trent, who tells him that she has changed her name from Louise Harvey in order to pursue a gang of jewel thieves. The murder of her brother, a Scotland Yard man, unites Temple and Steve in their determination to unmask the Knave of Diamonds. That achieved, they create crime fiction history by deciding to marry—thus securing a quick return to the airwaves in *Paul Temple and the Front Page Men* in the autumn of 1938 and thereafter cementing their position as a mainstay of the BBC.

The early Paul Temple radio serials were adapted as books from the outset, but Durbridge's first five novelisations were collaborations with another author because at that time he regarded himself as essentially a writer of dialogue, a scriptwriter rather than a novelist. *Send for Paul Temple* was published by John Long in June 1938, so it was presumably written while the radio serial was being broadcast and was intended to capitalise on the serial's success. It was described in newspaper advertisements at the time as 'the novel of the thriller that created a BBC fan-mail record', and it was made Book of the Month by the Crime Book Society. The co-author was identified as John Thewes, although today it is widely believed that this was a pseudonym of Charles Hatton (who used his own name when collaborating on the next four Paul Temple novels). There is further evidence that Durbridge saw the wider potential of *Send for Paul Temple*, because he adapted it as a stage play produced in Birmingham in 1943 and also co-wrote the screenplay of the 1946 film version.

The Paul Temple serials proved to be Durbridge's most enduring work for the radio, and they continued until 1968. One could easily assume that in the twenty-first century they might be regarded as *passé*, but today the Temples have been re-introduced to radio listeners through repeats of the surviving original recordings and new productions of the 'lost' serials, and there is a continuing market in printed books, e-books, CDs, DVDs and downloads. A new generation, together with those feeling nostalgic, can follow the exploits of the urbane detective who is constantly faced with bombs concealed in packages or booby-trapped 'radiograms', who deplores violence except in self-defence, and who never uses bad language but regularly utters the oath 'By Timothy!' The appeal seems undiminished, irrespective of the fact that the Durbridge *milieu* of Thames houseboats, expensive apartments, luxury sports cars and sophisticated cocktails must surely be alien to the lives of many among his present day audience.

The Temples were by no means the only protagonists created for radio audiences by Francis Durbridge. Among others was Johnny Washington, who appeared in eight episodes from 12 August to 30 September 1949 entitled *Johnny Washington Esquire*. This was not a serial, but a run of complete thirty-minute plays described as 'the adventures of a gentleman of leisure', with a young American scoring barely legal coups in Robin Hood style at the expense of London underworld characters. Of particular interest was the fact that Johnny was played by the Canadian actor Bernard Braden, who before his move to the UK had played the title role in the Canadian radio version of *Send for Paul Temple* in 1940.

Given Durbridge's astuteness in maximising the commercial opportunities provided by his plot ideas, he would have wanted to get *Johnny Washington Esquire* into book form while its success on the radio was still fresh. His problem was that the radio series would be unsuitable as a novel, as it consisted of eight separate stories. The popular central character could nevertheless still be used in a full-length book, which resulted in John Long publishing *Beware of Johnny Washington* in April 1951.

Rather than produce a new and original novel, Durbridge

took his 1938 book *Send for Paul Temple* and re-wrote it, with every character name changed and Johnny Washington instead of Paul Temple joining reporter Verity Glyn instead of Steve Trent in the hunt for her brother's killer. In the 'new' book, Johnny is framed by a gang of criminals who leave visiting cards bearing his name on their crime scenes. Although usually an object of police suspicion, Johnny has to side reluctantly with the law in order to clear his name, protect the threatened Verity and identify the ruthless gang leader who calls himself Grey Moose.

So why did Durbridge re-cycle his earlier book in this way? It is unlikely that he was so dissatisfied with *Send for Paul Temple* that he made a purposeful attempt to improve upon it, because it had already achieved a classic status and had been reprinted several times (and indeed is still in print today). The obvious answer must surely be that Durbridge needed to use the Johnny Washington character before the name was forgotten, given the fact that he was to write no more Washington plays for the radio, and it was therefore necessary to act with the minimum of delay. It is also likely that he was trying to widen his appeal to the reading public, and was keen to secure recognition for more than his creation of the Temples. There could even have been a degree of insurance against the slim possibility that after five Paul Temple novels some readers might have begun to tire of them, which was one of the factors that from 1952 onwards encouraged Durbridge to create a brand of record-breaking television serials that deliberately excluded the Temples.

In the case of his novels, he was nevertheless careful to keep all his options open. Paul Temple books continued to appear from 1957 to 1988 (three were original and five were based on his radio serials); sixteen of his television serials were novelised between 1958 and 1982; and he wrote two stand-alone novels (*Back Room Girl* in 1950 and *The Pig-Tail Murder* in 1969) plus several novellas as newspaper serials. In addition it must be said that *Beware of Johnny Washington* was not the only example of re-cycling, as his novels *Design for Murder* (1951), *Another Woman's Shoes* (1965) and *Dead to the World* (1967) were all originally Paul Temple radio serials that became non-Temple books with recycled plots—although only one of these, *Beware of Johnny Washington*, had also appeared as a separate Temple book.

In spite of its history, or perhaps because of it, *Beware of Johnny Washington* remains of considerable interest to Durbridge enthusiasts. It is a good solid thriller with many of the author's typical elements and trademark twists and turns, written in a smooth and readable style that improves upon the slightly stilted early Temple novelisations. While it follows the storyline of *Send for Paul Temple*, it is more than just a straight transcription with new character names. Sub-plots are changed and developed, while Washington himself is given a personality and lifestyle that clearly distinguishes him from Temple.

Above all, unlike most of Durbridge's other novels, *Beware of Johnny Washington* has not been available since its first publication over sixty-five years ago. For the host of Durbridge fans, that is a big attraction.

MELVYN BARNES
February 2017

CONTENTS

CHAPTER I

AN OBVIOUS CLUE

'ANOTHER gelignite job,' said Chief Inspector Kennard, folding his arms and gazing moodily through the tall window of the deputy commissioner's office.

'Eight thousand pounds' worth of diamonds,' added Superintendent Locksley in a worried tone. 'Gloucester this time—we never know where they'll turn up next.'

The Deputy Commissioner, Sir Robert Hargreaves, pulled a stack of variously coloured folders towards him and selected a grey one. For a minute or two he thumbed over the papers without speaking. His subordinates eyed each other a trifle uncomfortably and waited for him to speak.

They watched him turn over one report after another, scanning them briefly and stopping twice to make a pencilled note on the pad at his elbow. Meanwhile, the cigarette he had been smoking slowly burnt on the ash-tray beside him.

A man in his late fifties, Sir Robert had attained his present position by a reputation for his capacity to digest facts rapidly and methodically and, having done so, to arrive at a rapid decision which usually proved to be the right one.

The smoke from the chief's cigarette tickled Locksley's nose and he felt a sudden craving to light one himself, but would not dare to do so without Sir Robert's invitation. There was an air of discipline about this plainly furnished office which one did not associate with tea-drinking and cigarettes. When you went to see Sir Robert you gave him your information, received his instructions, and left to put them into operation.

However, the gelignite robberies were in a class of their own and on a scale that had not been encountered at the Yard for some years. A lorry load of gelignite which had been dispatched to the scene of some mining operations in Cornwall had never arrived at its destination, though the driver was discovered lying senseless at the side of the road in the early hours of the morning. All he remembered was climbing into his cab after calling at an all-night pull-up near Taunton, and receiving a blow on the head which resulted in slight concussion. He had not even caught a glimpse of his assailant.

A week later, the safe at a large super cinema at Norwich was blown open with gelignite, and the week's takings, amounting to about one thousand five hundred pounds, were stolen. This was presumably in the nature of a try-out, for the gelignite gang almost immediately went after bigger game. They began with a jeweller's safe in Birmingham, which yielded over five thousand pounds' worth of diamonds, pearls and platinum settings. After Birmingham came Leicester, Sheffield, Oldham and Shrewsbury. The aggregate value of the stolen goods was now in the region of five figures.

The deputy commissioner looked up from the report of the raid on the Gloucester jewellers, which he had been scanning carefully.

'What about this night watchman?' he inquired.

'I'm afraid he's dead, sir,' replied Locksley. 'He was pretty heavily chloroformed and according to the doctor his heart was in a bad state to stand up to any sudden shock.'

Sir Robert frowned.

'This is getting extremely serious,' he murmured. 'We shall have the papers playing it up worse than ever; then some damn fool will be asking a question in the House. Was this night watchman above board?'

Locksley shook his head.

'I'm afraid not, sir. He'd only been with the firm about a month. He joined them under the name of Brookfield, but we soon found he had a long record as Wilfred Hiller, alias Burns. Everything from petty thefts to smash and grab.'

'Humph! He might have been part of the set-up,' grunted Sir Robert. 'Pity they gave him an overdose . . .'

'It was one way to make sure he didn't talk—and to avoid paying him his cut,' Kennard pointed out quietly.

Sir Robert nodded. 'Who was in charge down there?' he asked.

'Inspector Dovey had already arrived when we got there—you remember we recalled him from the Special Branch to work on the gelignite jobs,' replied Locksley. 'He was questioning the constable who had discovered the robbery, a young man named Roscoe. Roscoe's only been in the force two years, but he's quite a good record. He was apparently passing the jewellers on his beat and noticed that the side door was open a couple of inches, so he went in to investigate.'

'What about fingerprints?'

'Nothing we can trace, except Hiller, the night watchman's, and they were nowhere near the safe,' replied Locksley. 'It was the same on all the other jobs. There's somebody running the outfit who knows his way around.'

Sir Robert shrugged and went on reading the report, a tiny furrow deepening between his eyebrows, and his lips tightening into a thin line.

'What did Dovey have to say?' he inquired at length.

Kennard smiled. 'He didn't seem to know whether he was coming or going. Talked about a large criminal organization—I think he's been meeting too many international spies.' A note of contempt in his voice prompted Hargreaves to ask:

'Then you don't think it is a criminal organization?'

Kennard shook his head most decisively, a flicker of a grin around his thin mouth.

'We're always reading about these big criminal set-ups,' he said sarcastically, 'but I've been with the police here and abroad for over fifteen years without coming across a sign of any really elaborate organization. Crooks don't work that way; it's every man for himself and to hell with the one who's caught. Of course, we had the racecourse gangs a few years back, but that was different—not what you'd call scientifically planned crime. If you ask me, these jobs have been pulled by a little bunch of old lags.'

Sir Robert swung round in his chair and stubbed out his cigarette.

'What do you think, Locksley?' he demanded. The superintendent glanced across at his colleague and shifted somewhat uncomfortably in his chair.

'I'm afraid I don't agree with Kennard, Sir Robert,' he admitted at last. The inspector looked startled for a moment and appeared to be about to make some comment, but he changed his mind, and Locksley went on: 'I thought the same as Kennard for some time, but I've come to the conclusion this last week or so that these jobs are being planned to the last detail by some mentality far and away above that of the average crook.'

Hargreaves gave no sign as to whether he was impressed by this argument, other than by making a brief note on his pad.

'Did you see the night watchman before he died?' he asked. Locksley nodded.

'Yes, sir. He was in pretty bad shape, of course, and I thought he wouldn't be able to say anything. But the doctor gave him an injection, and he seemed to recover consciousness.'

'Well, what did he say?' urged Hargreaves with a note of impatience in his tone.

The superintendent rubbed his hands rather nervously.

'I couldn't be quite sure, sir,' he replied dubiously, 'but it sounded to me rather like "Grey Moose".'

There was a sound of suppressed chuckle from Kennard, but the deputy commissioner was quickly turning through his file.

'Here we are,' he said suddenly. 'A report on the Oldham case—you remember Smokey Pearce died rather mysteriously soon after. He was run over by a lorry—found by a constable on the Preston road—there was an empty jewel case on him from the Oldham shop.'

'That's right, sir,' said Kennard. 'But we couldn't get him to talk . . .'

'Wait,' said Hargreaves. 'He did manage to get out a couple of words before he passed out . . . "Grey Moose".'

'The same words exactly,' said Locksley, his eyes lighting up. 'But what the devil do they mean? It might be a brand of pressed beef—'

'Or one of these American cigarettes,' put in Kennard.

Hargreaves waved aside these interruptions.

'It must mean something,' he insisted. 'Two dying men don't speak the same words exactly just by coincidence.'

Locksley nodded slowly.

'I see what you're driving at, sir,' he said. 'You think these two were in on those jobs, and the gang wiped 'em out so as to take no chances of their giving the game away. They sound a pretty callous lot of devils.'

'I should say that it's the head of this organization who is behind these—er—liquidations,' mused Sir Robert. 'They are quite obviously part and parcel of his plans.'

'Then you agree with Locksley that there is an organization,' queried Kennard abruptly.

Sir Robert rubbed his forehead rather wearily with his left hand while he continued to turn over reports with his right. At last, he closed the folder.

'That seems to be the only conclusion, Inspector,' he said, with a sigh. 'If they were just the usual small-time safe-busters, like Peter Scales, or "Mo" Turner or Larry the Canner, the odds are we'd have got one or more of them by now. They'd try to get rid of the stuff through one of the fences we've got tabs on, and we'd be on to them. But the head of this crowd has obviously his own special means of disposal.'

'That's true,' agreed Locksley. 'We haven't traced a single item in all those jobs yet.'

'He could be holding on to the stuff till it cools down,' suggested Kennard.

'I shouldn't imagine that's very likely,' said the deputy commissioner, thoughtfully tracing a design on his blotting pad with his paper-knife. 'I can't help agreeing with Locksley that we're up against something really big, and we've got to pull every shot out of the locker. Now, are you absolutely sure there was nothing about the Gloucester job that might give us something to go on?'

He looked from one to the other and there was silence for a few seconds. Then Locksley slowly took a bulging wallet from his inside pocket and extracted a small piece of paste-board about half the size of a postcard.

'There was this card,' he said, in a doubtful tone.

Sir Robert took the card and examined it carefully.

'Where did you find it?' he asked.

'In the waste-paper basket just by the safe at the Gloucester jewellers. As you see, it was torn into five pieces, but it wasn't difficult to put it together.'

Sir Robert picked up a magnifying glass and placed the card under it. On the card was printed in imitation copperplate handwriting:

With the compliments of Johnny Washington.

'So that joker from America has popped up again,' murmured Sir Robert. 'Where's the catch this time?'

During the past year or so, Scotland Yard had come to know this strange young man from America, with the mobile features, rimless glasses and ingenuous smile rather too well. For the presence of Johnny Washington usually meant trouble for somebody. As often as not, it was for some unscrupulous operator either inside or on the verge of the underworld, but the police were usually none too pleased about it, for the matter invariably entailed a long and complicated prosecution, even when Mr

Washington had presented them with indisputable evidence. And what particularly annoyed the police was the fact that Johnny Washington always emerged as debonair and unruffled as ever, and often several thousand dollars to the good. The Yard chiefs had experienced a pronounced sensation of relief when Johnny had informed them that he had bought a small manor house not far from Sevenoaks, and proposed to devote his energies to collecting pewter and playing the country squire.

'Where's the catch?' repeated Sir Robert, turning the card over and peering at it again.

'In the first place,' replied Locksley, 'Johnny says he has never set foot in Gloucester in his life.'

'Well, you know what a confounded liar the fellow is,' retorted Hargreaves. 'Have you checked on him at all?'

'The jewellers say they have never set eyes on him,' said Locksley.

'I don't suppose they've set eyes on any of the gang that did the job,' grunted the commissioner. 'Did you find out if he had an alibi?'

'Yes, he had an alibi all right. He was up in Town for the night to see a girl named Candy Dimmott in a new musical— seems he knew her in New York. He stayed at the St Regis—got in soon after midnight. According to the doctor, the night watchman had been chloroformed about that time—and the constable found him soon after 2 a.m. So Washington simply couldn't have been in Gloucester then.'

'You never can tell with that customer,' said Kennard dubiously.

'I questioned the night porter at the St Regis—he knows Washington well, and swears he never left the place while he was on duty,' said Locksley. He turned to his chief again. 'There's another thing about that card, sir.'

'Eh? What's that?'

'There are no fingerprints on it. I used rubber gloves when I put it together, and whoever tore it up and put it in that waste-paper basket must have done the same. Now, if Mr Washington left that card deliberately, why should he go to the trouble of using gloves?'

'He might have been wearing them anyhow,' pointed out Kennard.

Locksley shrugged.

'Yet again, if he wanted to leave a card, why tear it up?' he demanded earnestly.

Sir Robert rested his chin on his hand and gazed thoughtfully at the fire.

'I begin to see what you're driving at,' he murmured. 'You think this card business is a plant—presumably to distract attention from the real master mind.'

'That's about it, sir,' agreed Locksley. 'Washington's name has been in the papers several times—and there was that silly article about Johnny being the modern Robin Hood. It's given somebody an idea.'

Sir Robert picked up a wire paper fastener and very deliberately clipped the card to the report of the Gloucester robbery.

'You haven't seen Washington?' he asked.

'No, sir. I spoke to him twice on the telephone. He seemed a bit surprised, then amused. But he helped me all he could about the alibi when he saw how serious it was.'

'Alibi or not, I think we should keep an eye on that gentleman,' suggested Kennard.

'That sounds like a good idea,' replied Hargreaves. 'You know him fairly well, don't you, Locksley?'

'I certainly saw something of him in the Blandford case.'

'All right, then you can pop down to his place and have a talk to him as soon as you can get away from here today. And if you get the slightest hint that he is the brains behind this gang, don't take any chances. Just tell him you are rechecking his alibi.'

'It isn't easy to fool Johnny Washington,' said Locksley, slipping his little black notebook back into his inside pocket.

'I must say, sir, I'm not convinced that it is a real organization we're up against,' insisted Kennard. 'What makes you so sure about that?'

Sir Robert began to pace up and down between his desk and the fireplace.

'It's more a hunch than anything,' he confessed. 'For one thing, they've tackled such a variety of jobs—the average safe-buster sticks to one line as a rule and goes after the sort of stuff he can get rid of without much trouble. This gelignite gang have already robbed a cinema, a bank, two jewellers and a factory office. It takes a very unusual brain to plan such a variety of jobs in a comparatively short time.'

'A brain like Johnny Washington's?' queried Kennard.

Sir Robert Hargreaves did not reply.

CHAPTER II

CALDICOTT MANOR is a sturdy four-square white house standing about half a mile outside the village of Caldicott Green, near the junction of the main road to Sevenoaks, which is some four miles away.

From the moment he set eyes on it in an agent's catalogue, the manor had intrigued Johnny Washington, who had been suddenly overcome with the idea of retiring into the heart of the English countryside and getting back to nature for a spell after his exciting but profitable incursions into the London underworld.

He also liked the look of Caldicott Green, with its small stream running parallel with the main street and draining into a large pool near the manor which offered possibilities for fishing, one of his favourite forms of relaxation. Mr Washington was burdened with over-large and slightly troublesome feet which debarred him from most forms of sport. Angling, however, was ideal, for it allowed him to relax at full length for long periods on sunny afternoons, taking the weight off his pedal extremities. Johnny claimed that many of his best ideas had come to him while sitting beside a placid stream, hopefully awaiting a bite that never materialized.

His enemies were wont to declare that Johnny suffered with his feet because he was too big for his boots, and there was possibly something in this accusation, for this young man from America could have bluffed his way into the secret councils of the Atomic Control Commission as nonchalantly as if he were the man who originally split the atom.

But the secret of his success lay in the fact that he never

over-estimated himself; his bluffs were always a part of a coolly calculated scheme and designed for a specific purpose.

Naturally, having enriched himself to some considerable extent at the expense of a wide variety of social parasites, he had made a number of bitter enemies, so he was not in the least surprised to hear of the attempt to implicate him in the jewel robbery at Gloucester. It was by no means the first time such a thing had happened; in fact, he was often surprised that it did not occur more often.

Johnny Washington lay on the enormous settee in his draw-ing-room (that was what the previous tenant had called it) awaiting the arrival of his nearest neighbours, Doctor Randall and his niece, Shelagh Hamilton, with whom he had scraped acquaintance at a nearby point-to-point meeting. They had promptly invited him to lunch, and he was now about to return their hospitality. Johnny had not planned to intermingle with the local country folk, but he had to admit that the doctor and his niece rather intrigued him. The niece in particular. Shelagh, who bore not the slightest resemblance in features to her uncle, seemed right out of place in the heart of the Kent countryside. Johnny had met plenty of her type in the night spots of New York; in fact she awakened vague murmurings of nostalgia inside him.

Blonde, brittle, perfectly made-up, exquisitely manicured, Shelagh looked as if she had been born with a lipstick in one hand and a drink in the other. She had a lively turn of conver-sation which amused Johnny; she was a cynic to the tips of her blood-red fingernails and he liked meeting people who had no respect for those who sat in the seats of the mighty. But he found it hard to believe that she was Doctor Randall's niece, and found it idly intriguing to speculate upon their exact relationship.

Randall was a man in his early fifties, a very energetic type, somewhat wizened by many tropical suns, for he had told Johnny that he had worked on the Gold Coast for some years before his retirement, and he certainly talked knowledgeably about certain parts of the world, so that he made a very agreeable dining companion. But there was again an air of mystery about him; he ran a couple of large cars and horses for himself and Shelagh, and to all outward appearance seemed to live at the rate of about ten thousand pounds a year.

Johnny was pondering upon these and other minor matters while he smoked one of his favourite Chesterfields, when the telephone rang in the hall, and his butler, Winwood, came in to tell him he was wanted.

Johnny had always had a yearning for the genuine type of old English butler he had seen in so many indifferent British films. He had interviewed over thirty men for the job, and Winwood came nearest to the genuine article. This was possibly because Winwood had played such a part in no fewer than sixty-eight films, and was now driven to play it in real earnest as a result of the parlous condition of the British film industry!

Winwood had carefully omitted to mention to his employer that his experience had been largely upon the sound stages of Denham and Pinewood, rather than the stately homes of England, but Johnny was not over-fussy about details of domestic routine, as long as his butler looked the part. And he delighted to watch him throw open a door and announce in nicely modulated tones as he was doing at this moment:

'There is a Superintendent Locksley who would like to speak to you on the telephone, sir.'

Johnny gave Winwood an appreciative grin, then slowly placed his slippered feet on the floor.

'O.K. Winwood, I'll be right out,' he nodded.

Superintendent Locksley, wanted to know if he might drop in a little later that evening, and Johnny assured the detective that he would be delighted to see him. He was just replacing the receiver when the front door bell rang and Winwood opened it to usher in his guests. Apologizing for his slippers, he led them into a tiny conservatory he had converted into a cocktail bar.

Johnny commented on the fact that Shelagh was looking particularly attractive.

'I adore you Americans,' she laughed. 'You always say exactly the right thing at the right moment. Now I feel that the three hours I spent at the hairdresser's wasn't entirely wasted.'

Johnny grinned.

'If only I'd known, I'd have invited some more people,' he assured her. 'You're worth a much bigger audience!'

She accepted a cocktail and sipped it appreciatively, but Doctor Randall preferred whisky, and drank three before dinner, explaining somewhat apologetically that it was the sundowner habit he had developed in the tropics. This was the doctor's cue for a series of stories about his adventures which lasted half-way through dinner, despite cynical comments from Shelagh.

Winwood served the meal impeccably and poured coffee from the silver coffee-pot with such dignity that, as Johnny whispered to Shelagh, you expected to see a curtain go up at any minute and find yourself starting on Act Two.

The doctor went on drinking whisky which appeared to evoke longer and more lurid reminiscences, until at last Johnny turned to Shelagh and pleasantly inquired:

'What about *your* past, Miss Hamilton? Haven't you ever had any hair-raising adventures?'

'I dare say,' she replied non-committally, 'but I guess I know when to keep my mouth shut.' She looked across at her uncle meaningly, and he seemed to take the hint, for soon afterwards he announced that they must be going. It was after nine-thirty and there was still no sign of Superintendent Locksley, for which Johnny was secretly thankful, for he was not particularly anxious for his country neighbours to suspect that he had any dealings with the police—he was well aware how rumour distorts and magnifies in the rural areas.

Still discoursing upon the origins of sleeping sickness, the doctor vanished into the night, holding his niece's arm rather more tightly than would have appeared necessary. Ten minutes later, Winwood announced Superintendent Locksley with the quiet aplomb of the trusted retainer who is acquainted with every skeleton in the family cupboard.

Johnny had seen Locksley quite frequently when they were concerned with the mysterious dope smuggling that had been centred upon the police station of the little Thames-side town of Blandford, which Johnny had eventually traced, by what he modestly termed a stroke of luck, to the police sergeant of the station, who had been using his lost property department as a distribution centre.

Starting by disliking each other to some extent, Johnny and the superintendent had been mildly surprised to discover they had mutual interests, such as fishing and American cigarettes, and a weakness for unorthodox methods. Locksley had risen to his present rank by reason of his alert mind that showed a genius for bypassing routine procedure and getting quick results.

Johnny favoured the same methods, but was the first to admit that it was much easier for him to apply them, for he did not have to contend with a massive list of rules and regulations. Since their first meeting, they had occasionally enjoyed a drink together at the hostelry just round the corner from New Scotland Yard, comparing notes about their mutual acquaintances in the underworld and elsewhere. They were slightly startled to discover how many times they had reached exactly the same conclusions.

Johnny waved Locksley to the most comfortable arm-chair and asked if he had had any food.

'Thanks, Johnny, I snatched a quick supper on the way down—that's why I'm a bit late,' said the Superintendent.

'Well at least you'll let me give you a drink— Winwood, a whisky for Mr Locksley.'

Winwood took the drink over to Locksley, then crossed to Johnny and murmured discreetly:

'I'm sorry, sir, but we are almost out of whisky. The doctor was—ahem—a trifle heavy on our last bottle.'

'Good lord!' exclaimed Johnny. 'Is it as bad as that? I must nip down and see Harry Bache at the Kingfisher.' He turned to Locksley. 'Perhaps you'd like to run down to the local with me. The landlord there lets me have the odd bottle of my favourite brand now and then. We can have a quick one while we're there—it's not a bad old pub, and there's a stuffed pike in the "snug" that will interest you . . .'

Locksley smiled and nodded. Winwood withdrew and closed the door silently behind him. Johnny carefully placed his feet on his favourite fireside stool and grinned at the superintendent.

'Well, Locksley, is somebody still trying to put the smear on me?'

Locksley took an appreciative gulp at his whisky and leaned back in his chair.

'It's still the same smear,' he replied. 'The chief isn't altogether happy about your alibi.'

'Well, that's just too bad,' murmured Johnny, rubbing his chin with his long sensitive fingers. He reached for a package of Chesterfields and flicked one over to Locksley. 'You tell your boss he's darn lucky to find me with such a good alibi. It isn't once in a blue moon I stay the night in Town; I wouldn't have done this time if I hadn't taken my girl friend on to a night spot.'

'She could corroborate all that, I suppose, if necessary?'

Johnny frowned.

'Say, what's going on now?'

'You didn't take her home, I suppose?'

'I put her into a taxi in Piccadilly just on midnight—we'd have stayed on later but she'd had a hectic day and wanted some sleep. Then I went straight back to the hotel, just as I told you. You don't think I'm pulling a fast one, do you?'

'No, no, of course not, Johnny,' said Locksley with a worried expression. 'But these gelignite robberies have got us all a bit rattled. Close on one hundred thousand pounds' worth in a few months.'

Johnny pursed his lips thoughtfully.

'Chee, somebody's thinking big for once in a while,' he commented. 'Looks like they're trying to nationalize the crime racket.'

'So you see, Johnny, the D.C. is out to follow up every clue like grim death. He's convinced—and so am I, for that matter—that this is a large organization under the direction of a master mind. And if we can take a short cut to the master mind, the sooner we'll clear up the business.'

Johnny blew out a large cloud of smoke.

'Are you trying to tell me that your boss suspects that I'm the big black chief?'

'He wants to make absolutely certain that you're not,' said Locksley earnestly. 'After all, he knows you're pretty cute, and you've been around quite a bit on both sides of the Atlantic. You're the sort of unknown quantity that might well be in charge of a gang of this sort—not that I think for a moment—' he added hastily.

'I appreciate that!' grinned Johnny.

'But you see,' went on Locksley, 'he's got to eliminate as many possibilities as he can. Also, he thought you might be able to give him some inkling as to who would be likely to want to plant the Gloucester job on to you.'

Johnny shrugged.

'It might be any of the boys and girls—Princess Vaniscourt, Skeff Larabie, Billy Sorrell; they'd murder their own mother if they thought they could frame me.'

Locksley took another gulp of whisky and looked round the room for a minute without speaking. Then he said somewhat cautiously:

'This is a very nice place you've got here. You've done nicely for yourself, Johnny.'

Johnny grinned again.

'Meaning where did I get the doh-ray-me? Do we have to go into all that? Maybe you'd like to see a signed statement from my accountants.'

'No, no, of course not.' Locksley looked distinctly uncomfortable. 'I'm sorry, Johnny, but we're all a bit nervy about this business. There hasn't been anything this big for some years now, and I dare say one or two of us will be out of a job by the time it's over.' He leaned forward in his chair and looked directly at his host.

'Are you quite sure you haven't any ideas about it, Johnny?'

Johnny Washington flicked the ash from the end of his cigarette.

'To tell you the honest truth, old man, I've hardly given it a thought. I've been concentrating on rusticating these past few months.'

Locksley took out his wallet and passed over the visiting card, with the copperplate inscription.

'Can't you think whose work that's likely to be?' he demanded seriously.

Johnny flicked the card with his fingernail.

'Your guess is as good as mine,' he said.

'You've never had any cards like that yourself?'

Johnny shook his head.

'I've never bothered about visiting cards—always thought they were kinda old-fashioned.'

'You haven't sent anyone a present with a card like that enclosed?'

'No; in that case I'd use my own handwriting.' He paused for a moment, then asked: 'If you've come here to collect my fingerprints to see if they tally with those on the card, go right ahead, brother.'

Locksley gloomily shook his head, and took another drink. 'There aren't any "smudges" on the card; at least there weren't when I found it,' he said. 'That's what made me suspicious. If you'd wanted to advertise the job as your work, you wouldn't have taken the trouble to bother about fingerprints.'

'Nor would I have bothered to tear up that card,' ruminated Johnny. 'And if I had really wanted to get rid of the card I wouldn't have been such a mug as to leave it lying around in a trash basket.'

'It might have led us on a pretty involved false trail if you hadn't happened to have that alibi,' said the superintendent. 'I'd have had to set a couple of men on to tail you night and day.'

Johnny laughed and passed the card back to Locksley, who replaced it in his wallet.

'This gelignite gang interests me,' said Johnny Washington, wriggling his toes inside his slippers. 'I always like meeting people with new ideas. Tell me more about the set-up, that's if it isn't top secret.'

Locksley filled in the details of the chain of robberies very rapidly, but there was little that was new to Johnny, who had read most of the accounts in the newspapers. When Locksley had finished, Johnny poured the remainder of the whisky into his guest's glass.

'About this night watchman at Gloucester,' he murmured. 'Did you see him before he passed out?'

'Yes,' said Locksley. 'He was an old lag named Hiller, and he'd had a heavy dose of chloroform; too much for his heart.'

'Then he didn't say anything?'

'Well, he did come round just before the end, and he whispered two words quite distinctly—"Grey Moose". For a minute I thought perhaps he might be talking nonsense, then I remembered.'

'What did you remember?'

'Just after the gang pulled the Oldham job, we picked up a man named Smokey Pearce, run over by a lorry on the Preston road. Just before he died, he said the same two words.'

'Grey Moose,' repeated Johnny thoughtfully. 'It might mean anything . . . some sort of password maybe . . .'

'It doesn't suggest anything to you?' queried Locksley, eyeing him closely.

'Not a thing—except that I seem to have seen the words somewhere—can't call it to mind right now. It might be some sort of trade name.'

'We've been into all that,' nodded Locksley. 'But you'll agree that when two dying men say the same thing it must have some sort of significance, specially as they were both suspected of being linked with the gelignite gang.'

'You got something there,' agreed Johnny thoughtfully. 'I wish I could help you, brother, but I guess I've had enough of the crime racket to last me for a while. All I want to do is mooch around, a little fishing, a trip to Town once in a way, a lot of relaxing and a drink at the local . . . and that reminds me; we better get going if we don't want to be shut out.'

He fumbled for his shoes and put them on with a certain amount of effort.

'How far is this pub?' asked Locksley.

'It won't take us five minutes in the car,' Johnny told him. 'I think you'll like the Kingfisher—it's a fairly old inn—oak beams and all that—dates back quite a way. We Americans are always suckers for tradition.'

'You're also suckers for Scotch whisky,' said Locksley with a faint smile as they went out.

Johnny's car was an enormous American roadster, but the engine seemed to be cold, and missed on two of its cylinders all the way to the inn.

'I guess the plugs are getting clogged up,' frowned Johnny as they drew up in front of the Kingfisher Inn. 'I'd better run her round to the back and take a quick look at 'em. It won't take a minute; you go in and order the drinks—be sure to tell Bache they're on me.'

Locksley got out and Johnny ran the car into the little car park at the back of the inn, where he manœuvred it until the bonnet was exactly under the solitary electric light. Then he took out the offending plugs and carefully cleaned and replaced them. He was a little longer than he had anticipated because an elusive blob of grease on one of the plugs was more than usually obstinate.

He had replaced the bonnet and was just about to switch off all the lights, when there was a shout from inside the Kingfisher. Then a door opened and there was a sound of running feet. Washington immediately recognized the diminutive figure of Harry Bache, the landlord of the inn.

'I thought it was your car, Mr Washington,' he gasped breathlessly.

'Anything wrong, Harry?' asked Johnny noting his obvious distress.

'Was that feller with you—the bloke what just come in?'

'Yes, of course. Didn't he tell you to put the drinks down to me?'

'That's right—but I was a bit suspicious like, as I'd never seen him before. And then, while my back was turned, it happened . . . My God, it's awful!'

'What happened?'

'Why he . . . shot himself!' The little innkeeper's eyes seemed to bulge right out of his head, and he clutched at the mascot on the front of Washington's car as if he were about to faint.

CHAPTER III

GREY MOOSE

WASHINGTON reached inside the car and took out a silver flask from one of the side pockets. He unscrewed the top and passed it to Harry.

'Drink this,' he ordered. The innkeeper took the flask in a shaking right hand, gulped down a mouthful of brandy and passed it back. Johnny slipped it into his pocket ready for further emergencies.

'All right, Mr Washington,' the landlord said hoarsely. 'We'd better go in now and see if there's anything we can do.'

'O.K. then, come on. No time to be lost.'

They went in through the back door, along a short passage and into the saloon bar.

'I've locked the front door, sir,' breathed Harry Bache's hoarse voice behind him as Johnny went into the room. He stood for a moment on the threshold as if to establish a clear impression of his surroundings.

The body of Superintendent Locksley was almost the first thing he saw, for his attention was directed to it by an overturned table and stool in a far corner of the saloon. The body lay nearby, with a trickle of blood flowing from the head and a revolver clasped in the left hand.

On Washington's left was the small service room, which was connected to the saloon by a small enclosed counter, and opened out into the bar which was usually patronized by local farmworkers. Apparently the house had been empty of customers at the time, for it seemed quite deserted now. Washington was not altogether surprised at this, for Harry Bache was always grumbling about the lack of custom, although the brewery had spent a considerable sum upon refurnishing the saloon with small tables, imitation antique settles and small stools.

Washington went over to Locksley, placed a finger on the neck artery, then turned to Bache.

'Anyone else around?'

'I told the missus to stay in the kitchen. And there's a Mr Quince upstairs . . .'

Washington took in the room—the little service counter with its rows of bottles on their shelves, the new chromium-plated beer engine, the cash register, the advertisements for cigarettes and soft drinks, the recently built brick fireplace, the reproduction oak settles, the heavy china ash-trays, the solitary siphon at one end of the counter . . .

Harry Bache shifted uncomfortably from one foot to the other.

'Can't think what made 'im do it, Mr Washington,' he burst forth at last. 'Never known such a thing in all me born days—'e comes in and orders two double whiskies and the moment I turn my back—'

'Can I use your telephone?' asked Johnny somewhat abruptly.

Harry Bache nodded in the direction of the passage, where Johnny found the instrument in a small alcove. He was connected with the police station and spoke to the sergeant in charge. The police surgeon was not available. Washington suggested that the sergeant should get Doctor Randall, who was comparatively near at hand.

Harry Bache was still standing nervously in the doorway of the saloon bar; he had obviously overheard the telephone conversation.

'What did you mean, Mr Washington, when you said as 'ow it *might* be suicide?' he demanded with an aggressive note in his voice. Washington ignored him and went over to the body of Locksley, stooped and examined the revolver for a minute, then turned to Harry Bache.

'What were you doing when this man came in?' he asked.

'A crossword,' was the prompt reply. 'The place was as quiet as the grave—I 'ave to do something or I'd go barmy.'

'You were standing behind the bar?' asked Johnny.

'That's right. He come in and ordered the whiskies—said they was to be charged up to you—and just as I was going to pour 'em 'e asked me if I could change a pound note. So I went off into the sitting-room to get the money, and when I gets back 'e's lying there just like 'e is now, with that gun in 'is 'and. Give me a proper turn it did—thought for a minute I was goin' to pass out. I 'ollers to the missis to stop where she is, and comes out to see if you was 'ere like 'e said.'

'How long were you out there?' inquired Johnny.

'About three or four minutes I dare say. I 'ad a bit of an argument with the missis about 'arf a dollar she'd borrowed from the petty cash.'

Johnny thrust his hands deep into his trouser pockets and sat down on one of the stools.

'I suppose someone could have come in here while you were in the sitting-room,' he suggested.

Harry Bache rubbed the back of his head with his rather dirty hand. 'I reckon they might,' he conceded. 'They could 'ave come from upstairs or through the front door.'

'What about that door yonder?'

Johnny indicated a door to the right of the bar.

'That's the club room—only used one night a week by club members. I always keep it locked, on account of the stuff in there.'

'What sort of stuff?'

'Oh, you know—robes and chains of office and all that tomfoolery.'

Johnny Washington walked over to the door and tried the knob. The door was locked. Johnny paced back to the bar and picked up one of the two empty glasses, which were standing side by side, and poured into it a generous measure of brandy from his flask. Then he glanced inquiringly at the landlord, who shook his head.

'No more for me, Mr Washington.'

Johnny sipped the brandy thoughtfully. A solitary car went past outside. They could hear the clock ticking in the public bar. Suddenly, Harry Bache said:

'Funny I never 'eard that gun go off. Nor the missus neither or she'd soon 'ave—'

'Not much mystery about that,' replied Johnny absently. 'If you look at the gun you'll see it's fitted with a silencer—that cylindrical gadget fastened to the end of the barrel. There'd only be a sort of quiet pop.'

'Cor, 'e didn't 'arf make a job of it, and no error!' ejaculated the innkeeper. 'But it beats me what 'e wants to come 'ere for—never set eyes on 'im in me life before.'

'You're quite sure about that?' said Johnny quietly.

'Course I'm sure. Who is 'e, anyway?'

'Oh, just a friend of mine. By the way, did you say there was someone upstairs?'

'That's right. An old gent, name of Quince. Bit of a queer bird if you ask me. Got 'ere yesterday afternoon—says 'e's on a tour of the county—asked me all sorts of questions about this 'ere place. There wasn't much I could tell 'im, I've only bin 'ere six months myself.'

'I think you'd better ask Mr Quince to come down here,' decided Johnny.

Harry Bache seemed surprised.

'What do we want the old geezer nosin' about for?' he asked.

'The police sergeant will be sure to want to see him when he gets here, so we might as well break it to him gently.'

Harry Bache shrugged.

'O.K. with me if you say so, Mr Washington!'

Johnny watched him go out muttering towards the stairs in the passage. He had always felt a vague dislike for this little man, but had tried to be friendly, as he had been with most of the folk round about. But there always seemed to be something lacking about the atmosphere at the Kingfisher Inn; there was none of that warm bonhomie one associated with the typical British country pub. Which was, no doubt, the reason why most of the locals patronized the other inn which was in the centre of the village.

When he heard the landlord's footsteps at the top of the stairs, Johnny swiftly crossed over to the till, cautiously rang up 'No Sale', opened the drawer, examined the contents and closed it again. Before doing so, he stood apparently lost in thought for quite a couple of minutes, until he could hear distant voices from the stairhead.

However, Bache returned alone, and said that Mr Quince would be down in a minute.

'I broke it to 'im,' he went on, 'and he took it as if I was passin' the time of day. Never turned a blinkin' 'air. If you ask me 'e's as tough as the Office o' Works and Board o' Trade rolled into one!'

Johnny lit a cigarette and wondered how much longer the police would be. For the first time, the full implications of the death of Locksley impressed themselves upon him. The superintendent had come to see him about his possible connection with the gelignite gang; he had brought him down here for a drink and he had either committed suicide or had been murdered. Scotland Yard were going to be very difficult from now on, and it looked as if he was going to be involved with this case whether he liked it or not.

A sound outside the door cut short his reflections, and he swung round to see Mr Quince standing in the doorway. He was a man in the late seventies, neatly dressed in a dark blue suit but with, curiously enough, a fancy waistcoat. Johnny saw Quince take one look at the body then turn away again. After introducing himself, he led the old man to the settle where he sat facing away from the body.

'As the dead man was a friend of mine, Mr Quince, I thought

perhaps you wouldn't mind answering a few questions, just for my private information. Of course, the police will probably ask you much the same questions, so it may help you to get things straight in your mind.'

'I'll be only too pleased,' replied Quince with a little smile, 'but I'm afraid I can't help very much. What is it you want to know?'

'Well now,' said Johnny, 'I wonder if you could remember what time it was when you went to your room tonight.'

Mr Quince hesitated a moment, then said: 'It was just on ten o'clock, because I remember thinking the place should be closed. I sat reading for a short while; I happened to come across a most interesting book about this part of the world—'

'Quite so,' put in Johnny suavely, hoping to head the old boy off what was obviously a favourite theme.

'This affair must be quite a shock for you, Mr Washington,' he went on. 'The idea of a friend committing suicide is very distressing, an act of sheer desperation that is beyond the comprehension of many of us—'

'Mr Quince,' Johnny interrupted again, 'what makes you so certain that this is suicide?'

For a moment he seemed a trifle bewildered.

'What makes me so certain?' he repeated in a puzzled tone. 'What else can it be, Mr Washington? Unless, of course, Mr Bache shot your friend.'

There was a faint clatter from behind the bar as Harry Bache dropped a glass he had been wiping back into a bowl of dirty water.

''Ere! What are you gettin' at?'

His voice sounded unduly harsh, and the back of his neck turned a deep red. He came from behind the bar, still clutching the towel. He drew himself up to the full extent of his five feet two inches and glowered down at Mr Quince.

'What should I want to kill 'im for? Never set eyes on the cove in my life.'

Mr Quince stood up and peered at the body.

'There doesn't seem to be very much blood, Mr Bache,' he announced a trifle wistfully.

'There's enough to give me the willies,' retorted Harry Bache in a grating tone. 'This ain't no laughin' matter, I can tell yer. Blokes 'ave lost their licence over affairs like this before today.' A thought seemed to strike him and he swung round and confronted Quince.

'If it comes to that, you might 'ave done it yourself. You wasn't in bed when I knocked at your door.'

'That's quite true, Mr Bache,' he said calmly. 'I happened to be reading.'

'Have you decided to stay here long?' interrupted Johnny, conscious of the passing of the valuable minutes.

'I haven't quite made up my mind,' replied Quince. 'Most probably until the end of the week.'

This was the cue for Harry Bache to intervene once more.

'You didn't say nothing about that when you signed the register,' he reminded him. 'You said it was only for one night.'

But Mr Quince was in no way dismayed. He treated Harry Bache rather like a recalcitrant child.

'It was my original intention to remain here only one night, but I found this part of the world so extremely interesting.'

'You don't say?' exclaimed the landlord with heavy sarcasm.

'Indeed I do. This inn must be at least five hundred years old—I refer to the outside walls of course—and the beams; they are quite magnificent.'

'You can 'ave 'em,' sniffed the landlord. 'I been 'ere six months too long for my likin'.'

'I'm sure it all seems quite snug,' said Quince politely. 'I should have thought you would get quite a number of tourists . . .'

Harry Bache did not deign to reply. He looked across at the body once again and shivered.

'Them police are a long time gettin' 'ere,' he muttered. 'Wish they'd 'urry up . . . it fair gives me the creeps to see 'im lyin' there starin' at nothin'.' He turned to Washington.

'Couldn't we cover 'im up, sir? Just till the police come . . . it wouldn't do no harm.'

'Good idea,' agreed Johnny.

'All right. I'll get an old sheet from the linen cupboard,' nodded Bache, as he hurried out of the room with some alacrity, obviously relieved to get away from the sight of the corpse. He went off upstairs, and they could hear him opening a cupboard.

Quince sat quite still for a minute without speaking. Then he slowly walked round the room, pausing for some seconds to peer at the body. Presently, he said:

'Was he a very great friend of yours, Mr Washington?'

Johnny shrugged.

'I hadn't known him more than a year or so. But he was a good guy. We got along.'

Quince nodded.

'I thought for a moment his face was familiar, but I see now he's quite a stranger to me.'

'His name was Locksley—he was a superintendent at Scotland Yard.' Mr Quince was suitably impressed.

'Scotland Yard?' he repeated. 'Dear, dear, that makes it even more serious, doesn't it?'

'It certainly is very serious,' agreed Johnny.

Quince walked over to the door which led into the club-room and bent down to examine the floor.

'Is it my imagination, Mr Washington, or is there a damp patch here by the door?'

He went over to him.

''M, it could be,' he agreed. 'Perhaps somebody spilt their beer.'

'There's hardly been anyone in all evening,' Quince told him. 'This—er—moisture is quite recent—as if someone had cleaned up a mess of some sort.'

'You mean,' said Johnny quietly, 'it could be blood.'

'I'm not saying so,' replied Quince hastily, 'but it must be *something*.'

Johnny measured the distance from the body with his eye. It was quite ten feet . . . and if the blood came from the body why should anyone wish to clear it up before the police arrived? Johnny shifted his weight from one foot to the other and stared pensively at the locked door.

When Harry Bache returned with the sheet and covered the body, Johnny said quite casually:

'Have you got the key to that club-room handy?'

A shifty look came into the landlord's eyes.

'I'm not supposed to let anybody in there,' he replied defensively.

'Somebody goes in to clean the place?' queried Johnny softly.

'Of course they do—the missus does it. But it's a private room. What d'you want to go in there for?'

'Mr Quince and I thought we'd like to take a look round.'

Harry Bache was obviously reluctant to comply with Johnny's request.

'There's nothing to see in there I tell you—just a table and some chairs . . .'

'In that case,' said Johnny, 'there can be no possible harm in our taking a look.'

He hesitated a moment, then said meaningly: 'The police will almost certainly want to see in there.'

'I don't see why.'

'It's fairly obvious I should have thought,' said Johnny. 'A murderer might have left some trace.'

'Murderer!' gasped Bache. 'Mr Washington, you don't think—'

'I think you'd better give me that key,' replied Johnny smoothly. Mumbling to himself, the landlord went over to the till, opened the drawer as far as it would go, and took out the key. Then he joined Johnny and Quince at the door of the club-room. The

key fitted easily; he opened the door and switched on the light
. . . As he had said, it was just a bare room as far as furniture was
concerned, apart from a small table and about a dozen chairs.
Opposite the door, a large cupboard occupied almost half the
length of the wall. Johnny nodded in its direction.

'What's in there?' he asked.

'Oh, their robes and chains of office and all that sort of
rubbish,' sniffed Bache. 'Like a lot of kids they are, playing
dressing up.'

The room smelt strongly of disinfectant Johnny noticed as
he crossed over to open the cupboard. As the landlord had said,
it was full of shapeless robes and decorations. Meanwhile,
Quince had crossed to the fireplace and was stooping to examine
the floor again. Washington joined him at once, and turned to
Harry Bache.

'When did you say this room was last used?' he asked.

'Why—on club night—last Tuesday,' said Bache.

'Then how do you account for this damp patch on the floor?'

Bache was on the defensive again.

'There's always damp coming through the floors in this
place,' he almost snarled. 'I can't help that, can I?'

Johnny looked round for an ally in Quince, but found the
old man studying an insignia mounted above the fireplace.

'Founded in 1756,' he was murmuring to himself, 'how very
interesting . . . Mr Washington, have you seen this? It's a sort
of coat of arms. . .'

He went across and read the inscription under his breath.

'Loyal Antediluvian Order of Bison . . . Grey Moose Lodge
1478 . . . Grey Moose . . .'

CHAPTER IV

A JOB FOR THE POLICE

JOHNNY looked round cautiously, somewhat apprehensive that his low whisper might have been overheard. But Quince gave no hint of having noticed anything unusual, and Harry Bache was moving over towards the door, as if to hurry them out.

'I must remember to make a note to look into these ancient orders,' Quince was saying. 'I'm sure one could write a whole book about them. I'm quite certain it has never been done before.' He turned to the landlord.

'Can you tell me who runs this—er—lodge?' he asked him. Harry Bache sniffed.

'Yes, it's a feller named Dimthorpe—keeps a greengrocer's in the village. And you won't get much out of *him*,' he added in a surly tone.

While Quince gossiped to the landlord, Johnny peered at the shield above the fireplace, with its second-rate reproduction of a moose's head and somewhat faded gilt lettering. Of course, it might be just a coincidence that the gelignite gang had some connection with a Grey Moose Lodge—there must be scores of others in various parts of the country. But he could not help feeling that Superintendent Locksley's death had some connection with this room. Maybe he had been inside himself and seen someone; Harry Bache could have been lying about the place always being locked. He suddenly realized that Quince was talking to him.

'May I ask if you have any information about the history of these ancient orders?' he was asking. Johnny came back to earth with a start.

'Me, sir? Why not very much I guess. I went to one or two

31

Elks' dinners when I was in the States, but I can't say I ever really belonged.'

'What exactly is the purpose behind these organizations?'

Johnny shook his head.

'You have me there, brother. I had some good times with the Elks, but I don't remember anyone performing any good deeds.'

A fleeting expression of annoyance flitted across Quince's features, but he obviously had no intention of abandoning the idea.

'There must be some source where one can obtain such information,' he mused. 'After all, secret societies are against the law . . . at least I think they are . . . Or would that be one of those Defence Regulations?'

Johnny broke open a new package of Chesterfields and offered Quince one. The old man refused, and Johnny lit one for himself. He didn't know what to make of this old boy, but he was hardly a sinister type. All the same, the strangest people got mixed up in murder, folks who looked as if the sight of the merest scratch would send them into a dead faint.

Johnny was suddenly conscious of a car approaching in the distance; its engine came nearer, roared for a few seconds then stopped. Two doors opened and slammed and there were foot-steps outside. Harry Bache hurried off to open the front door, and Johnny and Mr Quince returned to the saloon, closing the club-room door behind them.

Almost at once, they heard voices, the suave tones of Doctor Randall mingling with the richer country dialects of Sergeant Hubble and the constable with him. It seemed that the doctor had picked them up in his car, and there had been a slight delay in locating the constable. Johnny knew them both by sight, but had never done more than pass the time of day with them.

While Doctor Randall examined the body, the sergeant questioned Harry Bache, the constable slowly taking down his replies in long-hand. The sergeant had already been acquainted with the dead man's identity, and fairly bristled with self-importance. Year after year he had patiently awaited the call to Scotland Yard, the big assignment, the congratulatory pat on the shoulder from the Commissioner. Now his probation was over. Scotland Yard had come to him!

Sergeant Hubble was out to show his superiors just how a job like this should be handled; all the evidence very much to the point, nothing overlooked, and no nonsense from any of the witnesses! This case was going to be run exactly as Sergeant Hubble wanted it.

While the constable took down one or two minor details from Harry Bache, the sergeant strolled across to where Doctor Randall was kneeling beside the body.

'Ah, revolver in the left hand,' noted Hubble at a quick glance, making a mental note of the fact. The doctor had pulled away the sheet and began his examination, first asking for as much light as possible. Harry Bache went out into the passage and pressed down two more switches. Having made certain that there were no other visible signs of violence upon the body, Randall turned his attention to the head wound which was undoubtedly the cause of the death.

Sergeant Hubble began to take a few notes on his own account, concerning the position of the body in relation to the rest of the furniture, a description of the Luger clasped in the dead man's left hand, and the exact position of the wound in the head.

Apparently, he did not leap to the conclusion that Locksley had committed suicide, for he sent his constable to make a thorough investigation of the other rooms for trace of a possible intruder.

Meanwhile Johnny Washington and Quince sat patiently at the far corner of the bar, awaiting their turn to be questioned. For some reason best known to himself, the sergeant had apparently decided to defer this until the doctor had completed his examination. From time to time Quince went on prattling, half to himself, about the history of friendly societies, craftsmen's guilds and similar institutions, while Johnny puffed moodily at his cigarette and said very little.

At length, Doctor Randall replaced his instruments in his worn attaché case and rose somewhat painfully to his feet.

'The man has been dead nearly half an hour I should say,' he announced. 'He must have died almost instantaneously. The bullet penetrated the brain.' He turned to the sergeant. 'Would you like me to make a full written report?'

'If you'd be so good,' nodded Hubble. 'The police surgeon won't be back for a few days; it was lucky you were available, or I'd have had to telephone Sevenoaks.'

The doctor signalled to Harry Bache and asked for a strong whisky, which was very quickly poured out. With a keen sense of his responsibilities, the sergeant refused a drink. However, Johnny accepted one, and while he was sipping it the sergeant came over to him.

'I understand that the deceased was a friend of yours, Mr Washington,' he began respectfully.

'Not exactly a friend,' returned Johnny with equal politeness. 'Let's say a close acquaintance. He'd come down to see me on a matter of business.'

The sergeant's bushy eyebrows were raised at that.

'You mean Scotland Yard business, Mr Washington?'

'That is so.'

Hubble bit his pencil, hesitating how to frame his next question.

'Could that business have had any connection with this unfortunate affair?' he asked, with a certain deliberation.

'It could have,' replied Johnny, his tone remaining as noncommittal as before. 'That is, if this turns out to be a case of murder.'

'Then you don't think it might be suicide?' persisted Hubble somewhat portentously.

Johnny shook his head.

'The superintendent seemed like the last man in the world to commit suicide.'

'You don't happen to know if he's been suffering from ill health?'

'Not to my knowledge. They'll tell you more about that at the Yard, I dare say.'

The sergeant paused to make several notes, and Johnny sipped his whisky. Quince sat with an air of polite attention, as if he were listening to a lecture.

'Did you come here for any particular reason tonight?' continued the sergeant.

'The usual reason,' answered Johnny with a faint grin. 'I'd run out of whisky at home, and we wanted a nightcap before closing time. I stayed to clean up the plugs in my car and the superintendent came in ahead of me to order the drinks. Mr Bache here has told you the rest.'

'All this happened just before ten o'clock, I take it?'

'Yes,' nodded Johnny. 'About five to, I should think.'

The sergeant jotted down some further notes, then turned to Harry Bache.

'I'd like you to go over your statement again, Mr Bache,' he said pleasantly. 'Just to make sure that nothing has been left out and so the doctor can hear it.'

With a certain reluctance, Harry Bache agreed.

'I was standin' behind the bar 'ere doin' me crossword puzzle when this fellow comes in and orders a couple of whiskies and says put 'em down to Mr Washington. Then 'e asks me if I could change 'im a quid. so I goes off into the sitting-room to get the money. When I gets back I sees him lyin' there, just like 'e is now.'

'You are quite sure there was no one else in any of these rooms?'

'Only the missus in the back, and Mr Quince upstairs. I never saw anyone else.'

'And you heard nothing?'

'Not a sound—there's a silencer thing on that gun,' added the landlord confidentially. 'They only makes a noise like a kid's popgun.'

'How d'you know that?' snapped the sergeant.

'I goes to the pictures when I get the chance!' retorted the landlord with a certain acerbity.

'All right, there's no need to be funny,' growled Hubble. 'We got enough trouble here as it is, without you puttin' in any back answers. Don't forget you're the most important witness, and I'll warn you that you'll have to keep your wits about you.'

'I've told you the truth, and that's all there is to it,' replied Harry Bache obstinately. 'You know as much about it as I do now.'

The sergeant looked round the room.

'Is this gentleman staying here?' he inquired.

'Yes, Sergeant,' said Johnny. 'This is Mr Quince.'

For the first time the sergeant became really conscious of the keen brown eyes of the gentleman in question. He crossed over to Quince, and stood with his arms akimbo.

'Well, sir, can you help us to throw a little light on this affair?'

'I'm afraid not, Sergeant,' replied Quince meeting his gaze quite confidently. 'This sort of thing is rather outside my province, you know. In fact, I can't recall ever having set eyes on a dead man before in my life.'

'Where were you when this happened?' interposed the sergeant, to forestall any possible reminiscences.

'In my room reading. Mr Bache came up to tell me what had occurred, and naturally I was extremely upset.'

Harry Bache sniffed. 'You didn't look very upset to me.'

Quince turned to him with an injured air.

'One does not always display one's emotions to strangers,' he murmured. 'You may remember my saying that I would follow you downstairs in a few minutes. I needed a little time to collect myself.'

There was something slightly pathetic about Quince's

dignified restraint, and Johnny found himself feeling rather sorry for the poor old boy. At the same time, he had to admit that Quince appeared comparatively unruffled and dispassionate about the tragedy that had just been enacted. He imagined that he was a retired school teacher, for he was treating the sergeant's inquiries with the same patience one would display towards an over-persistent pupil. Nevertheless, the sergeant found him a far more agreeable witness than the landlord, for he made cool and accurate replies to his questions, with no hint of blustering or concealment.

'How long have you been staying here, Mr Quince?' he inquired.

'I arrived yesterday afternoon—I am making a short tour of these parts.'

'Could I have your full name and permanent address?' he asked.

'Horatio Quince, 17 Quadrant Row, Bayswater, London,' he announced, and the sergeant wrote it down very solemnly.

'You may be needed as a witness at the inquest, Mr Quince. I'll let you know about that later, when I've had a word with the inspector.'

'Have you any idea when that will be?'

'Probably tomorrow afternoon.'

At that moment the constable returned to report that he had discovered nothing unusual in any other room in the house, and that he had made a thorough search of any possible hiding-places both inside and outside.

The sergeant was frankly puzzled. He was very dubious that an exalted official of Scotland Yard would commit suicide in a small country inn: on the other hand, nobody seemed to have seen any murderer. He went over to Johnny and checked that he had seen no one leave from the back of the inn while he had been in the car park. And the landlord had seen no one else enter or leave through the front. All the same, he was not entirely satisfied about Harry Bache, and presently tackled him again.

'Now, Mr Bache, I want to get this little matter cleared up. Think carefully—could anyone have come in here while you were in the back room getting that change?'

Bache rubbed the back of his head.

'Yes,' he decided. 'They could 'ave come in 'ere either from upstairs or the street.'

'What about the back door?'

'I reckon I'd 'ave 'eard anyone who came in that way. The door sticks and makes a jarrin' sort of noise when you open it.'

'And you didn't hear anyone come downstairs?'

'I didn't hear anyone,' replied Bache, 'though I'm not sayin' anyone might not 'ave crept down very quiet like.' He looked meaningly in the direction of Quince, who was, however, gazing thoughtfully into the fire, apparently quite unconscious of any insinuation. Somewhat baffled, the sergeant instructed his colleague to telephone for an ambulance to take the body to the mortuary, then recollected himself and abruptly cancelled the order. The inspector would probably want to see everything exactly as it was; he was inclined to be fussy and unwilling to accept a report from an inferior officer, no matter how detailed or reliable it might be. Besides, he might even decide to call in Scotland Yard.

Sergeant Hubble, somewhat lamely, ordered the constable to telephone Inspector Martin at Sevenoaks. It would have been nice to be able to present the inspector with an open and shut case, but things very rarely worked out that way in real life; only in those cheap thrillers his fourteen-year-old son was always reading. Anyhow, there wasn't much more he could do, for he was certain that if this was a case of murder, the person responsible was no longer on the premises.

There might be some sort of clue in the way of fingerprints, but they were going to take a bit of sorting out in a public room of that sort which was used by all and sundry for eight hours a day. The 'smudges' on the gun itself would almost certainly prove to be those of the dead man.

The constable returned to say that Inspector Martin would be at the station in twenty minutes, and would the sergeant meet him there.

'I'll run you back if you like, Sergeant,' volunteered Johnny, and the sergeant gratefully accepted the offer. Johnny went off to start his car, saying he would pick the sergeant up outside the front door. Hubble gave instructions to the constable, who was to remain in charge during his absence, then turned to thank Doctor Randall for his help. The doctor cut short Hubble's apologies for troubling him.

'I'm only too glad to have been able to give a hand, Sergeant. It reminded me of old times on the Gold Coast. I remember once when I—'

But the appearance of Washington cut short his reminiscences, and as he was going the sergeant turned to speak to Quince.

'It will be all right for you to go back to your room, sir,' he said respectfully. 'I doubt if the inspector will want to see you tonight.'

Quince permitted himself a circumspect little smile.

'Thank you, Sergeant, and you, too, Mr Washington,' he murmured gratefully and wished everyone good night. Johnny smiled politely and watched him until he was out of sight. Quite frankly, Quince puzzled him. He hardly looked a sinister type, but you could never tell with these odd eccentric little characters.

Johnny and the sergeant made a move towards the door, but Harry Bache called after them.

'What am I supposed to do about that?' He indicated the body. 'We can't just leave 'im 'ere all night.'

The sergeant waved aside the interruption.

'I'll attend to that presently. Pearman will look after things here till I get back.' He turned to the constable and ordered him to keep a close watch on the front door.

'Don't let anyone in.'

'You want me to wait and see the inspector?' queried Doctor Randall.

'If you wouldn't mind, Doctor. Just a formality.'

'I'll be delighted.'

The doctor looked as if he meant it, for he had settled down in the most comfortable chair with another glass of whisky. Outside, the engine of Johnny's saloon roared for a moment, doors slammed, gears changed and the sound of the car slowly receded into the night.

What seemed to be an oppressive silence fell upon the house. The constable went over to the body, pulled the sheet further over the head, and perched on a stool.

A minute or two went by, then Harry Bache suddenly said: 'Why don't we go into the back room? There's still a good fire—looks more cheerful.'

'Good idea!' approved the doctor, getting to his feet.

'What about you, Mr Pearman?' asked the landlord.

The policeman shook his head.

'I think I'd better stop in here if you don't mind.'

'Please yourself. We'll be out there if you want us.'

Harry Bache and the doctor went out along the short passage to the little back sitting-room, where a small but lively fire was burning between the two old-fashioned hobs. The doctor set his glass, still half-full, on the table, and made himself comfortable in a well-worn rocking chair, while Harry Bache closed the door with some care.

'Where's your wife?' asked the doctor, as soon as he was settled. Harry Bache made an upward gesture with a grimy thumb.

'Packed 'er off to bed out of the way,' he answered. They began to talk in low voices.

'I don't like this business, Doc,' said Harry Bache, in a hoarse, apprehensive voice. 'I ain't never been mixed up with anything like this before.' His Cockney origin became more apparent than ever in his agitation.

'Don't be a damned fool!' snapped Randall in low tones. 'Everything's turned out all right. You've only got to keep your wits about you.' His face was redder than usual, possibly because of the quantity of whisky he had drunk that evening. Harry Bache leaned against the mantelpiece and looked into the fire.

'It's tricky, Doc. I can't think what the devil brought 'im 'ere—of all places. D'you think 'e'd found out anything?'

'Well, nobody'll know the answer to that now,' replied Randall grimly.

'It's a nasty business,' repeated Bache. 'I don't like the looks of that Mr Washington. E's a queer bird, if you ask me.'

'Yes,' nodded the doctor. 'I've read one or two things about him in the papers; we'll have to keep an eye on him.'

'What's 'e want to come and live in these parts for?' demanded Bache curiously.

'He's very fond of fishing.'

'That's what he *says*. But I don't trust 'im. I've got a feeling 'e's up to something.'

'Pull yourself together,' said Randall, taking a gulp at his whisky. 'It's quite simple. Locksley came down to see him because of that card left behind on the Gloucester job.'

'Card? What card? I don't know anything about—'

'Skip it, and give me another drink. You don't have to worry about Johnny Washington. We'll look after him.'

The landlord opened a cupboard, took out a bottle and filled two glasses.

'I thought for a minute 'e'd got wise about the club-room—'e asked to go inside—and found a damp patch on the floor, where I wiped up the—'

'You damn fool! What did you want to let him go in for!' The doctor was on his feet now, towering above the little innkeeper.

'I 'ad to let 'im in. 'E said the police would want to go and 'ave a look round . . . it'd 'ave looked fishy if I'd tried to keep 'im out.'

The doctor sat down again.

'He never mentioned anything about the club-room,' he reflected. 'Maybe he didn't attach any importance to whatever he saw there.'

'Anyhow, 'e can't prove nothing,' nodded the innkeeper. 'I'm the only witness, and I got my story.'

'Of course you have,' rallied the doctor. 'There'll be no trouble.' For a minute or two they drank in silence. Then Bache said suddenly:

''Eard anything about the next job?'

'Yes,' nodded the doctor. 'Brighton.'

'Ah . . .' Harry Bache nodded several times. 'Plenty of stuff down there if you know where to lay 'ands on it.'

'It's practically settled,' Randall told him. 'We'll be meeting on Thursday.'

'Not here?' queried the landlord in some alarm.

'Why not? This business will be all over by then. It'll be safe as anywhere.' The doctor drained his glass for the ninth time that evening.

'This is a big job at Brighton,' he went on. 'One of the biggest we've taken on yet, and we've got to leave nothing to chance.' He got up and went over to the door, opened it a few inches and closed it again before adding in a low tone:

'I had the tip this morning that Grey Moose may be coming down here himself.'

CHAPTER V

INQUISITIVE LADY

'How ever did I get on without you, Winwood?' lazily demanded Johnny Washington, levering himself into a slightly more comfortable position in his arm-chair. His butler smiled politely without vouchsafing any reply.

It was just after nine on the Thursday morning after the death of Superintendent Locksley, on whom the coroner had returned an open verdict. There had been plenty of sensational headlines during the past few days, but the police did not seem to be much nearer establishing the exact cause of their colleague's death. Crime reporters with varying degrees of imagination speculated upon the case from a number of angles, and two or three 'played up' Johnny Washington's connection with it. They would not readily forget the young American's comparatively recent exploits amongst the strange characters in and around the London underworld, and as it was known that Locksley had been investigating the gelignite robberies, the natural inference was that Johnny Washington was in some way linked up with that gang. With the result that a number of brisk young men, usually wearing shabby raincoats, had been seen in the district of Caldicott Manor during the past two days. Most of them had called at the house, but had been duly repulsed by the faithful Winwood, who, having performed just such an operation some forty times in a wide assortment of film productions, was able to command a variety of techniques suitable for any emergency.

Johnny gazed out of his french windows across a vista of Kent orchards, while Winwood methodically read reports from all the morning newspapers of the inquest on Superintendent

Locksley. His own evidence was detailed quite fully, but gave no clue as to the reason the superintendent had visited him on that fatal evening. As he had caught sight of Inspector Dovey from the Yard in close consultation with the coroner just before the inquest, Johnny guessed that this omission had been carefully arranged.

All the reports of the inquest so far had proved reasonably discreet, until Winwood turned to the melodramatic pages of the *Daily Reflector*, with its lively display of two-inch headlines and bathing beauties on each alternate sheet.

'This is a little more sensational, sir,' began Winwood with a slight apologetic cough, deferentially inclining his head exactly as he had done in some long-since forgotten epic. He started to read a report with the by-line, 'By Our Crime Correspondent'.

'Playboy Johnny Washington was a guest of New Scotland Yard chiefs last night, when he discussed with Chief Inspector Kennard the incidents leading to the tragic death of Superintendent Locksley at the Kingfisher Inn, near Sevenoaks, which was the subject of today's inquest. Further sensational disclosures may be expected in the near future.'

Johnny wriggled his toes inside his very comfortable slippers and asked Winwood to pour him some more coffee.

As the butler passed the cup to Johnny, he said quietly:

'I forgot to tell you, sir, that a gentleman called to see you when you were in London yesterday.'

'Really?' said Johnny with some interest. 'Did he leave his name?'

'Yes, sir. It was a Mr Quince.'

'Quince?' repeated Johnny thoughtfully. 'Now I wonder what he wanted?'

'He didn't say, sir. He seemed quite a pleasant gentleman, but he wouldn't leave any message. He said he might call again if you didn't get in touch with him. He's staying at the Kingfisher.'

Johnny nodded absently and deftly extracted a cigarette from the silver box on the small table beside him. As he lit it, Winwood asked:

'Shall I go on reading the reports, sir?'

'No, that'll do for now, Winwood. You'd better run along and see cook about lunch—or whatever you do at this time of morning.'

The butler hesitated.

'I'm afraid several of those reporters are likely to call again this morning, sir. You won't be making any statement to the press?'

Johnny unlatched the french window and opened it to admit the cool morning breeze.

'No, Winwood, I guess we won't be making any statements just yet awhile. As far as the press boys are concerned, I've always found it pays to say as little as possible.'

Winwood nodded approvingly. He rather enjoyed rebuffing the gentlemen of the press.

Johnny perched on the top stone step, which was already quite warm from the early morning sunshine, and gazed out across the orchards. A tractor was chugging away busily somewhere nearby, and there was something vaguely reassuring about the neatly shaven lawns and trim, well-kept borders.

'This is the life, Winwood,' he murmured. 'Folks are crazy to stifle themselves in towns . . . what is it some poet fellow says about a flask of wine, a loaf of bread and thou . . .?'

'Yes, sir, that reminds me,' said Winwood, who was still hovering near the window. 'One of the reporters who called yesterday was a young lady—a most attractive young lady.'

Johnny wagged an indolent finger.

'Now, Winwood, take it easy.'

'She was most insistent, sir. In fact, she refused to take "No" for an answer.'

'That's too bad,' murmured Johnny. 'Blonde or brunette?'

'I beg your pardon, sir?'

'I said was she dark or fair?'

'A sort of chestnut I think would describe her colouring, sir.'

'Very nice, too. Did she leave a name?'

'Yes, sir. She was a Miss Verity Glyn.'

'Verity Glyn,' repeated Johnny thoughtfully. 'I've seen that name some place.' He went over to the pile of newspapers and found a copy of the *Daily Messenger*. Folding back the pages, he turned to a column headed: "Feminine Fancies", and there at the foot of the column was the name he sought.

Johnny chuckled.

'I've been in some queer places in my time, Winwood, but I've never been in a heart-throb column before. Well, I guess it's all experience, as the chorus girl said when she stepped into the crinoline.'

'Quite so, sir. And if Miss Glyn calls again, am I to tell her to—' He was interrupted by the peal of the front door bell.

'That's probably Inspector Kennard,' said Johnny, as Winwood went off to open the door. 'Better show him in here, Winwood.'

Johnny wandered back to the french windows. The morning sunshine was very tempting. He stepped out and stretched himself, yawned mightily, felt for the inevitable package of cigarettes in his jacket pocket, and was about to extract one when he was distracted by the sound of raised voices inside the house. Winwood seemed to be expostulating with a girl who was displaying some signs of persistence.

'I'm sorry, madam,' he heard the butler say. 'But Mr Washington is expecting someone else.' Johnny could not catch the girl's reply, but Winwood went on: 'I'll ask Mr Washington, but he's very busy . . .'

The door opened and Winwood came into the room and crossed to where Johnny was standing by the window.

'It's the young lady I mentioned just now, sir,' he said in a low voice. 'Shall I tell her to wait until after the inspector has gone?'

Johnny frowned thoughtfully for a moment, then said

quickly: 'No, I'll see what it is she wants right now. All right, Winwood, let her in.'

A voice from the doorway called out:

'Don't bother—I'm in already.'

For some seconds Johnny stood and appraised her from her trim chestnut curls down to her slim nylon-clad ankles.

'Well, well,' he murmured at last, 'I guess you're one of those girls who knows her way around.'

She smiled as if she really meant it and moved forward a couple of paces with an elegance he could not fail to note.

'I'm sorry,' she said frankly, 'but it really is terribly important.'

'If you're going to tell me the old one about being flung out on to the hard pavements of Fleet Street unless you go back with a story, skip it!' advised Johnny. 'I used that one myself when I was a cub reporter first year out of college.'

'You've given up reporting?' she asked.

'I guess I was flung out one day when I didn't go back with a story,' he admitted with a rueful grin. 'But you'd better sit down now you've come all this way.' He dismissed Winwood with a casual nod and indicated an arm-chair for the benefit of his visitor. He opened the silver cigarette box and indicated the English and American brands in their separate sections. He was slightly surprised when she chose the American.

'Well, he's certainly a throwback to the good old days,' she smiled, indicating the departing butler. Johnny snapped his lighter and held the flame to her cigarette.

'Yes, he kinda makes me feel good,' he told her with an understanding nod. 'Worth every cent I pay him.'

She settled back in her arm-chair and puffed out a stream of smoke very deliberately. Johnny admired the dark green dress she was wearing beneath her swagger coat. Not a day over twenty-five, he told himself; a girl who'd be exciting to take around or come home to. He found himself trying to get a glimpse of her left hand, and experienced a slight feeling of relief to note there was no ring on the slim, well-manicured fingers.

'You'll be Miss Verity Glyn?' he inquired politely as he lit another cigarette for himself.

She nodded.

'Well, this is an honour,' went on Johnny in a suave tone. 'Will you be wanting to write a piece about this fine old English manor with its Tudor chimneys and—'

She shook her head decisively.

'No, Mr Washington, I've come to see you about something much more serious than that. I shouldn't be here at all really; I should be at the office. I'm very conscientious about my job, so you can guess I wouldn't come running down here without a very good reason.'

'Then your visit has nothing to do with the *Daily Messenger*?'

'Not a thing. I'm afraid I rather misled your butler—I used the paper's name because I was so anxious to see you. I'm sorry if it upset you in any way.'

'Think nothing of it,' said Johnny with a lazy gesture. 'There's nothing I like better than being kept out of the *Daily Messenger*!'

She threw her head back against the chair and laughed. It was an infectious little laugh. But she became serious again almost immediately.

'Well, I'm rather busy this morning,' Johnny told her. 'I had some thought of going fishing. I suppose that's a bit outside your sort of column, Miss Glyn, though I shall be glad to show you—'

'Mr Washington,' she interrupted in an earnest tone, 'do you think Superintendent Locksley committed suicide?'

Johnny paused in the act of flicking the ash from the end of his cigarette.

'Really, Miss Glyn, that's what your English lawyers call a leading question, isn't it?'

But Verity Glyn was not to be diverted.

'I'm serious about this, Mr Washington.'

He suddenly realized that there were tears in the grey eyes. Even so, he wasn't particularly impressed. Johnny had met far too many women who switched on the tears as easily as they powdered their shapely noses. He particularly recalled a pretty little confidence trickster who 'worked' the trans-Atlantic luxury liners with just such a display of ready emotions which had relieved many a dollar millionaire of a nice little bunch of travellers' cheques.

For all Johnny knew, the very personable young lady who sat opposite might be a tool of the gelignite gang, sent to pry into his affairs or plant some new evidence against him. For all he knew, she wasn't even Verity Glyn. She might have simply picked on that name and called herself a newspaper woman . . .

The girl seemed to guess what was passing through his mind, for she suddenly opened her bag, fumbled in it for a moment and passed over a neat red card to him.

In some perplexity he looked at it. The card testified that Miss Verity Glyn of the *Daily Messenger* was a paid-up member of the National Union of Journalists, and requested that she should be afforded full facilities available to members of the press. Still looking somewhat bewildered, Johnny passed back the card.

'I don't get it,' he said. 'Have you turned crime reporter or what?'

Once again, she fumbled in her handbag, and this time produced a postcard photo.

'I have a very strong personal interest in this case,' she said. 'Now, will you look at this . . . then take another look at me.'

He recognized the photo at once; it was one of Superintendent Locksley, taken some fifteen years ago he estimated. Locksley wore an open-necked shirt and a sun-helmet, and the buildings in the background looked rather like a South African farmhouse.

Johnny glanced across at the girl. The resemblance was obvious.

'Gerald Locksley was my brother,' she said simply. 'Now do you believe me?'

With a sigh, Johnny passed back the photo.

'I believe you,' he said slowly.

'Then will you answer my question? Did he really commit suicide?'

Johnny hesitated. At last he said: 'Just between ourselves, I'm not at all satisfied about your brother's death. When he came to see me he was certainly very worried about this gelignite gang, but he certainly wasn't in the desperate sort of mood one associates with suicide.'

'Then it *was* murder!' she exclaimed emotionally. 'I knew they'd get him. I knew it!'

Her hands trembled in nervous excitement as they fingered the clasp of her handbag. She was leaning forward and trying hard to fight back her tears.

'I always warned Gerald . . . but he never took me seriously . . .'

Johnny went over to the sideboard, opened it and took out a decanter of Napoleon brandy, from which he carefully poured about a dessertspoonful into a liqueur glass, which he carried back to her.

'Drink this first; then we'll talk,' he said briefly.

She took several sips and the colour which had drained from her face began to surge back again. Then she set the glass on a small table nearby and said quietly:

'I need your help, Mr Washington, more than anything I've ever needed in my life before.'

Johnny slowly sat down and propped his feet on a footstool.

'Then your real name is Locksley?' he queried.

'That's right. Everybody knows me as Verity Glyn—it's part of the paper's publicity stunt to boost the column—I'm not supposed to give away my real identity.'

'It's a very nice name—Verity Glyn,' decided Johnny, saying it slowly, a syllable at a time.

He lit fresh cigarettes for both of them, then said:

'All right now, tell me what you meant when you said you knew they would get your brother.'

She hesitated a moment, then said: 'It's rather a long story. Will you answer me one question first?'

He nodded encouragingly, and she went on:

'What did my brother come to see you about the night he died?'

Johnny blew out a ring of smoke and thoughtfully watched it rise.

'I shouldn't tell you this,' he said, 'but your brother had reason to believe I might be implicated in one of these gelignite gang jobs. He came down to ask me one or two questions. Unfortunately for the gang, I had rather a good alibi for the night the affair occurred.'

'And he didn't mention any of his theories about this gelignite gang?' she inquired.

'We didn't get very much time. I rushed him off to the Kingfisher for an extra bottle of whisky, and I thought we'd probably have a good talk when we got back.'

'You don't know anything about my brother's earlier experiences abroad?'

'Not very much. He wasn't a particularly talkative character; you know that as well as I do,' he murmured, wondering vaguely when she would come to the point.

'About eight years ago,' she began, 'Gerald was attached to Service B.Y.—a special branch of the Cape Town Constabulary, who were very busy at that time with a series of daring raids—mostly on jewellers and diamond warehouses. My brother and another officer were in charge of the investigation, and it was very tough going. After several months they discovered the leader of the organization was a man who went by the name of Max Fulton.'

'I seem to remember reading about that affair,' nodded Johnny. 'Go on.'

'This man Fulton was a very shrewd customer—well-educated and widely travelled. He knew the underworld in half a dozen countries, and he stopped at nothing. But the police pulled in several members of the gang; one of them told all he knew, and so they found out quite a lot about Max Fulton. But

Fulton had provided for that emergency and when the police made a big round-up of the gang, he managed to escape.'

'That's right,' put in Johnny, 'I seem to remember hearing about him being in Chicago the following year.'

'Not long after he had fooled the police,' continued the girl, 'the officer who had been working with my brother on the case was murdered. It wasn't a very pleasant murder. Almost immediately after that, there were two attempts on my brother's life.'

Johnny whistled softly. There was a strained look in her eyes as she recalled those distressing days with an obvious reluctance. 'I suppose there was no evidence against Fulton?' he queried.

'Not a trace. The police officer's body was found by a farmer lying in a roadside ditch. He had been terribly beaten up by someone who had apparently kidnapped him and dumped him out in the country.'

'Looks to me as if this Fulton guy's got a nasty kink in his imagination somewhere,' mused Johnny. 'What about the attacks on your brother?'

'They might have been accidents. I don't think he was taking any chances with Gerald, because the police were very much on his tail by that time. He tried to get Gerald just outside Cape Town one day—a large saloon car swerved and Gerald only just leapt clear in time. He couldn't see the driver—and there was no back number plate. The other time, Gerald was walking along one of the main streets when a large wooden crate weighing about a ton crashed down on the pavement a few feet away. They swore the rope had slipped, and Gerald couldn't prove otherwise, but I can still remember how suspicious he was about the whole business. He was terrified that Fulton would find out that he had a sister. I was living with relatives then, and he made me adopt an assumed name, and when things were very tense he wouldn't even telephone me in case the line was tapped. He knew Fulton would stop at nothing. There was something quite devilish about the man;

it was as if he rejoiced in evil for its own sake as well as for the money it brought him.'

Johnny leaned over and flicked the ash off his cigarette. There was no mistaking this girl's sincerity, but he had a feeling that she might be a little overwrought, which was quite natural, of course, in view of her brother's sudden death.

'You said this Max Fulton got clear from the country just in time?' he murmured quietly.

'Yes. But Gerald had a letter from him soon after, saying that Fulton would get even one day, and ever since he's received threatening letters at irregular intervals. The last was just before this gelignite gang started its activities, and right from the moment Gerald was put on the case he's had a feeling that he was up against Max Fulton. He warned me weeks ago that I must lie low and use the name Verity Glyn on every possible occasion.'

It was Johnny's turn to look worried.

'What made him think it was Max Fulton?' he demanded.

'I don't quite know. Just a sort of hunch he had. Maybe he found something similar between the way the gang worked and the old set-up in Cape Town. Gerald's hunches in that line were usually pretty reliable, and he became more and more certain as time went on. It was he who finally convinced the Scotland Yard chiefs that they really were up against a big organization.'

Johnny reached out and rang a bell at the side of the fireplace, and when Winwood promptly appeared asked him to bring some coffee. As the butler closed the door silently behind him, Johnny said:

'I could kick myself for letting your brother out of my sight that evening. I had a feeling he was going to spill something . . .' He sighed. 'Well, I guess we all make mistakes and pay for 'em. The question is—where do we go from here?'

'Then you do believe me? You believe I'm telling you the truth?' There was a note of relief in her voice.

'I believe you, ma'am,' replied Johnny evenly, 'but I don't know if that helps very much. We've got no proof that Fulton is behind this gang, or that he killed your brother. We don't even know what he looks like. I suppose your brother never met him?'

She shook her head.

'That's just the awful part about it. Max Fulton has always escaped the police records in every country he's visited. Some other poor devil has always taken the rap for his crimes, and the international police haven't even as much as a photograph.' There was a trace of bitterness in her tone. 'Gerald used to tell me that Fulton built up a completely new identity for himself in every country; sometimes he'd spend more than a year doing it before he planned a new coup.'

'Looks like this guy knows the answers even before he hears the questions,' mused Johnny. 'All the same, I wish I knew why he picked on me over that Gloucester job. I've never done him any harm . . . at least, none that I know of.'

'But don't you see,' she urged. 'He probably thinks you're a friend of Gerald's. He may have seen you two together—suspected you were working against him, and decided to get in the first blow.'

Johnny stubbed out his cigarette with a decisive gesture.

'Young lady, this business is gettin' a darn sight too complicated for my liking,' he pronounced. 'I'm a peace-loving guy—oh, I'll admit I've had my hectic moments with the crooks and cops, but right now all I want to do is relaxin' and fishin'. I've kinda got used to this pleasant country routine; it's in my blood now. I don't go for the big-time skulduggery any more.' He paused with a far-away look in his eyes and added: 'Why, if I could happen across a real nice girl I might even think of getting hitched up . . .'

She flung her cigarette end into the fireplace and leaned forward impulsively.

'Mr Washington, you know as well as I do that Gerald was murdered, and you've got to help me.'

He sighed again. There was something very pleasant about the large grey eyes, the quivering lips.

At that moment, Winwood came in with a large pot of fresh coffee, a silver jug of milk and a plate of Johnny's favourite biscuits. Verity Glyn's expression was noticeably less strained now, and she drank her coffee with obvious enjoyment, complimenting her host on its quality. When he had refilled her cup, he suddenly returned to the subject they had been discussing.

'D'you happen to know if your brother had any sort of a dossier on Max Fulton?' he inquired.

She shook her head a trifle dubiously.

'Not to my knowledge. Of course, he knew an awful lot about him, but he'd never put it on paper. The day before he died, he seemed to have some sort of presentiment. He telephoned me at the office and asked me to meet him on the bridge in St James's Park. We sat on a seat nearby and he told me all he knew about Max Fulton.'

Johnny jerked his feet off the footstool and sat bolt upright.

'This is pretty serious,' he exclaimed, 'or it would be if Max Fulton knew about it. It puts you in a very awkward spot—you realize that?'

'That's exactly why I came to see you. Gerald told me to come to you in case of any trouble.'

Johnny looked doubtful.

'You know, honey, I've a feeling I should pass you on to the police and tell them you need protection.'

'I can look after myself,' she insisted sturdily. 'I'm not planning to run into danger unnecessarily. At the same time, I won't rest until the person who killed Gerald pays for it.'

'Looks to me like you're heading for trouble,' observed Johnny with a worried look.

But Verity appeared comparatively cheerful now she was assured of his co-operation, for her brother had described Johnny as 'the dark horse that's always first past the post', and she had implicit faith in his judgment.

In fact, she seemed far happier about the present position than Johnny was himself. He didn't really want to become involved with the gelignite gang, and the prospect of having to keep a watchful eye on a comparatively helpless female to boot wasn't nearly as inviting as the two or three months' fishing which he had planned. All the same, he was upset about Locksley's death, and he would like to help his sister . . .

He toyed with the silver cigarette lighter, and presently asked:

'Did Gerald know any special personal details about Max Fulton? A birthmark, for instance?'

Almost at once she answered:

'He has a small mark, caused apparently by a burn, just above the left elbow; and there's a girl named Sonya who frequently travels around with him.' She paused for a moment, then added in a tone that was rather more tense:

'And he never uses anything but a Luger.'

Johnny Washington clasped the arms of his chair. He could still see the figure of Superintendent Locksley, stretched full length, with a dark stain of blood from the wound in his forehead, and his left hand clutching a dull black Luger revolver.

CHAPTER VI

As Chief Inspector Kennard did not arrive when expected, Johnny decided to stroll over to the Kingfisher Inn before dinner. He knew that Kennard had been busy there and hoped to find him still on the job.

Since the removal of the body of the unfortunate superintendent, the Kingfisher had become famous overnight. Motor-cars, char-a-bancs, cyclists and hikers arrived in multitudes, and Harry Bache had twice telephoned his brewery in Sevenoaks for fresh supplies of beer. Without any exception, the visitors betrayed a similar thirst for the gory details of the discovery of the body, and the landlord's voice had become quite husky as he retold the tale, even though he made frequent pauses for liquid refreshment.

Not many of the visitors paid much attention to the men in somewhat sombre raincoats who sat quietly in a corner of the public rooms, taking stock of the visitors and comparing notes from time to time.

Kennard had drafted in these plain-clothes men, telling them it was unlikely they would be lucky enough to spot the murderer's return to the scene of his crime, but they were nevertheless to keep their eyes open just in case. After seeing them installed, he went off in a police car, presumably to make further contact with the local police. When he returned several hours later they had nothing to report, apart from the shortage of beer, and Kennard went off again, saying that he would look in later.

It was during his absence that Johnny Washington called in at the Kingfisher, to find the saloon bar crammed with a very mixed collection of humanity. Having left a message with Harry

Bache to the effect that he would be home all evening if the inspector wanted to see him, Johnny strolled thoughtfully back to the Manor, pondering upon many things, including that strangely attractive young lady, Verity Glyn. He was a little troubled as to what he was going to do about Miss Glyn; her work took her all over London and also into the provinces, and he couldn't always be there to keep an eye on her.

Indeed, it seemed that Verity Glyn was going to provide an unexpected complication in this affair. At first Johnny had planned to keep out of it; now he didn't see how he could. The only way to dispose of the danger to Verity Glyn was to put paid to the gelignite gang and its leader—supposing that leader to be Max Fulton.

Johnny had another important reason for wishing to steer clear of this case. He couldn't see what he stood to get out of it; hitherto he had consorted with criminals and skated very near the edge of the law himself only when he stood to gain very substantially. He didn't object to taking risks and exercising his ingenuity when he was well paid to do so, but he knew full well that the man on the side of the law rarely reaps any big returns. All the same, he could not forget Verity Glyn . . .

Later that evening, when the Kingfisher Inn had relapsed into its usual state of desolation, the thick black curtains of the club-room were drawn across the windows, and the door was locked from the inside. Three men sat round a shabby card-table examining a large-scale plan of the centre of Brighton.

Doctor Randall, who seemed to be in charge of the proceedings, held a pencil in his pudgy right hand, while he addressed himself mainly to two young men in flashy suits. Harry Bache hovered somewhat uncertainly in the background.

The room, which was lighted by a solitary bulb, smelt of stale tobacco smoke and disinfectant. Apparently, the doctor was more than a trifle conscious of this, for he seemed to be pressing on with the business in hand as if there were no time to be wasted.

'Now, have you got it all clear, Cosh?' he asked the chubby-faced young man in the cheap, flashy suit, who had a grubby hand holding down one corner of the map. 'We don't want any slip-ups on this job, or the Yard will be on us like a shot. How does the set-up look to you, Slim?'

He turned to the taller of the two men, a swarthy individual with piercing black eyes and a thin, cruel mouth.

'I reckon it wouldn't do any harm to go over it again,' he rasped, relighting the cigarette that hung from his lower lip.

With an impatient sigh, the doctor returned to the map.

'Shelagh will be parked here, just round the corner from West Street. All you have to do, Cosh, is get the stuff out to her as fast as you can—hand it over and then go back and mix with the crowd. Whatever you do, keep with the crowd until the police move them on. That's very important.'

Cosh nodded understandingly. 'I looked the joint over this morning,' he said casually. 'Reckon I ought to be out in five or six minutes.'

'Then that's all right,' said Doctor Randall. 'Now, let's go over your piece, Slim. This is the first time we've done a daylight job, and the chief's a bit fussy about it all going off to schedule. In fact, it's got to look as if it wasn't our job at all; that's one of the main reasons for this new layout. It's all got to be spot on and through like clockwork, and then there'll be no come-back.'

Slim Copley signified his attention by the merest shrug of the shoulders. Since the war, Slim had never been able to settle down to normal civilian life. On leaving the army, he had, amongst other things, ridden a motor-cycle in the familiar 'Wall of Death' attraction with travelling fairs, then had moved on to work for an organization of stunt men, who doubled for film stars in the hair-raising sequences of productions which involved high risks to life and limb. But he grew tired of earning his money by law-abiding methods and linked up with one of the South London gangs, very soon acquiring a reputation for bringing off daredevil coups.

He placed a lean forefinger on the map.

'That's where she parks the car?'

'That's correct, Slim. You see the jewellers' and the gown shop the moment you come charging round the bend—at three-forty on the dot. There'll be a good crowd in the street then. Now, the chief is most particular that you shouldn't take any extra risks—we don't want a manslaughter rap pinned on to us. Got that?'

'Sure,' he replied indifferently, as if this sort of job was really beneath his consideration. 'Maybe I'll have to run some of the mugs down though—he wouldn't want me to let up just because some damn silly woman leaves a pram or something—'

'No, no,' put in the doctor hastily. 'You keep the horn going and they'll clear; then we want a real job made of that dress shop window. The glass is almost down to the ground, so you shouldn't have much trouble. And as much noise as you like.'

'Don't worry,' growled Slim. 'I'll wake up half the blasted town.' He dropped his cigarette end on the floor and twisted his shoe over it. 'I handed over the doings for the lorry last night; it's all fixed. We can have it any time, and enough juice to take us down there.'

'Then that's all settled,' said the doctor in a relieved tone.

'Thank Gawd I ain't drivin' that lorry,' said Harry Bache.

Slim laughed. 'It's a cakewalk,' he sniffed.

'As long as it looks a genuine job, the chief will be satisfied,' said Randall.

'It'll be so genuine, you can claim the insurance,' Slim told him.

Cosh fidgeted uneasily.

'There's just one thing, Doc. Do I have to wait till I hear the smash before I get busy?'

Randall shook his head.

'The chief says get going right away. You won't have any time to play with, but it shouldn't take any longer than the

Gloucester job. Once you're inside, you can work to the usual routine.'

'I'll be out of the place in no time,' grinned Cosh. 'Have you got a list of the stuff?'

'I'm expecting Shelagh with it.' The doctor glanced at his wrist-watch. 'She should be here any minute. The chief got the full list of stuff this morning . . .'

There was silence for a few seconds, then Harry Bache licked his lips and said rather nervously in a hoarse whisper:

'You mean Grey Moose?'

The doctor inclined his head.

'Who is this bloke who calls himself Grey Moose?' persisted Slim. 'He's been around over three months now, and we're no wiser. I reckon we got a right to know the feller we're working for. How do we know he won't double-cross us?'

Cosh contradicted him with an expressive gesture.

'I don't worry who the cove is,' he announced. 'He's cut me in over three thousand quid since I been in this racket, and when I get that sort of money I don't bother to ask questions.'

'I'm not grumblin',' nodded Slim, perching on the back of a chair. 'I'm just sort of curious. You see, I'm used to knowin' the bloke I work for. There's never been any harm in it yet.' His tone had become slightly more aggressive, and Doctor Randall hastened to pacify him.

'Don't blame me, Slim—it's all part of the chief's idea. When we've made our last big clean-up, he'll let us all in on everything. Up till then, he doesn't want to take a chance on anybody recognizing him at the wrong moment.'

Slim muttered something under his breath; he was obviously by no means completely satisfied. But Cosh distracted his attention by asking further questions about the Brighton job.

'What happens after Shelagh gets away with the stuff?'

'She brings it back to my place here; then I take it to the airfield. It'll be in Amsterdam by Saturday.'

'And when will the payout be?' inquired Slim.

'One day next week, I should imagine.'

'Any idea how much the stuff will be worth?' asked Cosh.

'I'm not sure,' replied the doctor. 'They carry a heavy stock at Dollands. We know there's a ring worth six thousand pounds, and two sets of pearl ear-rings that run pretty high. I dare say Shelagh might know more about it. But the chief told me that they carry insurance for close on fifty thousand pounds.'

Cosh whistled softly.

'It's a blinkin' marvel how he finds out these things.'

'Ah, he has his own ways of doing it,' said Randall in a tone of mingled satisfaction and mysteriousness. 'He's got sources of information that would startle Scotland Yard if they knew.'

The doctor began to fold up the map very deliberately, and all the others lighted cigarettes. They were discussing the Brighton job in low tones when there came two distinct raps from behind the wall near the cupboard.

'That'll be Shelagh,' nodded the doctor, and went over to open the tall cupboard door. There was a sound of a sliding panel, and a moment later Shelagh stepped from behind a grey robe which concealed the hidden panel. She was wearing a long evening cloak, on which there were some traces of dust and cobwebs.

Harry Bache went to close the panel, but Shelagh stopped him.

'Leave it,' she said quietly. 'The chief will be along in a few minutes.'

The announcement caused something of a sensation. The men looked at each other with some uncertainty; then the doctor asked:

'The chief's coming here?'

'Yes, I had a telephone message just before I left.'

'But I thought he said—'

'He's changed his mind,' interrupted Shelagh. 'He's decided that this job is so important that he's got to talk it over with us himself. Also, he's got the money from the Gloucester job; it came through this morning.'

'Blimey! That's quick work!' exclaimed Slim, who had now lost all trace of indifference. 'I reckon there ought to be a nice packet for all of us . . .'

'There will be,' promised the girl, placing several chairs in position around the table. She turned to Harry Bache. 'Will you get a gin and vermouth for the chief? The same for me . . .'

The others murmured their orders and Harry Bache went off into the bar to fulfil them.

'The chief's takin' a bit of a risk comin' down 'ere so soon after that Locksley job,' murmured Cosh. 'The village is full of plain-clothes men.'

Shelagh smiled. 'Don't you worry about the chief,' she advised. 'He can take care of all Scotland Yard if he puts his mind to it. But remember, everybody—if anybody talks about this job or squeaks about the chief, he'll get 'em just as sure as he got the others.'

Harry Bache returned with the drinks just in time to catch the last sentence, but nobody made any comment upon Shelagh's threat, except Cosh.

'It's all right, Shelagh,' said Cosh reassuringly. 'We know when we're well off. As long as the chief plays it on the level with us, we're sticking to him.'

'You can rely on the chief,' she insisted, opening the small evening bag she carried and taking out two sheets of mauve notepaper. She passed the notepaper over to the doctor, who looked through them carefully, then handed them on to Cosh.

'That's the Brighton stuff,' he explained.

Cosh took the paper and studied the typewritten list of valuables, each with a price against it. Harry Bache put down the tray of glasses and joined Slim, who was peering over Cosh's shoulder.

'They must be mugs to keep all this stuff about the place,'

breathed the landlord, frowning at the list. 'It must amount to thousands . . .'

'We've seen to it that they've got the stuff,' Shelagh blandly informed him. 'Just lately, they've been getting a lot of inquiries which meant bringing down some of the best stuff in London.'

'You see?' queried Randall with some satisfaction. 'The chief takes care of everything.'

Cosh refolded the notepaper carefully and tucked it away in his inside coat pocket.

'This is going to be some job,' he declared with a hoarse chuckle. He picked up his glass of beer and called out: 'Here's to us and the Brighton job!'

The others had also taken their glasses and were about to drink when there was a sound outside the door.

'Who's that?' asked Slim in some alarm.

'It's all right,' breathed Harry. 'I locked it when I came in.'

'If it's one of those damned detectives . . .' whispered Cosh, taking a pace forward.

The doctor pushed him aside.

'I'll handle this,' he snapped, his hand going to his coat pocket. But Shelagh interposed.

'Don't be damned fools. Get out of sight through that panel. Leave this to Harry and me.'

The door rattled.

'All right, Harry,' nodded the girl. 'Open up—and if it's a stranger tell him he's made a mistake . . .'

With some hesitation, the landlord went to the door and turned the key. He opened the door about a foot, and said in an uncertain voice:

'I'm sorry, there must be some—'

But Shelagh's rippling laugh interrupted him. 'It's all right, Harry. This is the chief!'

She turned to the men inside the room and called out:

'It's all right, you can come out.'

They came from their hiding place and saw the silent figure standing in the doorway.

'I thought you said the chief was—' began Slim to be interrupted by Cosh's exclamation:

'This ain't the chief—it can't be Grey Moose!'

Doctor Randall smiled.

'I warned you fellows,' he said. 'I warned you.'

CHAPTER VII

A CALL FROM SCOTLAND YARD

On Saturday morning, at the end of an eventful week, Verity Glyn sat in her plainly furnished office at Fleet Street House ruefully contemplating a pile of letters. She did not always come to the office on Saturday, for her secretary had the day off. But there had been a rush of correspondence during the past two or three days following a question she had raised in her column, and she began to sort out the letters that could be easily answered, placing the others in a little pile to themselves.

She was busily making pencil notes on the letters for the benefit of her secretary when her telephone rang and a familiar voice said:

'Miss Glyn—remember me?'

Her face lit up as she tried to speak in a level tone.

'Of course, Mr Washington. I was wondering if you'd phone.'

'You're pretty busy, I guess?'

'Pretty busy.'

'No time to help cement the ties of Anglo-American relations?'

'It rather depends what that involves.' There was a flicker of amusement around her mobile mouth.

'I thought maybe we could have lunch some place,' he suggested. 'It'd do you good to get away from the grindstone.'

She considered this for a moment, then said: 'Where d'you think?'

'If it's all the same to you,' he replied after a moment's hesitation, 'I'd like to make it Sevenoaks. I have special reasons for wanting to stick around these parts for a day or two, and there are some things I want to talk to you about. Can you make it?'

'I could be down there about one-thirty, if that suits you.'

'That'll be fine. There's an hotel just along from the Post Office called the Star and Garter. You can't miss it. I'll be waiting in the lounge. Sure you can make it O.K.?'

'I'll be there,' she promised, pushing the stack of letters into a folder with one hand as she replaced the receiver with the other.

Verity knew that the art of getting into the depths of Kent with maximum speed and minimum wear and tear on nerves lay in choosing a route which avoided the London tram-lines as far as possible, and half an hour later she was following her own favourite course through the leafy roads of Dulwich. It was a sunny day, with a cool breeze stirring the treetops, and there were signs of activity on many of the sports fields she passed as the groundsmen made their preparations for the afternoon.

She reached the Star and Garter with just over five minutes to spare, and ran her car into the car park at the back of the hotel.

In the lounge, Johnny was talking to an elderly farmer, whom he deserted as she came through the door.

'Right on time,' he murmured approvingly. 'I guess you're just about the first punctual woman I ever met. I was expecting to wait another half-hour at the very least. We ought to have a drink to celebrate.'

They sat in a corner of the lounge and sipped their drinks.

'What happened about those damp patches on the floor of the club-room?' she was anxious to know. 'You said you were going to mention them to Inspector Kennard.'

Johnny shook his head.

'Afraid there was nothing much in that,' he told her. 'Kennard said he'd had the experts look at the patches but they couldn't find any traces of blood. If there had been any blood there, someone had cleaned it up pretty thoroughly.'

Verity sighed.

'We seem to come up against a dead end whichever way we turn. But I still think that Gerald was murdered.'

He rose and took her empty glass.

'Come in to lunch,' he suggested. 'We'll feel more like coping with life's little problems after a good meal.'

They went into the long oak-panelled dining-room, with its low beams, glistening cutlery and bleached tablecloths. True, there was no deferential head waiter, but the young lady who deputized filled the breach very competently, and brought them a meal that was obviously home-produced and cooked to perfection. The soup was innocent of any contact with tin; the chicken had not ranged its run for a day over ten months; the vegetables might have been picked from the garden an hour previously, and the tart was smothered with rich blackcurrant jam that had never been inside a factory.

Johnny seemed determined not to discuss their present problems over lunch. He asked her a number of questions about her job, her experiences as a young reporter on a suburban paper in Cape Town; he discussed the shows that were on in Town, with passing reference to Miss Candy Dimmott, which somehow made Verity feel vaguely uncomfortable. He even launched upon a long story as to how he had persuaded a notorious woman confidence trickster to pay several thousand pounds for a necklace that was practically worthless under the impression that she would more than double the price of it.

'You seem to meet some very peculiar people,' she observed, as they sat drinking their coffee.

'Yes, I'm not what you'd call a highly respectable guy, I'm afraid,' he sighed. Verity laughed.

'If you were highly respectable, you'd probably be running a canning factory in Chicago.'

'And then I'd never have had the pleasure of meeting you. I guess I like things the way they are.'

They went on to talk about the differences between the American and English viewpoints, the ending of Marshall Aid, the strange anomalies of the film industry, the short-comings of UNO, the privileged position of the Arts Council, and the colour bar in the tropical countries. Anything, in fact, but the activities of a certain Max Fulton. Johnny seemed strangely reluctant to discuss the sordid realities of crime with his guest, who in her turn appeared quite content to let the conversation drift pleasantly and await his leisure before turning to sterner topics.

After lunch, at his suggestion, they took a short stroll through the ancient main thoroughfare as far as the entrance to Knoll Park, pausing occasionally to peer into antique shops or examine an inscription on a tombstone in the churchyard.

When they got back to the hotel, it was decided that, to save Verity's petrol, they should go on to Caldicott Manor in Johnny's car, and that he should bring her back to the hotel in the late afternoon. He drove in leisurely fashion through the winding Kent lanes which wound over the wooded hill-sides and down into the spacious valleys. It was after three o'clock before they had settled themselves in the familiar drawing-room, where the afternoon sun was streaming in through a smaller window beside the fireplace.

Verity sat by the open french window and looked across the smooth lawns to the orchards beyond. A solitary blackbird perched on the low wall that enclosed the little courtyard and gazed at her curiously.

'I asked you to come down here, Verity—by the way, is it O.K. to call you Verity?'

'Of course. What were you saying?'

'I was going to say that I wanted to see you because I've been thinking pretty hard about what you said about your brother—'

'And about Max Fulton?'

'That's right. Especially about Max Fulton. I reckon if he really is this fellow Grey Moose who's behind these big robberies, then you ought to tell Sir Robert Hargreaves all about it.'

'He'd never believe me,' she interrupted.

'Don't be too sure about that. Sir Robert's listened to a heck of a lot of stories in his day, and he only got to his present job by being able to sort out the truth more than once in a while. He's no fool.'

'But they don't even believe Gerald was murdered,' she declared impulsively. 'You heard the statements at the inquest. And when I talked to Inspector Kennard afterwards he obviously seemed to think I had a bee in my bonnet.'

Johnny lazily reached out for an ash-tray.

'Supposing,' he said quietly, 'that I have a certain amount of proof—enough to satisfy me at any rate—that your brother was murdered?'

'You mean you can prove it to them?'

He hesitated. 'It's a small point,' he said at length. 'But it seems to me pretty convincing.'

'Well?'

'Why should your brother want change for a pound when he'd charged the drinks to me and had over eight shillings in loose change in his trouser pocket?'

Verity's smooth forehead furrowed in thought.

'And there's just one more point,' said Johnny, 'that calls for a little clearing up.'

'What's that?'

'Your brother was holding that gun in his left hand.'

'That's true,' she agreed, looking puzzled. 'But Gerald was left-handed.'

'Of course, he was.'

'I don't see what you're getting at.'

'I'm trying to tell you, Verity, that your brother was murdered by someone with a little too much imagination, and not quite enough intelligence. You didn't identify the body, but I can tell you that your brother never inflicted that wound on himself; it was physically impossible.'

She rose to her feet in some agitation.

'Why are you telling me this, Johnny? If my brother was murdered, why do the police think it was suicide?'

'Hold your horses, honey,' said Johnny quietly. 'Maybe the police ain't so sure about that suicide after all.'

'But it's been in all the newspapers, and even at the inquest they never even asked for an adjournment.'

'All the same, I've got a hunch they aren't satisfied.'

'Then why don't they *do* something?'

Johnny shrugged.

'I guess they've got their own ways of working,' he hazarded. 'Maybe they're not the F.B.I.'s ways, but you've got some mighty peculiar laws in this country that are liable to trip up anybody, including the police, if they don't keep to strict procedure. I dare say they've a pretty good reason for holding off a murder charge just yet awhile—there's a chance they may be waiting to get two birds with one stone. It doesn't always pay to call the bluff too soon when you're dealing with some of these crooked characters. They're liable to hop a plane and vanish.'

'Yes,' she mused quietly, almost to herself. 'Max Fulton has done that before today.'

The door opened to admit Winwood carrying a heavily loaded tea tray. They noticed it was after five o'clock.

'On the table by the window,' said Johnny.

The butler set down the tray and quietly withdrew.

Johnny eyed the tea-tray somewhat quizzically and said to his visitor:

'I can't get used to this afternoon tea set-up. Maybe you wouldn't mind . . .'

'Of course,' smiled Verity, taking up the milk jug, and pulling the cups and saucers towards her. 'How d'you like it?'

'I guess it's all much the same to me. Pretty strong and fairly sweet. I tried suggesting to Winwood that he should give me coffee, but I thought he'd pass through the floor.'

Verity laughed and dropped two lumps of sugar into his cup. 'You'll get used to our quaint old English customs in time,' she assured him.

Johnny sipped his tea and pulled a face.

'By the way, did you notice that quaint old customer at the inquest?' he asked.

'You mean the little old man who was staying at the Kingfisher—what was his name?'

'Horatio Quince. He's a sort of antiquarian, specializing in old inns, but dabbling in anything ancient that he happens to come across. Quite a character.'

'You don't think he had any connection—?' she hesitated.

'He could have, I suppose. He was the only other person in the place except Bache and his wife, as far as we know.'

'I've a feeling we don't know everything by a long way,' she said grimly. He passed her a plate of home-made scones, then said quietly:

'I noticed something about the Kingfisher that rang a bell somewhere. In fact, it was old Quince who indirectly drew my attention to it. Try another of those scones . . .'

He passed the jam, helped himself to another scone, then went on thoughtfully:

'If you read the reports of the robberies at Preston and Gloucester that gelignite gang pulled off, there was a man killed each time. And before they died, each man whispered the words "Grey Moose". Your brother had been telling me about it that night he came to see me . . .'

'Yes, I know about Grey Moose,' interposed the girl. 'Gerald said he was quite sure Max Fulton was using that name over here. Of recent years he has taken to using names like that—in Canada he was known as The Spider; in Brazil they called him Black Visor. Gerald always used to say he liked those fancy names because he was very vain, and it made him sound daredevil and romantic. It also helped him to command a certain amount of respect among his supporters; some of them never knew his real name, so they couldn't give him away if the police questioned them.'

'The more I hear of that customer,' mused Johnny, 'the less I like him.'

'He's a danger to any civilized community,' said the girl, and the note of bitterness in her voice was more pronounced than it had been. Then she suddenly became conscious of her duties and asked if he would like some more tea.

'No, sir!' exclaimed Johnny piously, reaching for a cigarette, then replacing it in the box when he noticed that his guest had not finished.

'About this Grey Moose I was telling you . . .' he went on. 'Over at the Kingfisher they hold a weekly meeting of the Antediluvian Order of Bison in a special club-room.'

'There's nothing very unusual about that,' commented Verity. 'Most of these pubs are headquarters for Buffs or Foresters or some queer society.'

'Hold your horses, honey,' begged Johnny. 'The point about this set-up is that it's called the Grey Moose Lodge. Now, does that strike a chord?'

'Grey Moose Lodge . . .' she repeated, her eyes widening the merest fraction. 'You think they might be meeting under the cloak of these Bison or whatever they call themselves?'

'Stranger things have happened,' said Johnny. 'Looks to me as if it would be a pretty good cover.'

'Couldn't Scotland Yard keep the inn under observation?'

'Surely. The place is swarming with plain-clothes men. Inspector Dovey's hovering around too—Kennard has handed over to him.'

'Inspector Dovey? Oh, yes, he was working on the case with Gerald. Is he a friend of yours?'

'Not so's you'd notice it,' grinned Johnny. 'We've had one or two friendly arguments in the past. Still, I got a soft spot for Charles Montague Dovey. He's unorthodox—we've got that in common. Maybe if he hadn't been quite so rude to his superiors, he'd have been a really big shot.'

'Did you go inside this club-room?' she inquired, a note of eagerness in her tone.

'Oh, yes, I made Harry Bache unlock it. He didn't seem very

pleased. But we didn't find anything in there, except the coat of arms, or whatever they call it, and some chairs and one or two small tables. And a lot of robes and chains and things in a large cupboard. It didn't get us very far, but I still have a hunch that . . .'

Johnny broke off as the telephone rang in the hall outside, and excusing himself he went out to answer it. When he returned there was a fresh glint in his eyes.

'I'll be coming back to Town with you,' he announced. 'That was the assistant commissioner. He says he particularly wants to see me.'

She replaced her cup and saucer on the tray and said with some deliberation:

'Johnny, does this mean you're really going to work with the police?'

He shrugged.

'Maybe—maybe not. I guess we'll both be pulling in the same direction. Whether we use the same tactics is anybody's guess.'

'Was that the assistant commissioner himself on the phone?'

'It was.'

'He must have been very persuasive.'

'Not particularly. He just gave me a bit of news.' He paused for a moment, then added in a casual tone:

'There's been a big robbery at Brighton, and it seems they've left another card around with my name on it.'

'Another robbery?' she exclaimed anxiously. 'Johnny, what does this mean?'

'It means,' replied Johnny Washington emphatically, 'that this affair is getting beyond a joke!'

CHAPTER VIII

LONDON BY THE SEA

THOSE pioneers who exploited the health-giving effects of sea-bathing on Brighton's placid beaches would, no doubt, have been a trifle startled to see the fungus urban growth that resulted, and the endless surge of traffic that snaked its way towards the town every Saturday afternoon.

Brighton's early-closing habits are somewhat erratic. A section of the shops close on Wednesdays for their weekly half-holiday, others on Thursdays and some on Saturdays. Dollands was a large Jewish family business that had always closed on Saturdays, and Grey Moose had selected it partly for this reason. It was also in a suitable position for his purpose, for it stood in the lower half of West Street below the ornate clock tower, and about half-way down a fairly steep incline.

Leaving herself plenty of time to spare, Shelagh Hamilton insinuated the long bonnet of her sports Harman-Grade into the stream of Brighton-bound traffic just beyond Purley, and swept along the trunk road at a steady forty miles an hour.

As she was well ahead of time, she turned off the main road just outside the town, and was presently meandering through the well-kept Regency squares in Hove. But she paid little attention to that dignified architecture; her brain was busy with the details of the adventure ahead. It seemed fool-proof, whichever way she looked at it. Every item had been checked and double-checked; everybody concerned knew exactly what he had to do.

They had all gone to Brighton by different routes at various times, so there could be very little risk of their being seen

75

together. Moreover, the odds were that the local police would be scattered and very busily occupied with the traffic on a Saturday afternoon.

Shelagh steered the car on to the smooth tarmac of the promenade and sniffed the tang of the salt air appreciatively. She was feeling beautifully keyed-up now, ready for any emergency. The six cylinders of the sports car purred with a suggestion of the eighty miles an hour they could produce in a matter of seconds.

Presently, she turned left into the town, and the clock at the cross-roads pointed to exactly twenty-five minutes to three as she slid to the side of the rose-tinted pavement just round the corner of North Street and throttled down the powerful engine until it was barely audible. This done, she sat back, and took a cigarette from her small handbag. There was not the slightest trace of emotion in her smooth immobile features. Even when the bulky form of a policeman stopped beside the car, she showed no sign of alarm.

The constable cleared his throat and said a little gruffly, 'Sorry, miss, you can't park here.'

Shelagh switched on her most seductive smile. He was a very young policeman.

'It's all right, officer, I'm only waiting for a friend inside the shop,' she pleaded, indicating a men's outfitting establishment.

But P.C. Talbot was not shaken off as easily as that; he had strict instructions about parking cars in the main streets. Some of these weekend trippers thought nothing of drawing into the kerb for half an hour while the family went off for a bathe. Of course, this exquisite young blonde was obviously no weekend tripper, but the sergeant invariably saw these things in rather a different light.

'There's a parking place just across the square, miss,' he said persuasively.

'But my friend promised he wouldn't be more than two minutes, and if I go off to a car park he won't have the least idea where I am.' Her eyes seemed large and luminous and eloquent in their appeal. P.C. Talbot hesitated.

'It won't have to be for more than a couple of minutes then, miss,' he stipulated. 'You wouldn't believe the trouble we have with this lot on a Saturday.' With an expressive nod he indicated the crowds of holiday-makers surging down towards the parade.

'I'm sure I don't know how you manage to cope with them,' said Shelagh admiringly in her most melting tones. 'I was only telling my friend this morning that the police of this country are dreadfully underpaid for the work they do and all the risks they have to take.'

She smiled at him a trifle wistfully, and P.C. Talbot for a moment felt that a policeman's lot was not entirely an unhappy one.

'Oh, it's not as bad as all that, miss,' he said with a depre-cating grin. 'Mind, I'm not saying we couldn't do with another pound or two . . .'

He broke off suddenly and straightened himself as there were unmistakable sounds of confusion coming from the upper part of West Street. In the distance and growing rapidly louder, was the strident blast of a motor horn. People were scattering in all directions to the safety of doorways and shop entries. A young woman pushing a perambulator screamed and rushed off down North Street with a scurry of flying heels.

The constable moved towards the cross-roads, but before he had gone many yards the lorry came into sight, swaying drunkenly at a speed far beyond the regulation twenty miles an hour. It was an old-fashioned five-tonner, which still had some traces of green paint on its body. To a casual observer, it seemed obvious that the brakes had failed and the vehicle was completely out of the driver's control.

Talbot caught his breath as the lorry seemed almost certain to rush full tilt into the clock tower, but the driver somehow contrived to send it skidding past and with yet another violent lurch it came jolting over the incline into the lower part of the street which was fairly free from traffic, though a small stream of cars had just that moment turned in from the promenade.

It seemed that the sight of these oncoming cars urged the lorry driver to a sudden decision, and he turned his front wheels into the kerb as if to check the vehicle. But the wheels mounted the pavement and with a deafening clatter the bonnet crashed straight through the plate glass window of the gown shop next door to Dollands, the jewellers. The driver was seen to shield his face with his elbow as splinters of wood and glass flew in all directions. Torn dresses and dainty underwear were draped grotesquely over the bonnet of the lorry, and two particularly elegant wax models were tilted tipsily against the driver's cabin.

An elderly lady, who looked like the proprietress, and an assistant, cowered helplessly behind the partition which divided the shop from a small office. They clung to each other, speechless from shock.

Now the pedestrians began running from the openings and shop entrances where they had taken cover—luckily there had been no one near the dress shop—and they surged round the scene of the accident, ignoring P.C. Talbot's well-meaning attempts to clear the pavement. Someone rushed off to telephone for an ambulance, and above the din of the motor horn another man was heard to shout something about the driver.

'Out of the way there! Out of my way!' called P.C. Talbot for the tenth time, as he elbowed his way through the crowd. But most of the spectators stood their ground with the morbid expectation of some grisly spectacle which seems to grip so many onlookers.

This time, however, they were to be disappointed. Indeed, the least perturbed person present was the driver who slowly forced open the door of his cab, and clambered down quite unhurt. The constable yelled something at him, but he did not seem to hear. Standing amongst the shambles of torn dresses he reached into his cabin for a screwdriver, then with the policeman's help managed to lift the bonnet, and after a minute or two the din from the horn abruptly ceased. It was replaced by the clang of a burglar alarm.

'It was the brakes, constable—I only got the lorry yesterday, and they told me they were all in order—the swine!' Slim was complaining. He broke off for a second, knowing only too well what was the cause of the bell. He tried to divert the constable's attention.

'I must have bashed through the wires of the burglar alarm,' he said quickly, and the officer nodded. He went over to the women in the office and called out above the din:

'You all right?'

The older woman nodded a trifle dubiously, and Talbot cupped his hands and shouted:

'Can't you switch off that bell?'

The woman shook her head tearfully, disclaiming all know-ledge of the source of the commotion. In another second, the constable would have realized that the noise came from next door, but at that moment the ambulance came rushing up with yet another bell reverberating heavily, and bringing an extra fifty or sixty spectators rushing behind it. By this time, the crowd had swelled right into the roadway and was seriously threatening to hold up the traffic. Two more policemen arrived on the scene and began to push back the people, while Talbot assured the ambulance men that their services were not required after all.

Slim Copley leaned against the lorry, looking somewhat dazed, while Talbot started to take down some details in his notebook. He purposely hesitated in answering the questions, hedged now and then, and then talked much more than was necessary.

By now, the other two policemen had realized that it was the jeweller's alarm bell that was ringing, but they did not attach any serious importance to it. They readily accepted the theory that the terrific jolt to the adjacent premises was entirely respon-sible. One of them went to telephone the private house of one of the partners while the other climbed up and muffled the clapper of the bell with a large handkerchief.

The clock in the tower pointed to three forty-five as Cosh emerged from a side alley in North Street and handed Shelagh a small cheap brown attaché case.

'Everything O.K?' she asked.

'It was a hell of a crash,' he whispered, looking round furtively. 'I hope Slim was all right.'

'Don't worry about that,' she advised, stowing the case away under the front seat. 'You get off back there as quickly as you can.' He nodded and slammed the car door. There was hardly anyone in sight as Shelagh slammed the gears and the car roared off.

Cosh watched the car until it was out of sight, then turned and made for the crowd which was still surging round the dress shop. He displayed such enthusiasm for his new role of curious onlooker that P.C. Talbot singled him out almost at once, and thrust a retaining elbow across his chest.

'Here you, take it easy! It's folk like you who make all the trouble!' declared P.C. Talbot with unconscious irony.

CHAPTER IX

THE fact that they each possessed a car was introducing a chain of complications into the lives of Verity Glyn and Johnny Washington, in that they desired nothing so much as to travel in the same car together.

On the evening of the Brighton robbery, they were anxious to return to London in such intimate fashion, but it was only after a considerable amount of discussion that they finally evolved a plan. Johnny was to take them to Sevenoaks in his car, which he would park at the hotel. From there, they would travel to Town in Verity's, and he would spend the night at the St Regis, as it looked like being a late session at the Yard.

She invited him to lunch at her flat the following day, conscious that it was high time she returned some of his elaborate hospitality, and she had already telephoned her housekeeper, Mrs Todd, to warn her that there would be company to lunch. They hadn't quite decided how Johnny would get back to Sevenoaks, but he assured her that there was an excellent train service, and hundreds of hire cars available in the event of emergency.

They started almost at once, and as they slowed down to emerge from the gates of the manor into the main road, a shining Harman-Grade sports car swept past, and the girl at the wheel raised an indolent hand in greeting.

'Friend of yours?' inquired Verity, hoping her voice sounded more indifferent than she felt.

'Sort of,' grinned Johnny. 'More of a neighbour really. She's the niece of the doctor who lives along the way. I fish in their pond once in a while.'

'She's a very attractive girl,' persisted Verity.

'I guess so,' replied Johnny indifferently.

'Don't you agree?'

'I operated too long in night-club circles maybe . . . anyhow I seem to be kind of allergic to blondes nowadays. They don't remind me of zephyrs in the cornfield any more.'

She laughed, then looked thoughtful.

'I'm sure I've seen that girl before somewhere,' she murmured, as they came into the outskirts of Sevenoaks. 'I wish I could think where.'

'Probably at some dress show—or maybe a party,' he suggested. 'I dare say you get around quite a bit in that job of yours. You must tell me more about it some time. I'm such a lazy so-and-so, I enjoy hearing how people work for a living.'

She looked at him for a moment, then said with a slow smile: 'You don't fool me, Mr Washington.'

'Honey, I'd be scared even to try,' he solemnly assured her, as he manœuvred the car towards the hotel garage.

With Verity driving her own car they were heading for Town five minutes later, and as there was comparatively little traffic until they approached the more thickly populated South London area, they did the journey in remarkably good time.

'Where would you like me to drop you?' she asked, as they crossed Lambeth Bridge.

'But you're not shaking me off just like that,' he protested. 'I guess I'll be needing you as an alibi; you're about the only person who can testify that I haven't been into any mischief all afternoon.'

She hesitated a moment, then said: 'Oh, very well—if you really think it's as serious as all that.'

'But it is,' he insisted. 'Didn't I tell you they'd found another of those cards with my name on it?'

'You didn't tell me very much else about this Brighton affair,' she reminded him.

'Because the Yard weren't doing much talking over the

phone. You know as much as I do about it.' He paused a moment, then said in a dubious tone: 'Of course, if you had a date for this evening . . . well, I guess they won't gaol me for a day or two.'

Verity smiled. 'I'd hate to see anything like that happen to you,' she said. 'Are you going straight to the Yard?'

He nodded, and she swung the car in an easterly direction along the Westminster Embankment.

'Grey Moose seems to be quite determined to blow my small reputation to shreds,' ruminated Johnny, as he watched her steer her way deftly between two buses.

'Have you upset him in any way in the past d'you think?'

'I don't even know the guy. But there's always a chance I might have pulled a fast one across one of his buddies. That's the worst of keeping bad company; it's liable to catch up on you when you least expect it,' he told her seriously. 'You might care to remember that and put it in your column some time when you're writing a piece about juvenile delinquents.'

'I'll keep that in mind,' she promised, as she manœuvred into position in a line of cars parked in a side road near the Yard. Johnny was laboriously extricating his large feet when he noticed a familiar figure emerging from the next car but one ahead.

'Hi, there, Dovey!' he called.

The sturdy young man in his middle-thirties turned and recognized Johnny at once.

Inspector Charles Montague Dovey would not have been readily recognized as a plain-clothes detective, a factor which had proved of considerable assistance to him in his career. He was well dressed in a dark suit which set off his trim masculine figure to its best advantage.

Johnny introduced him to Verity and at once Dovey was on the alert.

'You're the woman who writes for the *Daily Messenger*?' he queried, for Dovey always believed in keeping in with the press, holding the theory that carefully controlled publicity could go a long way to smashing any crime racket. He was even ready to make friends with the editor of a boys' comic paper just in case he might come in useful one day.

Verity acknowledged her Fleet Street connections and Dovey immediately suggested that they should adjourn to the tavern nearby for a drink.

'They're expecting me at the Yard,' Johnny told him.

'You mean about the Brighton job?' said Dovey. 'Yes, I'm due for that little pow-wow as well. They can do without us for ten minutes while we give each other the low-down.'

'Have you come from Brighton then?' asked Johnny, as the inspector led them to the pub in question.

'No, I've come from near your place at Sevenoaks. I've been keeping a pretty close watch on the Kingfisher. So close, in fact, that I haven't had a chance to call in on you.'

They found a fairly remote table in a corner of the lounge and a barman came and took their order for drinks.

'I've telephoned you twice, Johnny, to find out just how far you were involved in this business,' said Dovey, having made quite sure they could not be overheard.

'Looks to me like I'm in it just up to the ears,' said Johnny. 'So is Miss Glyn, here.' He went on to give the inspector a brief outline of everything that concerned them, and Dovey eyed Verity with new respect.

'So you're Locksley's sister, eh? Your brother was a great scout, Miss Glyn. He did me a couple of good turns in my early days, and I haven't forgotten. I'd hoped to pay him back some time; now it seems the only thing I can do is to get the swine who shot him.'

'Then you think it was murder?' she queried eagerly.

'It was murder all right,' declared Dovey confidently. 'We're pretty sure of that over at the Yard, though we can't prove anything—yet. But I don't like the look of that Kingfisher place. I don't like the landlord, nor some of the characters I've seen hanging around there.'

'Such as?' put in Johnny casually.

'Well, one of my men bumped into a cove named Slim Copley there yesterday. Just caught a glimpse of him going out of the back door; then he seems to have vanished.'

'Slim Copley?' repeated Johnny. 'I remember him—he used to be a film stunt man—then something to do with a travelling fair—since then he's been mixed up with one or two smash-and-grab set-ups. Used to have the nerve of the devil himself.'

'You've got a pretty good memory yourself, Johnny,' said Dovey, eyeing him shrewdly.

'Absolute card-index,' Johnny assured him cheerfully. 'It's the best thing a feller can have when he's in my racket.'

'And what's your racket now?'

'I'm not operating at the moment,' grinned Johnny, refusing to be drawn. 'But it looks as if I'll soon be pulled into something pretty big, and on the side of law and order for once in a way.' He lifted his glass. 'Well, here's to the spice of life!' he pronounced.

'What would Slim Copley be doing in the heart of Kent?' he went on presently. 'I guess that's a pretty serious question you should ask yourself, Inspector—and here's hoping you get the right answer. Your man should have tailed him.'

'He didn't get a chance,' said the inspector. 'There wasn't a sign of him after he went out of the back door—and, of course, the landlord had never heard of him.'

'I don't trust that landlord,' said Johnny, and went on to relate the incident concerning the changing of Locksley's pound note. Dovey frowned thoughtfully when he had finished, then said:

'It's beginning to dawn on me why they've picked on you for a sort of scapegoat, old man.'

'You mean this gang are probably using the Kingfisher as headquarters, and they think if it should be traced, then Johnny living just by will—'

'Immediately arouse the suspicions of the police,' Dovey

finished for her. 'You're pretty smart, Miss Glyn. That's exactly what I was thinking. Nobody could be blamed for putting such an obvious two and two together.'

Johnny broke open a package of Chesterfields and passed them round. 'It certainly looks like I've got to play in with you boys for once in a while,' he said presently. 'I've been trying hard this last week to think of some other way out, but this Grey Moose seems to have 'em all nicely sealed off.'

Dovey thumped his fist on the table. 'Certainly, you've got to help us, Johnny—and there's Miss Glyn here; we've got to keep an eye on her. If Grey Moose finds out about her . . .'

'Did you check on that little guy named Quince?' put in Johnny hastily, anxious that Verity should not be in any way alarmed.

'Oh, yes,' replied Dovey. 'He seems all above board as far as I can make out. He's a retired prep school master—lives alone in a Bayswater flatlet. Spends a lot of time at the British Museum, so he told me. Calls himself an antiquarian.'

'That might cover a multitude of sins,' murmured Johnny. 'F'r instance, he might be mugging up ancient Egyptian poisons that could come in handy—'

'He said he was mainly interested in English inns, though he's lately been dabbling in Roman villas,' grinned the inspector. 'I think he's a pretty harmless old bird myself.'

'You wouldn't have been reading *Good-bye Mr Chips* just lately?' queried Johnny, with the merest twitch of his expressive mouth, and Verity caught his eye and smiled. 'You've got to admit that it's queer the old boy should be on the spot the night of that murder. They don't get a guest at the Kingfisher once in three months, except right in the middle of the summer, so the locals tell me,' continued Johnny, signalling the barman to bring another round of drinks. 'I guess we've got to think twice before we write off the old boy as harmless.'

Dovey stubbed out his cigarette.

'Have it your own way, Johnny,' he grunted. 'I'll have the

boys keep an eye on him. We can't afford to leave anything to chance. All the same, if that old bird's a master criminal, I'll pack up and go and lecture at Hendon!'

Johnny laughed.

'I guess things aren't quite as bad as that, Inspector. But I'd like to know what's been going on at Brighton this afternoon. Sir Robert wouldn't say much on the phone.'

'It's in the stop press of most of the evening papers,' said Dovey. 'Though they haven't got the full story by any means. Seems the gang decided to try their hand at a daylight job for a change, and they got away with it very nicely. It must have been pretty thoroughly planned, right down to the last detail.'

'Any idea how much stuff was there?'

Dovey looked round cautiously, then dropped his voice. 'Getting on for fifty thousand pounds, Sir Robert said when he phoned me. It was Dollands, the jewellers, and they were carrying a much bigger stock than usual. They've had several apparently genuine inquiries during the past week for expensive rings and necklaces, so naturally they got the stuff down on approval from Town. It was all worked out very neatly, including a lorry crashing into the shop next door to cover the noise when they blew the safe.'

'Pretty smart,' commented Johnny, taking a gulp at his whisky.

'And it seems they even had time to plant one of your cards before they made a getaway.'

'Not one of my cards,' Johnny corrected him. 'A card with my name on it that I didn't pay for. And you needn't give me that funny look, Inspector, because I can quite easily prove that I was at home all afternoon.'

'Glad to hear it, old man,' said Dovey, though there was a trace of false heartiness in his voice.

'I'm getting a little tired,' went on Johnny, 'of having to establish alibis like this. Maybe there'll come a day when they'll pull one of these jobs when I spent the whole day by myself fishing. Then I'll be in a spot. This business is getting on my nerves, and I object to anything that gets on my nerves. I'm kind of touchy about little things like that.'

He lit another cigarette and thoughtfully watched a large cloud of tobacco smoke rise towards the ceiling.

'Inspector,' Verity said suddenly, 'what's happened to the driver of that lorry that smashed into the shop?'

Johnny came back to earth abruptly.

'Yes, Inspector, what's happened to that driver?'

'Sir Robert said he'd got away when the police were coping with the crowd. They got his name and address—'

'That'll be phoney,' said Johnny quickly. 'Come on, Inspector, we'd better get round to the Yard. There's no time to be lost.'

The inspector looked puzzled and said: 'What are you up to, Johnny?'

'It stands out like Cleopatra's needle,' said Johnny Washington. 'Come on, Inspector—I think a special "all stations" call seems to be indicated.'

'An "all stations" call?' repeated Dovey, obviously bewildered.

'Sure, Inspector—for a guy named Slim Copley.'

CHAPTER X

WITHOUT any further delay, Dovey led his visitors through the front hall of New Scotland Yard, and along various corridors past the famous Information Room, with its three brilliantly lighted sections, to a room where a battery of teleprinters was busily clicking. Dovey phoned Brighton to check Slim Copley's description and a few minutes later they were sending it out to over a hundred principal stations.

'That's that,' declared Dovey with a sigh of relief. 'Now we'll go upstairs and see Sir Robert.'

The assistant commissioner was alone in his office engaged on what appeared an important telephone conversation and he motioned to them to be seated. When he eventually replaced the receiver, Dovey introduced him to Verity and gave him a brief account of her connection with the case. As soon as he heard that she was Locksley's sister, Sir Robert leaned forward in his chair and listened with keen interest. Presently, he opened a drawer and produced a silver cigarette box, which he handed round, and two minutes later Verity told her story for the third time.

Sir Robert made a note or two and asked her an occasional question. Once or twice he prompted her on minor matters, but for the main part she spoke without interruption. Towards the end, the assistant commissioner opened a file and cross-checked several facts she had mentioned, nodding quietly as he did so.

'That's very interesting, Miss Glyn . . . very interesting,' he murmured, as she came to the end of her story and stubbed out her cigarette with a hand that shook slightly. There had been traces of emotion in her voice when she spoke of her brother, and it was obvious to Hargreaves that she was completely sincere. He looked at her shrewdly for a few seconds, then said:

'You seem quite certain that from the very beginning your brother was under the impression that the brains behind these robberies was this man Max Fulton?'

'Quite sure, Sir Robert,' she replied with quiet emphasis.

He stroked his chin thoughtfully.

'I admit that Locksley seemed very positive about this being an elaborate criminal organization, but he never said anything about Max Fulton.'

'He wanted to be quite certain first,' she answered. 'You see, he had no evidence against Fulton . . . not even a photograph. He knew what a devil the man is, and he had to go very carefully.'

There was silence for a moment, then the assistant commissioner swung round in his seat.

'What do you make of all this, Mr Washington?' he asked. 'Have you ever come across Max Fulton in your wide and varied experience?'

Johnny grinned and shook his head.

'No, sir, but I heard quite a bit about him in the States. I guess he gave the F.B.I. boys a few headaches before he cleaned up fifty thousand dollars in some big Wall Street affair and vanished the next day. Yes, Maxie is quite a character.'

'That doesn't necessarily mean that he is running this organization.'

'That's quite true,' said Johnny. 'But it looks mighty like it to me. Locksley was convinced about it in his own mind, and Locksley was murdered all right.'

Sir Robert looked up sharply.

'What makes you so certain about that?'

Johnny said: 'Locksley was holding the revolver in his left hand, but he had been shot through the opposite side of his head. Locksley was left-handed all right, but I wouldn't say he was a contortionist into the bargain.'

'True enough,' agreed the assistant commissioner at once. 'I've been meaning to ask you about that doctor fellow who gave evidence, Washington. Is he a neighbour of yours?'

'Oh, yes,' replied Johnny. 'He was dining with me that evening.'

'You know him well?'

'I wouldn't say that.'

'H'm . . . well I've looked into the *Medical Directory,* and there doesn't seem to be any trace of him there.'

'I believe he took his degrees somewhere abroad,' said Johnny. 'He tells me he spent a lot of time on the Gold Coast.'

'Humph! Well, he certainly seems to have made a mess of this job. Any damned fool could see with half an eye that it wasn't suicide. There wasn't even a trace of a burn near the wound.'

'Perhaps I shouldn't say this,' began Johnny, 'but the doc had been drinking pretty heavily that night—and he had one or two more at the Kingfisher. He was certainly mellow.'

'Oh, well, perhaps that explains it,' shrugged Sir Robert. 'All the same, it was most unfortunate.'

Johnny smiled lazily.

'Maybe it'll work out better than we thought, Sir Robert.'

'Meaning what, exactly?' demanded Hargreaves.

'Well, if the gang take it for granted the police have accepted that suicide verdict, they're liable to relax their defences . . . and nobody in their position can afford to relax.'

The assistant commissioner nodded approvingly.

'Yes, you're right there, Washington. I don't propose to reopen the case of Locksley's death until we've got the man who killed him. You agree with that, Miss Glyn?'

'Oh, yes, Sir Robert.'

'When did you last see your brother?'

'Shortly before he visited Mr Washington.'

'Did he seem cheerful and in normal health?'

'Much the same as usual. He was worried about this case, of course, but he didn't seem depressed at all. We never saw very much of each other, Sir Robert. My work kept me very busy, and he was often in and out of town quite a lot.'

'Yes, of course.'

Hargreaves made several more notes, then, as he seemed to have completed his questioning, Dovey quietly intervened and told him about the all-stations call for Slim Copley. Sir Robert nodded his approval and began sorting through the contents of his grey folder.

Johnny looked across at Verity, smiled a trifle uneasily and shuffled his feet uncomfortably.

'Sir Robert,' he said at last, 'why did you ask me to come here tonight?'

The assistant commissioner deliberately closed his folder and placed it on one side.

'I've been waiting for you to ask me that, Mr Washington,' he replied in a pleasant tone. 'Why do you think I invited you?'

'In the first place,' hazarded Johnny, 'I guess you wanted to make sure I had a good alibi for this afternoon. Well, there she is. We've spent the entire afternoon together since one-thirty.' He nodded across at Verity.

'Is that correct, Miss Glyn?'

'Quite correct, Sir Robert. And if you want another witness, there is Mr Washington's butler.'

A vestige of a smile flickered across Hargreaves's deeply lined features.

'So you run to a butler nowadays, Washington?'

'A very respectable butler, Sir Robert,' replied Johnny imperturbably. 'He'd be quite horrified if he knew where I was at this minute.' Sir Robert permitted himself a grim chuckle.

'All right, Washington. I always suspected those cards were deliberately planted. Now, I want to talk to you two in complete confidence. Can you forget about that newspaper of yours for ten minutes, Miss Glyn?'

'I am only interested in seeing my brother's murderer punished, Sir Robert,' she solemnly assured him.

'And I'm gunning for the guy who's trying to roll my name in the mud,' put in Johnny. '"He who steals my purse steals trash, but he who takes my good name" . . .'

'All right,' interrupted Hargreaves hastily. 'Well, I don't mind admitting to both of you that this case has had us pretty badly rattled. We never know quite where this gang will break out next, and what method they will use. The man—or woman—at the head seems to be able to put his finger on all the weak spots in the police organization. In fact, they're apparently a couple of moves ahead of us the whole time.'

He picked up a large briar pipe from his inkstand and began to fill it slowly from a tin which stood on his desk.

'This is only a vague sort of idea of mine, Washington,' he went on with some hesitation. 'But I know you're a pretty unorthodox type, and you've a fairly wide knowledge of what the Sunday papers call the underworld. Now, I gather you're quite keen to help us on this case, and I thought if we gave you a free hand . . .' He placed the lid on the tin very carefully.

'How does that strike you?'

'Are you suggesting I should turn into a glorified—er—copper's nark I think you call it over here?' queried Johnny.

'I'm prepared to leave the plan of campaign to you. We'll either work with you or quite independently, whichever suits you better.'

'You embarrass me, Sir Robert,' said Johnny. 'I would sure like to help, but I haven't any plan of campaign right now, except to keep a close watch on the Kingfisher and ask a guy named Slim Copley a few awkward questions as soon as I can lay hands on him.'

'Later, perhaps,' nodded the Assistant Commissioner. 'At the moment, I am particularly anxious to discover how the gang gets the stuff out of the country—as they *must* be doing, because you can take it from me, Washington, that if it were still here, we'd have it back in less than a couple of days. Isn't that so, Dovey?'

'That's so, sir,' the inspector promptly corroborated.

'Now, that's one direction where you might come in useful, Washington,' continued the assistant commissioner. 'You're pretty used to picking up information about the valuable pieces of jewellery that are floating around the world. There was that affair of the Berkeley rubies, for instance, that very nearly landed you into a pretty mess.'

'It landed the man who stole them into a prettier one,' Johnny reminded him, 'I'm sorry, sir,' he went on, 'but I'm a bit out of touch with such goings-on these days. But I guess I'll take a look around one of these fine evenings and see what I can pick up.'

There was a soft buzz and Sir Robert lifted one of the telephone receivers on his desk. He listened for a moment then gave a couple of brisk orders and replaced the instrument. He turned to Johnny and said:

'You wanted a few words with Slim Copley?'

'I'll say I do!'

'All right, then, be here at ten sharp in the morning. They've just picked him up near Purley.'

With the rest of the evening to themselves, Johnny and Verity summoned a taxi in the Charing Cross Road, having decided that it was rather too late to go to a theatre. Johnny persuaded her to accompany him to a small club near the Marble Arch which he knew well enough to secure admission without any difficulty.

'You may see one or two characters there you could put in your column. I guess they'd be tickled to death!' he grinned, adding that there was no necessity for either of them to dress for the occasion.

'They've got a chef there who really knows his way around,' he concluded as a final recommendation.

As its name implied, The Bouquets Club had a late-Victorian atmosphere, with gilt and cupids very much in evidence.

In a far corner, surrounded by several palms, a trio of demurely dressed young ladies dispensed Victorian melodies on piano, violin and cello.

'There's somethin' kinda restful about this place,' murmured Johnny, as he passed the menu over to Verity. 'Other folks must find it so as well, because some of the biggest crooked deals of all time have been cooked up here. Mind you, the place is strictly above board; never been raided once, or I wouldn't have brought you.'

'I appreciate your thoughtfulness, Mr Washington,' replied Verity in a serious tone, though there was a suspicion of a twinkle in the grey eyes. A waiter came and took their order and Johnny nodded to a couple of people he knew. He began to describe some of the diners to her.

'The blonde dripping with ice over by the door'—he indicated a glittering fair-haired woman laden with jewels on every visible extremity—'she's tied up with a nice little racket in black market luxury flats. Started as a typist in an estate office; in next to no time the boss had taken a fancy to her—his wife divorced him—the blonde became more and more expensive— he had to go into the black market to pay her bills—and now she owns the business. It just shows what a girl can do if she keeps her wits about her!'

'Oh, dear,' said Verity. 'And I get so many letters from typists telling me the boss is in love with them. I'm beginning to wonder if I was right in advising them to look for another job.'

'You bet you were right!' replied Johnny emphatically, nodding in the blonde's direction. 'I wouldn't have a dog of mine step into her shoes.'

A stocky young man in a much too tightly fitting suit wandered over to the blonde's table and seated himself with a possessive air.

'Small-time crook,' explained Johnny. 'There's no depths a

woman of that type can't sink to. *And* he's kept her waiting at least twenty minutes.'

A waiter stepped on to the orchestra's rostrum and whispered something to the leader. Presently, they burst into a tinkling version of a famous galop.

'That's one of Tommy Belton's favourites—he's a sucker for Offenbach,' murmured Johnny, turning in his chair to get a glimpse of the man in question, a well-groomed elderly business man in the late fifties. He pointed him out to Verity as he applauded heartily at the end of the piece.

'He looks very respectable,' she commented.

'He's never been found out yet,' was the cryptical reply. 'Tommy has a very cosy little motor showroom in Great Portland Street, but nobody has ever yet managed to discover how he keeps a luxury flat in Park Lane, a large house near Ascot, a string of racehorses and an equally expensive string of girl friends.'

'Maybe he's discovered a new way of dodging super-tax,' suggested Verity.

'Say, I hope you're not going to print any of this in your column,' put in Johnny hastily, with vivid recollections of the American yellow press.

'There's such a thing as a law of libel,' she reminded him. 'And in any case, mine is a highly respectable column.'

'I guess I asked for that one,' he murmured as the waiter placed the celebrated chicken *à la* king before them. Suddenly, from behind the waiter a figure of an energetic man in the early forties loomed up and tapped Johnny on the shoulder.

'Hi, Johnny! Where have you been hiding yourself lately?' demanded a cultured voice with just the barest trace of a foreign accent.

'Well, well!' exclaimed Johnny, laying down his knife and fork. 'If it isn't Max Fabian. How's the world treating you?' He introduced Verity and invited the newcomer to join them. But Fabian shook his head.

'Sorry, old man, I'm expecting a certain party on a little matter of business. May see you later.'

And he went off to the table reserved for him, a trim figure in his dinner jacket and razor-creased trousers.

'Is he a great friend of yours?' inquired Verity, as they continued their dinner.

'Nobody in this joint is a friend of mine, or of anyone else's. They're not the sort of folk who make friends—only business acquaintances or sleeping partners,' explained Johnny patiently. 'The only friendship they're capable of forming is with a wad of banknotes.'

'How horrible!' said Verity with a little shudder.

'Oh, I guess you get used to it,' said Johnny philosophically. 'They're quite interesting characters in their way, and folks have always had a kind of fascination for me. Take Fabian, for instance . . .'

'You mean the man you just introduced to me?'

'That's right. Fabian is something new in the crime racket, a really international "fence", with headquarters in half a dozen countries.'

'You mean he's a receiver of stolen property?'

'In a very big way only. Fabian never bothers with the small-time crooks. I doubt if he ever makes a deal for less than ten thousand. Strictly big-time, that's Fabian.'

'What nationality is he?'

'His father was a clock repairer in a back street in Rome; his mother was a Greek servant girl. Fabian was a petty thief in Rome before the war, and during the war years he was right in the black market with both feet. The dollars that boy turned over must have upset the exchanges more than somewhat. Now, he's operating across half the civilized globe; Fabian's one of the penalties of civilization!

'And don't let that smiling boy act fool you,' went on Johnny. 'Fabian is ruthless with a capital R. He learnt it in the back alleys of Rome, and he'll never forget.'

The trio began to saw and thump its way through a Strauss waltz with somewhat surprising dexterity. The leader, a brassy blonde with a generous figure and ready smile, was obviously a great favourite with the male members of the club.

'You certainly know some colourful types, Johnny,' smiled Verity, as the waiter placed an enormous ice in front of her. 'Tell me some more about Fabian.'

'I guess there isn't much to tell. He's the biggest receiver of stolen gems in the world—has his own staff to break 'em up—fake 'em up—repolish 'em—and never makes less than a hundred per cent profit. You see, all his set-ups are operated under cover of a legitimate business, and nobody's been able to prove that it was anything but above board—yet.'

'Shouldn't you tell all this to the police?' demanded Verity, wide-eyed.

'Maybe I should,' chuckled Johnny. 'If it was as simple as all that. Maybe the police know in any case and wouldn't thank me for squeaking. Besides, there's no knowing when a guy like Fabian won't come in useful. I always say there's no point in upsetting people unless there's money in it.'

Verity laughed. 'That's one way of looking at things.'

The crowd in the club was getting thicker now; almost every table was occupied with the queerest assortment of humanity Verity had seen. There were dowager types who might have been Gaiety girls in their youth, thin middle-aged women with a nervous manner and abrupt gestures, and a sprinkling of very expensively dressed young ladies from gown shops, beauty establishments and film studios, whose purpose was obviously solely to entertain and bring prestige to their male escorts.

It seemed to Verity that the conversation had a slightly sinister buzz, perhaps on account of its polyglot nature. Waiters quickened the pace to and from the kitchens, and the trio began an extract from Verdi that was quite beyond its powers.

A tall, attractive girl, beautifully dressed in a dark gown stood in the doorway for a moment and caught Verity's eye. She

watched her move to a table where Fabian rose to welcome her.
As she sat down, Verity pointed her out to Johnny.

'Where have I seen that girl before?' she asked with a puzzled
little frown.

Johnny whistled softly to himself as he saw Fabian summon
a waiter to order a drink for his guest.

'You've seen her this evening,' he told Verity in a tone that
controlled any trace of surprise. 'You saw her outside my place
in a car . . . She's my neighbour—Shelagh Hamilton.'

CHAPTER XI

IF Johnny had been intrigued at the sight of a business meeting between Shelagh Hamilton and Fabian, he certainly did not allow it to interfere with his sleep, and it was not until he heard a heavy knock at his door and a voice informing him that it was nine o'clock that he returned fully to consciousness and recalled that he was due at the Yard in an hour's time.

He went down into the dining-room at the St Regis to be informed that breakfast was over, but as a great favour the waiter rescued a fillet of lukewarm sole and a couple of dejected pieces of toast for him. Coffee, it seemed, was right out of the question and orange juice unheard of. He asked for the head waiter to offer some protest at such hospitality, only to be told that gentleman never came on duty at breakfast. And the manager of the hotel was busy in another part of the building. Johnny gave it up, paid his account and set out for New Scotland Yard.

There did not seem to be many taxis about on this fine Sunday morning, and Johnny had a rooted objection to any more walking than was absolutely necessary. However, he eventually found one in Piccadilly, and was outside the main entrance to the Yard just before ten.

He was ushered into the assistant commissioner's office without any delay, and discovered Sir Robert already there chatting to Dovey and Kennard. A report from the Brighton police of the previous day's affair was on Hargreaves's desk and made none too pleasant reading.

'Well, what do we know about Slim Copley?' asked Johnny, as soon as they had exchanged greetings.

'We're holding him on a charge of being implicated with the

Brighton robbery,' replied Sir Robert, 'but I'm afraid it isn't going to be easy to make him talk—and if he did I'm not sure that he knows very much.'

'No harm in trying,' said Johnny. 'I see from this morning's papers that the robbery wasn't discovered until some time after the truck bashed into the shop.'

'That's so,' said Dovey. 'Actually, whoever did the job set off the burglar alarm, but the damn fools thought it was the lorry that had jolted it. They didn't find out any different till one of the partners came along with the keys.'

'I see. Has anybody tried to make him talk?'

'Yes, Dovey and Kennard have both had a go at him without very much satisfaction.'

'We found the nameplate on the lorry was a fake,' said Dovey, 'and he won't say if he was driving for anybody. His story is that he bought the lorry to go into business himself and the brakes were faulty. But we've had the brakes tested and they're quite O.K., so it was obviously a put-up job.'

'What's he say to all that?'

'He simply insists he's sticking to his statement.'

Johnny leaned against the window-ledge and thoughtfully watched a solitary tram swaying gently over Lambeth Bridge.

'There must be some way of making him talk,' he reflected, almost to himself.

'We'll see,' said the assistant commissioner. 'You'd better bring him in, Kennard.'

Dovey and Kennard went out, and Sir Robert turned to Johnny.

'How much d'you think he knows?' he asked.

'Enough to break up that outfit if we can get the truth out of him,' replied Johnny. 'D'you mind if I talk to him, Chief?'

Sir Robert hesitated.

'Well, it isn't usual, but it seems we've got to use unorthodox methods on this job. We don't want any of that American third degree stuff, mind.'

'Leave it to me, sir,' smiled Johnny. 'I'll handle him with kid gloves.'

Presently, the door opened and the two inspectors re-appeared, with a very sullen prisoner between them. Slim looked as if he had not slept well; his hair was dishevelled, his face badly shaved and his necktie carelessly knotted.

Kennard set down a letter-tray containing an assortment of small articles on the assistant commissioner's desk.

'These were found in his pockets, sir,' he said quietly, and Johnny moved across to take a look at them while Sir Robert seated the prisoner in a chair facing the strong light from the tall window.

In the tray were a new gold cigarette case, a wallet containing a driving licence and twenty-four pound notes, as well as several faded newspaper cuttings concerning the owner's speedway exploits, a cheap postcard photo of a girl, a dirty handkerchief, a small battered silver flask containing some sort of liquor, a large penknife, a ball-pointed pencil with a patent gadget for checking sparking-plugs, and a few shillings worth of loose change.

'What the 'ell's the big idea of all this?' rasped Slim Copley's unpleasant voice, as he looked round the room with a furtive air. 'I ain't a blasted criminal—I got my rights.'

Johnny Washington walked round and perched on the edge of the desk. He fixed Slim with an intense stare, then smiled lazily.

'Of course, you've got your rights, Slim,' he said softly. 'There's nothing to worry about—you and I are just going to have a little talk.'

Slim Copley licked his lips nervously and again looked round the little group of immobile faces.

'I got nothing to say,' he stammered. 'I want a solicitor here if you're askin' me questions . . .'

'I tell you it's all right, Slim,' interposed Johnny once more. 'This is just a little talk off the record. We know a bit more about this Brighton set-up than you think, Slim. It's for your own good we're giving you this chance to tell us what you know. You're mixing with a pretty tough crowd, Slim. They've already wiped out a couple of inside men who let them down. They've no time for failures, and it looks as if you're going to need protection.'

'I can look after myself,' said Slim sullenly.

'I dare say the other two had the same ideas about that.' There was a quiet intensity about Johnny's voice that compelled attention. Slim became more and more ill at ease; from time to time he shifted uncomfortably in his chair.

'We know you're connected with the Grey Moose gang because we've seen you at the Kingfisher,' went on Johnny, quite unperturbed. 'Was that where you planned this little coup?'

'I don't know what you're talking about.'

'Oh, yes you do, Slim. Just as well as you know those pound notes in your wallet there are part of the proceeds from the Gloucester job. We're catching up with the Grey Moose crowd pretty fast, Slim.'

'I got nothing to do with any gang!' growled Slim.

'Then all I can say, Slim, is I hope for your sake you're pretty fond of children.'

'What the 'ell has kids got to do with this? I didn't hurt no kids!'

'I'm trying to tell you how, Slim. I said I hoped you were mighty fond of children, because this time you're the sucker who's holding the baby. And, oh boy, what a bouncing baby it is! I shouldn't wonder if your share of the rake-off came to a couple of thousand, Slim. I told you that crowd has no time for failures—all you'll get will be a bullet in the guts, the same as the lorry driver at Preston and the night watchman at Gloucester. Of course, that's assuming you manage to wriggle out of taking the rap for this job—and it isn't going to be easy. They're piling up quite a bit of evidence against you, Slim, and you've got a record that's none too healthy. I don't suppose the judge'll feel any too brotherly towards you.'

Johnny paused for a moment to let Slim assimilate all the implications to the full, and he certainly seemed to find them none too comforting. He licked his lips nervously once more and ran a finger uneasily around the neck of his collar. He dropped his eyes and refused to meet Johnny's unwavering gaze.

'If you know what's good for you, Slim,' continued the soft remorseless voice, 'you'll start talking right now. You've nothing to lose except your cut on that job, and you'll never get that now. You're not playing with small-time crooks, you know; you'll need protection from the police till this gang is smashed, or they'll get you just as surely as they got the others.'

Slim Copley's hands were clenched so tightly that the whites of his knuckles showed, and his forehead was corrugated in a sullen frown. He was obviously weighing up the pros and cons of his present position and finding it none too happy. There was a heavy silence in the room, and everyone seemed to be experiencing a feeling of tension except Johnny Washington, who still perched on the edge of the desk with his arms folded. Slim's breathing became slowly more noticeable until he almost appeared to be gasping for breath.

'All right . . . I'll talk . . . but I got to have a drink first. I'm all shot to pieces.'

His distress was obviously genuine, and Johnny looked inquiringly at the other two, for he hadn't a notion where he would get a drink in New Scotland Yard at ten-thirty on a Sunday morning. Then it became obvious that Slim was referring to the small silver flask which had been taken from him when he was searched. At a nod from Sir Robert, Kennard passed it to Johnny, who held on to it for a moment.

'First of all, Slim, tell us something about this set-up that's responsible for the jewel robberies.'

'I—I don't know much about it . . . it's run by a bloke who calls himself Grey Moose . . . he looks after everything.'

'How does he get the stuff out of the country?'

'I don't know anything about that—I think it's by aeroplane . . . a private plane.'

'And the airfield?'

'I've never set eyes on it.'

'But you've seen Grey Moose? You'd recognize him again?'

Slim gulped hard, appeared to be about to say something, then suddenly grabbed the flask from Johnny's hand. For some ten seconds he noisily swallowed down the spirit—and Johnny judged the flask to have been well over half full. But almost before he had finished, the flask fell from his hands; he sank back in his chair, the blood draining from his face.

'Slim—what is it?'

Slim seemed to be struggling for breath.

'I—I—my throat—'

Johnny picked up the flask and sniffed it. Mingling with the smell of whisky was the unmistakable odour of carbolic acid.

'Where did you get this whisky?' he asked.

Slim's hands were still clawing at his throat, then he clutched his stomach, obviously in great pain.

'The Kingfisher—' he gasped, rolling forward on the floor. Dovey knelt and lifted his head, while Johnny felt his pulse. Sir Robert picked up the telephone and asked for a police surgeon immediately.

'It's too late,' said Johnny, looking up a minute later. 'He's dead.'

'Yes, he's dead all right,' repeated Kennard, in an almost expressionless voice. 'What was in that flask, Mr Washington?'

'Whisky mixed with enough carbolic acid to kill three men I should imagine,' replied Johnny. 'It might be an idea to send it down to your Fingerprints Department first and have it tested before it goes to the laboratory. There's just a chance there may be some smudges that would give us a clue.'

'He said he had it from the Kingfisher,' said Kennard.

'That was the whisky. It doesn't follow that the poison was put in at the same time.'

'That's true,' nodded Dovey.

'Are you sure it's too late?' asked Sir Robert anxiously. 'Perhaps if we could force an antidote . . .'

'You'd be wasting your time,' murmured Johnny.

'But it's—it's impossible!' exclaimed the bewildered Sir Robert. This was the first time in his long experience that anything like this had happened inside Scotland Yard, and he found it difficult to believe.

'We'd better try artificial respiration till the doctor gets here,' said Dovey, preparing to do so. But it was obviously too late. There was suddenly a sharp knock at the door.

'That'll be the doctor,' said Hargreaves. 'Come in!'

The door opened and the sergeant from the front hall came in with one of the familiar buff slips filled in by waiting callers.

'There's a gentleman to see you, sir,' he said to Sir Robert.

'I can't see him now! Tell him to phone!' snapped the assistant commissioner.

The sergeant hesitated, then said diffidently:

'He said it was rather important, sir, and he's made a special journey . . .'

'Oh, hell!' said Sir Robert. 'Who is it?'

'It's a Mr Quince, sir. Mr Horatio Quince.'

CHAPTER XII

'QUINCE?' repeated Sir Robert taking the slip from the sergeant. 'That's the fellow who is staying at the Kingfisher, isn't it?'

'That's right, sir. He's an antiquarian, so he says,' replied Dovey.

'H'm . . . maybe he's stumbled across something.'

'He's a cute old bird, sir,' put in Johnny. 'I guess it might be as well to see him.'

'All right, Sergeant,' nodded Sir Robert. 'Ask him to wait a few minutes. I'll phone when I'm free.'

The sergeant withdrew unobtrusively, and they turned to the body of Slim Copley again.

'Just our confounded luck,' growled Kennard. 'In another couple of minutes he'd have told us everything we want to know.'

'How did the poison get in the flask?' said Sir Robert, with a bewildered air. 'He certainly wasn't the type to commit suicide; I'm sure he didn't know the liquor was poisoned.'

'Whoever filled the flask at the Kingfisher could have done it,' Johnny pointed out. 'Or it might have happened any time since, if someone else had access to it.'

'You mean it might have been another arranged job—just as they liquidated the night watchman at Gloucester?' suggested Dovey.

'Could be,' said Johnny.

The arrival of the doctor cut short any further speculation. He lost no time in pronouncing that Slim Copley was dead and the body was quickly moved to the mortuary. The doctor was also shown the flask, and asked to be allowed to analyse the dregs as soon as possible. In the meantime, it was sent to the Fingerprints Department, who very quickly reported back that the only prints upon it of which they had any record were Slim Copley's.

Left alone with Johnny, while his assistant attended to the formalities, Sir Robert began brooding over his reports on the Brighton robbery. He seemed in no hurry to send for Mr Quince, and Johnny had no intention of leaving until he had done so. He refused one of the assistant commissioner's cigarettes and lit one of his own Chesterfields. Sir Robert went on turning over papers; Johnny puffed neat rings of smoke towards the fireplace, and neither spoke for two or three minutes. Then the assistant commissioner said:

'This business seems to get more and more involved. D'you think that poison was put in his flask at the Kingfisher, Washington?'

Johnny shrugged.

'Your guess is as good as mine, Chief. The point is he was rubbed out at just the right moment when he might have been some use to us. I guess we've just got to write him off the books and try something else.'

'Such as what?' snapped Hargreaves.

'Right now, I'm trying to dream up a little scheme,' replied Johnny, as if he did not wish to be interrupted. Sir Robert relapsed into a moody silence once more and read through a couple of pages. Suddenly he stopped and placed a finger on the paper to keep his place.

'There's rather an interesting point here, Washington. I don't know if it means anything . . .'

'Yes, sir?'

'It seems that a constable on his beat just before the robbery remembers talking to a girl in a smart sports car, and he's convinced that she had some connection with the affair. She insisted on parking just round the corner, although it was forbidden.'

'Then why didn't he move her on?'

'He says she promised she wouldn't be more than a couple of minutes; in fact, he was still arguing with her—so he says—when the lorry came charging down the hill.'

'Did he take the number of the car?'

'I'm afraid he didn't get round to that. But there's a fairly detailed description of the girl here.' He referred to the report once more, then went on. 'Yes—slim—wearing expensive tailor-made coat and skirt—fair hair, almost platinum—blue eyes—a set of golf clubs in the back of the car—no jewellery except a gold ring with a tiny diamond-shaped watch set in it.'

'A diamond-shaped watch?' queried Johnny sharply, his eyes catching Sir Robert's. 'Now, where did I . . .'

'Yes?' said Sir Robert expectantly. But Johnny shook his head.

'Can you recall seeing some woman wearing one of those ring-watches?'

'I can, but I guess there are hundreds about.'

'Who was it?'

'Oh, just a neighbour of mine in the country.'

'H'm . . . well, we've tried to trace the girl, but we haven't had any luck so far, and I'm beginning to doubt whether we will.'

'I guess you're right at that,' said Johnny, frowning thoughtfully as he called to mind the picture of Shelagh Hamilton passing his front gates in her Harman-Grade, with golf clubs in the back . . . But there must have been dozens of girls in sports cars carrying golf clubs. After all, it was Saturday, and he knew Shelagh was a fairly regular visitor to the Sevenoaks club.

Johnny carefully lighted another cigarette from the butt of its predecessor, which he stubbed out on the ash-tray.

'Sir Robert,' he began with some hesitation, 'I've got a kind of idea that might bust this racket open. It's taking a big chance, mind . . .'

'We've got to take risks, Washington. Things are getting pretty desperate. I had the Home Secretary on the telephone last night, hinting there might be questions in the House if we don't put a stop to this business quite soon. So if you've got any sort of an idea, for heaven's sake let's hear it.'

Still Johnny hesitated.

'It's pretty tricky, Sir Robert. The whole thing would have to be very carefully planned.'

'We can settle all that later. What is it you suggest?'

Johnny pulled at his cigarette.

'There's an old firm of family jewellers just round the corner from Bond Street called Trevelyans. Heard of 'em?'

'Of course.'

'I once did young Eric Trevelyan a good turn—he'd been having some trouble about a necklace bought by a distinguished member of the peerage whose lady friend professed to take a dislike to it and returned a fake in its place . . . but that's another story.'

'Go on,' urged Sir Robert with some impatience.

'Now supposing it became known that Trevelyans had a very valuable stone in their safe—the Brailsham Diamond for instance. It seems to me a sporting chance that our friends might be tempted to pay Trevelyans an unheralded visit—but in this case it wouldn't be entirely unexpected.'

Hargreaves drummed his fingers on his desk, and seemed to be deep in thought.

'We're pretty sure by now that these jobs the gang has pulled off have been very carefully planned,' continued Johnny. 'O.K. then. It's up to us to start planning ahead, too.'

'Just what do you mean, exactly?'

Johnny knocked the ash off his cigarette.

'Let's presume that our friends have heard that Trevelyans have the Brailsham Diamond, what's the first thing they do?

They take steps to make quite sure that the report is correct. They'll do that before they make a single move towards planning a robbery.'

He could see that Sir Robert was becoming interested.

'You mean they'll get somebody to make an inquiry in the ordinary business channels?' he queried.

'That's it,' nodded Johnny. 'And that's where my friend Eric Trevelyan comes in. I shall get him to let me have a full list of all inquiries about this stone, and maybe one of them will give us a clue.'

Sir Robert stroked his moustache as he considered the scheme. It certainly seemed a step towards carrying the war into the enemy's country. During the past month he had felt frustrated and baffled at every turn, for there seemed to be no way of anticipating any move from the gelignite gang. There was no knowing where they would strike next, and they covered their tracks so effectively that they had left very few clues. Furthermore, when they had enlisted the help of anyone with a criminal record they had taken good care to liquidate him before he could be made to talk.

He looked at Johnny Washington with new respect.

'Well, now, let's go into this seriously,' he began, settling himself back in his chair. 'Is your friend Trevelyan a man to be trusted?'

'Absolutely. What's more, Eric is always game to take a chance. But we've got to play this carefully, Sir Robert. That gang wasn't born yesterday; we haven't got to hand them this on a platter or they'll get scared right away. I reckon a short paragraph in the *Gem Trader* is all that's needed, and Eric will see to that. Of course, I can put it around to one or two contacts of my own—there's Fabian, for instance. I happen to know he's had his eye on the Brailsham Diamond for at least a couple of years.'

'He's the fellow we nearly pinned that receiving charge on in the Curzon Street affair—he got out of the country just an hour too soon, and took the stuff with him.'

'That's the guy,' said Johnny cheerfully. 'Fabian's a pretty smart operator, and he won't suspect anybody of making a tool of him. Not even me!'

'It wants careful handling,' temporized Sir Robert, liking the scheme better as it developed, and wondering if he could really trust the man who sat opposite him. It was against all his principles to call in outsiders upon even the most trifling affair, for it was his boast that he had a first-class staff who could deal with any emergency. But he had to face the fact that they had proved unequal to the gelignite gang, and his superiors were becoming impatient for results. This suggestion at least offered some opportunity for positive action.

'All right, Washington,' he said at last. 'I'll leave this to you for the time being, but keep me informed. And by the by, the fewer people who are let in on this, the better chance it will have of succeeding.'

'You've taken the words right out of my mouth, Sir Robert,' said Johnny fervently. 'I guess I shall only tell when it's absolutely necessary. In fact, I don't see any reason to let anybody in on it except Eric until we get an actual tip-off that the gang is interested.'

'That's settled then,' nodded Sir Robert. 'Now, I suppose I'd better see this Mr Quince. Maybe you should hang on, just in case he's got something that gives us a bearing . . .'

'Thank you, Sir Robert,' said Johnny, who had every intention of staying to meet Mr Quince unless he was bodily thrown out. Sir Robert picked up the phone and gave the necessary instructions, and presently the dapper little figure appeared in the doorway.

His somewhat chubby cheeks looked rosier than ever; there was a sparkle in his pale blue eyes, and he was obviously wearing his best suit with neat wash-leather gloves. In one hand he carried a copy of one of the more literary Sunday newspapers and a small Greek testament, with which he had been passing the time in the waiting-room.

'Why, Mr Washington!' he exclaimed, recognizing Johnny at once. 'How very pleasant to meet you again in such unique surroundings. This is the first time I have been inside this very remarkable building.'

Johnny smiled and introduced him to Sir Robert, who courteously asked him to take a seat.

'Would you like a cigarette, Mr Quince?' asked Johnny, opening his silver case and offering it to him. 'Those are Turkish on that side—or I've some American ones in my pocket if you prefer them.'

'Turkish!' echoed Mr Quince, selecting nevertheless a familiar English brand. 'A strange country, Mr Washington—Turkey, I mean. A most interesting history; I have made quite a study of their ancient architecture—a fascinating subject. We must have a chat about it some time.'

Sir Robert had been looking through the papers in his file and finally selected that which contained Mr Quince's statement.

'Are you still at the Kingfisher Inn, Mr Quince?'

'Yes, as a matter of fact, I am. I had intended to leave, but I was out for a walk one day this week in the Chevening direction when I came upon two young men who were excavating what they assured me was a Roman villa. It was really quite fascinating; I've been there every day since, so I decided to stay on for a while despite this deplorable affair.'

He was obviously prepared to ramble on in this vein indefinitely, but Sir Robert pulled him up with another abrupt question.

'Mr Quince, why have you come here to see me this morning?'

Mr Quince sat bolt upright for a moment, looked round the room as if to make sure there were no eavesdroppers concealed anywhere, then he leaned forward and said in a confidential tone:

'It's about that club-room, Sir Robert. I'm getting rather worried . . .'

'You mean the room where we found that damp patch on the floor?' prompted Johnny. 'Where the Elks or Rangers meet once a week?'

'The Antediluvian Order of Bison,' Mr Quince corrected him in his thin, precise voice. 'They meet once a week on a Thursday. I made inquiries about that. The point is, that room is being used on other nights by some other organization.'

'How d'you know that?' demanded Sir Robert.

'Because my bedroom happens to be immediately above it, and as is often the case with these old inns, the floor and ceiling are one and the same, so I can hear voices quite distinctly.'

'You mean you can tell what they are saying?'

'No, I can't hear the actual words. But the sound of the voices is loud enough to keep me awake—very annoying I assure you.'

'Then they keep pretty late hours?'

'Their last meeting went on till midnight.'

'But it might be a special committee meeting of these Bisons, or whatever they call themselves,' Sir Robert suggested. But Mr Quince waved the idea aside.

'No, no, I'm quite sure it's nothing of the sort,' he insisted.

'What makes you so sure of that?' asked Johnny with some interest.

'Because I made inquiries of the secretary, and he assured me that no feminine members are admitted to the Antediluvian Order of Bison,' explained Mr Quince solemnly. 'And one of the persons at those conclaves was most certainly a woman!'

CHAPTER XIII

AN UNEXPECTED PRESENT

It was nearly one o'clock when Johnny picked up a taxi in Charing Cross Road, for Mr Quince had proved a tenacious caller. Sir Robert, quite obviously, did not know what to make of him. On the face of it, he seemed merely a retired school master with a passion for antiques and ancient ruins, but one could never be quite sure nowadays, with so many apparently respectable people concealing mysterious illicit activities behind an outward appearance of middle-class prosperity.

If Mr Quince were really a staid little ex-dominie, would he really wish to stay on at the Kingfisher after that distressing evening? There were times when Mr Quince seemed to display an almost morbid interest in the death of the superintendent; at others he appeared to regard it as a mere incident in the day's routine.

Although Johnny found all this intriguing, it was obvious that Sir Robert had been a trifle worried. He checked over Mr Quince's statement with him, and found no flaw in it; he asked him more questions about the mysterious meetings without throwing any fresh light on the matter. Indeed, Mr Quince's main complaint seemed to be that his sleep had been disturbed, which robbed him of his concentrative powers when he wished to investigate the local antiquities the following day. Johnny professed to take a serious interest in the Roman villa, and urged the little man to stay on at the Kingfisher for a time. It would be useful to know where he was exactly, and if he were in no way involved, he would at least prove a thorn in the side of Harry Bache.

However, the party broke up at last. Mr Quince promised to keep in touch with Scotland Yard; Johnny exchanged a brisk farewell with Sir Robert, saying he would telephone him as soon as he had made 'the arrangements'.

Hargreaves nodded understandingly and saw them to the door.

Mr Quince departed for Charing Cross *en route* for Bayswater to collect a change of clothing from his flat, and Johnny walked round into Charing Cross Road to get a taxi, which took him to the address in Chelsea which Verity had given him.

He arrived soon after one, and found her on the fourth floor of a fair-sized block of flats. The sun was filtering pleasantly through the long window, transforming the room into a semblance of those interiors favoured by early Dutch painters.

He sank into one of the two comfortable arm-chairs and watched her putting finishing touches to the table in an alcove by the window.

'You've got yourself fixed up pretty nicely here,' he commented, his gaze wandering idly over the books packed tightly into the shelves beside his chair. He was surprised at the remarkable range of subjects they covered.

'You're certainly Little Miss Inquire Within,' he murmured, picking up a book on the history of South African diamond mining, and turning the pages until he came to a brief description of the discovery of the famous Brailsham Diamond. He closed the book and replaced it, then rose and said: 'Can I do anything to help? I should have asked.'

'That's all right,' smiled Verity. 'Mrs Todd will take care of everything. You can pour a drink if you like,' she added as an afterthought, indicating a cocktail cabinet near the fireplace.

'That's not a bad idea, either. I feel I've earned a drink this morning. What will it be?'

'Sherry for me, please—the light one.'

He poured out the sherry for her and mixed himself a gin and French.

'Has anything special happened this morning?' she inquired as she sipped her drink. He gave her a brief resume of the poisoning of Slim Copley, carefully omitting the more gruesome details.

She was not so upset as he had expected. For one thing she had known Slim Copley, and for another she could feel little remorse for any member of the gang which she was convinced was responsible for her brother's death. In fact, the only sign of emotion she betrayed was one of disappointment that Slim had died before he could enlighten them in any way about the gang's activities.

'This would have been a scoop for the evening papers on a weekday,' she reflected as they finished their drinks. 'I don't suppose a man has ever been poisoned inside Scotland Yard before.'

'And I should say it's pretty unlikely ever to happen again,' observed Johnny. 'I guess the morning papers will get the scoop instead. Sir Robert was on the telephone to the press bureau just before I left.'

'I wonder if I should phone our news editor, just in case the crime man doesn't get the tip,' mused Verity.

'Wait till after lunch,' he advised.

'Yes, of course. They won't be on duty until tea time.'

There was a gentle tap on the door, which opened to admit Mrs Todd, Verity's Scottish housekeeper, carrying a heavily laden tray. She was a plain little woman whose face was completely transformed on the comparatively rare occasions when she permitted herself to smile.

'Ye'd best get on with this while it's hot,' she ordered, laying the dishes on the table, for she was firmly convinced that Verity was underfed except when she was at home.

'M'm . . . this is what I call good home cooking,' said Johnny, wrinkling his nose appreciatively, thereby making Mrs Todd his friend for life. 'I just can't wait to get started.'

When Mrs Todd had disappeared, he said, 'You've certainly

got a treasure out there. I didn't think there were any like that left nowadays.'

'What about your Mr Winwood?' she smiled.

'Oh, Winwood's all right, I guess.'

'We'd better not introduce them,' said Verity, 'or they might marry and leave us in the lurch.'

'In that case, we'd just have to look after each other. And that might not be such a bad idea,' concluded Johnny with a speculative gleam in his eye. Hastily, she changed the subject and asked if there was any more news of the Brighton robbery.

Mrs Todd had brought in the coffee and left them sitting in the comfortable arm-chairs when she suddenly returned carrying a flat parcel.

'It's my memory again, miss,' she apologized, in an abject tone. 'It came while ye were out yesterday and I put it at the back of my sideboard and forgot all about it. I hope it's nothing urgent.'

Verity took the parcel and turned it over. There was no stamp or indication as to who had sent it.

'Wasn't there any message, Mrs Todd?' she asked.

'No, dear. One of them cheeky little errand boys brought it. He just said it was for you and ran off before I could get in a word. Isn't it somethin' ye've ordered, miss?'

Verity wrinkled her forehead.

'I can't recall asking for anything to be delivered.'

'You didn't sign for it, Mrs Todd?' asked Johnny.

'No, sir. The little devil was away before I could even turn round.'

'Maybe it's a present from an unknown admirer,' suggested Johnny lightly.

'Drink your coffee while I open it,' she said, dismissing Mrs Todd, who was obviously a little disappointed.

She produced a pair of scissors and snipped the string round the parcel, unfolding the paper and produced a very ordinary ten-inch record made by a well-known company. She looked inside the cover and searched through the outside paper, but there was no sign of any message.

'This is all very mysterious,' she said.

'Maybe some unknown admirer—too shy to put a note inside,' he suggested, sipping his coffee. Verity looked across at him.

'Johnny—it wasn't you, was it?' she asked.

He shook his head somewhat wistfully.

'No, Verity, I'm sorry to say it wasn't. I never seem to get any good ideas like that when I should.'

More intrigued than ever, she took the record from its cover and examined it.

'It's come from someone who knows me pretty well,' she decided. 'This is my favourite piano piece—Debussy's "Clair de Lune." It's the very latest recording, too, by that new Hungarian pianist.'

'Maybe someone at the office,' suggested Johnny vaguely, 'or even one of your readers.'

'Yes, I hadn't thought of that. I'm simply dying to hear it—I've already worn out three records of this piece.'

'Finish your coffee first,' said Johnny quickly, as she moved towards the large radiogram that stood near the window. He couldn't have told her why he suddenly felt anxious that she should not play the record immediately. However, she did as he suggested, returned to her chair and began to drink her coffee. When he had finished his own, Johnny set down his cup on a side table and walked over to the radiogram.

'This is a pretty nice little job,' he said admiringly. 'Looks as if it's a hand-made cabinet.'

'Yes, it is. My brother gave it to me for a twenty-first birthday present,' she replied, and there was just the barest perceptible catch in her voice.

Johnny walked round the radiogram, examining it from every angle, and was still doing so when she rose from her chair, opened the lid and slipped the record on the turn-table.

She was just about to press the switch, when he caught her hand.

'Wait a minute, honey,' he said. 'I've got a feeling there's a catch in this somewhere.'

'A catch in it?' she echoed. 'But that's just an ordinary record—what possible harm can there be—'

Nevertheless, he took her arm and gently pushed her back into her chair.

'Looks to me like we're walking right into something with our chins stuck out,' he mused. 'Whoever sent you this was sure you'd rush to put it on the gramophone so as to hear this wonderful new pianist . . .' He picked up the record and looked at it closely.

'This seems to be the genuine article all right; there's nothing sinister about it . . .' He put it back on the turn-table. Then he took a magnifying glass from his waistcoat pocket and looked at the needle in the sound-box. As far as he could see, it was quite harmless.

'That leaves the gramophone itself,' he mused. 'And whoever sent you that record obviously intended you to play it. By the way, is the radiogram in its usual position?'

She came over to him.

'It has been moved a little farther from the wall, but Mrs Todd might easily have done that when she was dusting.' She bent down and looked at the front of the cabinet.

'This gauze in front of the speaker seems rather more loose than usual,' she told him.

'All right,' he nodded. 'Now you go and sit down over yonder, well out of harm's way.'

Having checked the connections at the back of the set, and ascertained it was properly plugged in to the power supply, he turned the knob which switched it on and waited for some seconds until he heard a gentle hum. Then, standing well to the side of the cabinet, he lifted the tone arm and swung it over to the turn-table.

As he did so, there was a loud report and the tone arm jumped out of his hand to grind noisily across the record. A wisp of acrid smoke slowly filtered through the gauze in front of the speaker.

'Johnny!' exclaimed Verity starting from her chair. 'Are you all right?'

'Sure, I'm all right.' He walked across the room and noted that a bullet had chipped the top of a picture frame and buried itself in the wall. It had obviously had an upward trajectory from a revolver somewhere down inside the speaker, and had been fired by the movement of the tone arm.

'Lucky I wasn't standing right in front there, as you would have done if I'd let you start that record,' he told her. The girl shuddered.

'Thank goodness you were here,' she said.

He borrowed a screwdriver and removed a section of the radiogram, to reveal the revolver neatly clamped in position and connected to the tone arm by an ingenious spring device.

He whistled softly to himself as he worked, then said presently: 'I don't want to scare you, Verity, but we've got to be pretty careful from now on. This is a warning in more ways than one.'

She nodded understandingly.

'You mean,' she whispered, 'that Grey Moose knows my real name?'

CHAPTER XIV

A STRAIGHT TIP

With a hand that shook slightly, Doctor Randall depressed the lever of the siphon for a fraction of a second to send the suspicion of a splash of soda into his half-filled tumbler of whisky. By the time he had returned to his arm-chair he had already taken two large gulps. The doctor was plainly ill at ease.

He settled in his chair and lighted one of the black cheroots to which he was addicted, but even this did not seem to soothe his nerves. Ever since he had received a mysterious telephone call to inform him that the police had picked up Slim Copley, he had been irritable and on edge. This was the first time the Yard had managed to bring in one of the gang alive, and it had him slightly rattled. The mysterious caller had ordered Shelagh to meet him in the entrance to Charing Cross Underground station at 11 a.m., so she had taken her car and left for Town just after ten. Since then, he had heard nothing.

Though he had combed the Sunday newspaper reports of the Brighton affair, there had been no more reference to Slim than the brief intimation that 'a man was detained at Purley police station late last night'.

It was nearly two o'clock when there was a sound of hastily applied brakes outside, and presently Shelagh came in. She was obviously not in the best of tempers, peeling off her gloves and throwing them on the settee with an impatient gesture.

'For God's sake give me a drink!' she snapped, and he hastened to obey. While he poured it out, she went on:

'Has he telephoned?'

'Who?' he asked in some bewilderment.

'The chief, of course.'

He shook his head.

'I thought you went to Town specially to see him.'

She drank nearly half the contents of her glass before replying.

'I only know I walked round that blasted Underground station for over two hours,' she replied. 'There wasn't a sign of him.'

Randall looked more worried than ever.

'Then you haven't heard anything more about Slim?' he queried anxiously.

'Not a word,' she shrugged. 'They're still holding him as far as I know.' Randall emptied his own glass.

'I hope to God he doesn't talk,' he said, with a troubled frown. 'I always said he was told a damn sight too much.'

'He had to be told a certain amount,' she retorted.

'There was no need for the chief to let him know who he was.'

She went across to the sideboard and got another drink.

'It's too late to go into that now. Whether he talks or not, he'll be taken care of. You can rely on the chief for that at any rate.'

At that moment the door opened and Cosh Wilcox came in. His cherubic features were less cheerful than usual; it was obvious that he, too, was somewhat worried.

'Any news?' he demanded hoarsely.

'No,' replied Randall abruptly. 'And I've told you not to come here in broad daylight. We don't want to attract any more attention than we can help, with those plain-clothes men still hanging about the village.'

'I come the back way,' said Cosh. 'Not a soul set eyes on me. This place is quiet as the grave on a Sunday—fair gives me the jitters. Mind if I have a drink?'

'Help yourself,' said Randall shortly.

Cosh poured himself a generous measure of rum.

'You got the stuff out all right?' he asked Shelagh.

'As far as I know,' she replied somewhat distantly. 'It went off right on schedule.'

Cosh heaved a sigh of relief.

'That's all right then. If only that damn fool Slim hadn't let them get him, this job would have been plain sailing right from start to finish. As sweet a little job as ever I was mixed up in.' He fumbled in his pockets for a cigarette and lit it.

'Doc,' he went on cautiously, 'd'you think Slim will tell 'em anything?'

'Oh, shut up!' snapped Shelagh, whose nerves were plainly on edge. Cosh looked from one to the other apprehensively.

'What's the matter?' he asked. 'There's nothing gone wrong, has there?'

'We don't know—we haven't heard anything,' replied Randall. Cosh immediately began to look troubled again.

'Supposin' . . . supposin' they get it out of 'im who Grey Moose is,' he breathed. 'I reckon that'd just about bust the whole set-up. They'd hunt us down like rats in a hole—'

'Will you be quiet!' cried Shelagh, her eyes blazing. 'They'll never get the chief . . . never!'

'Maybe not,' sniffed Cosh. 'I dare say 'e's got 'is plans made for doing a bunk—we ain't all of us as lucky.'

'Oh, pull yourselves together,' said Randall abruptly. 'Things aren't as bad as that yet by a long way. Whatever they get out of Slim, they'll only have his word for it. They'll never get any real proof.'

This seemed to cheer Cosh up a little.

'Yes, and what's more they won't find it easy to make Slim talk,' he went on. 'That boy knows how to keep his mouth shut.'

He was about to enlarge on this when the telephone rang.

'I'll take it in the study,' said Shelagh quickly, going out of the room.

'That'll be him I reckon,' nodded Cosh. 'And about time, too, if you ask me.'

'Nobody is asking you anything at the moment,' said the doctor restlessly. 'Better have another drink and say as little as possible.'

So the two men lapsed into a moody silence that was unbroken for nearly five minutes until the door handle turned and Shelagh came back. For perhaps five seconds they looked at her without speaking. Then she said quietly:

'That was the chief.'

'Well?' asked Randall, moistening his lips.

'Slim Copley's dead,' she announced in what was almost a casual tone.

'Good God!' exclaimed Randall. 'How did it happen?'

She shrugged her elegant shoulders.

'He was just about to talk . . . but Grey Moose got him in time.'

'Was that why he didn't meet you?' inquired Randall.

'He didn't say. There were so many other things to discuss.'

'Such as?'

She went over and sat in a straight-backed chair beside the table.

'Cosh, have you ever heard of Trevelyans, the jewellers just off Bond Street?' she asked.

'Yes, of course I have. I was in a smash-and-grab job there about five years ago. Proper swindle it was—the ruddy commissionaire got in the way and we had to make a run for it empty-'anded.'

'Well, this time, there won't be any slip-ups like that,' she assured him.

'You mean the chief's planning a new job already?' Randall inquired.

'Yes, and you'll never guess where the tip came from.'

'Where?'

'Duke Leroy got it from our old friend Mr Washington. On

the phone. Of course, he gave the wire to the chief the minute he heard.'

'Is it something special then?' asked Randall.

'I'll say it is. Lord Brailsham's family estate are putting the Brailsham Diamond on the market at last—and it'll be on view at Trevelyans!'

Cosh whistled softly to himself.

'That'll be worth a packet! Best part of twenty thousand I shouldn't wonder.' He paused for a moment, then said:

'How the 'ell does Washington get to 'ear these things?'

'You know Johnny,' said Shelagh. 'He's got his nose in everybody's business. Leroy says he's after that diamond and the chief has other plans.'

Randall looked up suspiciously.

'Are you quite sure of this?'

'The chief was in no doubt about it on the phone.'

Randall seemed frankly incredulous. 'After all we've heard about Johnny Washington—'

'It's that girl,' put in Shelagh curtly. 'He's fallen for her. He needs more money to create an impression.'

'More likely it's those blasted cards I 'ave to leave around,' snorted Cosh. 'I always said that was a ruddy silly idea.' Shelagh swung round on him.

'You're paid damn well to do as you're told,' she snapped. 'You haven't done so badly out of it so far.'

Muttering to himself, Cosh went over to the sideboard and poured himself another drink.

'The chief is quite certain about Washington and this girl?' asked Randall.

'Of course.'

'Then why is he acting on his tip?'

'The chief is more than a match for Johnny Washington, whatever he may be up to,' retorted Shelagh. 'Besides, the tip was to Duke Leroy.'

'I see. Anything else?'

'Yes, the chief sent a special message to you. He says Johnny Washington has got to be taken care of. Can you handle it?'

Randall laughed mirthlessly.

'Leave Mr Washington to me.'

CHAPTER XV

AN INFORMAL VISIT

STANDING just round the corner from Bond Street, the old-fashioned family firm of Trevelyans specialized in antique jewellery. They had their own exclusive clientele, and bought up the heirlooms of many an impoverished county family.

Jonathan Trevelyan was a keen business man, but he appreciated the policy of paying a fair price that left him a reasonable profit and a satisfied customer who would recommend him to other profitable clients.

Eric did not approve of all his father's ultra-scrupulous transactions, nor indeed of some of his cautious business methods. He often complained that a shop of their repute should have a turnover of at least three times its present figure, but the old man would rebuke him sharply and tell him that all too few people left in the world concentrated upon quality nowadays, and Trevelyans had a duty towards their blue-blooded customers which must never be allowed to take second place to any get-rich-quick policy.

On the Thursday after the Brighton robbery, Eric rang up Johnny Washington just before lunch and said: 'About that little matter . . . could we meet some time fairly soon?'

'O.K.—see you this evening,' replied Johnny promptly. 'Not at the shop, though. Is there anywhere near we can talk?'

'There's my club—'

'No use—I want to bring a girl friend along, if you've no objection.'

'None at all. I'll see you at the Vine—it's the little pub in the next turning to ours, as you come from Piccadilly.'

'I'll find it,' promised Johnny. 'Six o'clock be O.K.?'

'That'll do nicely.'

Johnny replaced his receiver, then picked it up again to telephone Verity's office. She had not seen him for three days, but he had been telephoning her twice a day during the week to make sure she was all right.

He arranged to call for her at the office that evening and was waiting in the main hall promptly at five-thirty. A taxi dropped them outside the Vine just after six o'clock, and they found Eric Trevelyan lounging against the bar counter in the lounge. Noting with some satisfaction that the room was otherwise empty, apart from the barman, Johnny quickly introduced Verity and Eric, and they carried their drinks over to a distant corner.

'I had the devil's own job talking the old man into this little stunt of yours,' Eric confided, as they sat down. 'At first I thought I wouldn't say anything to him, but I knew it would come round to him in the end; then there'd be a real balloon ascent!'

Verity rather liked the look of Eric. He was a sturdy young man with friendly eyes and a forthright manner and when he smiled he displayed a perfect set of teeth which were white enough for a toothpaste advertisement.

'I'm sorry if I've upset the old man,' said Johnny.

'That's perfectly all right, old boy. He hasn't forgotten the good turn you did me last year, and as soon as I mentioned your name, he gave us his blessing!' Eric laughed again and buried his nose in his tankard. Presently, he set it down and delicately mopped his mouth with a large silk handkerchief.

'Well, we've certainly had some inquiries about the Brailsham Diamond,' he announced. 'I had them all referred to me personally, as you suggested, and it's kept me pretty busy, I can tell you. Most of the inquiries came from people in the trade; in fact, so far there have been only three outside people. One of them was Lady Tollitt, an old client, who makes it her business to nose into everything, though she hardly ever buys anything. Then there was a man we didn't know, who said he was a jeweller in Salisbury, and thought he might have a client for the stone. We checked up on him, and he's genuine.'

'And the third?' queried Johnny softly.

'The third was a girl . . .'

'Ah—' murmured Johnny, his eyes alight with interest.

'She came in this morning and asked to see some filigree silver brooches, and she actually bought one. Then, just before she left, she asked me if it was true we had the Brailsham Diamond, and could she possibly take a peep at it?'

'Go on,' said Johnny.

'I tipped off the commissionaire and gave the nod to a couple of the men behind the counter; then I fetched it for her from the safe. I felt a bit jittery at first, but I didn't see how a girl on her own like that could possibly hope to get away with anything.'

'And did she?' demanded Verity eagerly.

'No, of course not. She just took a pretty close look at the stone and admired it. Then she wished me good morning.'

Johnny broke open a package of Chesterfields and passed them round.

'What was she like?' he asked.

Eric's eyes glittered for a fleeting moment.

'Distinctly voluptuous type,' he declared appreciatively. 'Dazzling blonde—all the dangerous curves in exactly the right places—in fact, a real humdinger!'

'Yes, but don't you remember anything more definite? That description might fit any showgirl from the Palladium,' Johnny protested.

'Was she wearing anything special?' prompted Verity.

'Let's see now . . . she had a mink cape . . . and—and by jove, yes! I remember now. She wore one of those diamond-shape watches set in a ring. They're a French line—I begged the old man to handle them, but he looked right down his nose.'

'You're quite sure about that watch?' persisted Johnny.

'Quite sure because we once considered . . .' He suddenly stopped short and looked across at Johnny.

'I say, old man, d'you think you know this girl?' he asked eagerly.

'I guess so,' replied Johnny casually. 'The point is, Eric, would you recognize her again if I asked you to identify her some time?'

'You can bet your last dollar on that, Johnny,' grinned Eric Trevelyan. 'I'd know her in a million. She's got style . . . she's got that little bit extra . . . she's got . . .'

'Have a drink, Eric,' smiled Johnny, signalling to the barman.

'You really knew that girl?' asked Verity ten minutes later, as they walked towards Johnny's favourite restaurant.

'Didn't you?' he temporized.

'Well, yes, it sounded rather like that girl we saw at the night-club—your neighbour . . .'

'Shelagh Hamilton. I noticed that ring with a watch in it when she and her uncle dined with me a fortnight ago. It is rather unusual—even that officer at Brighton remembered it.'

He did not say any more until they were seated in the restaurant and had given their order. Then he said slowly:

'I guess it's high time we dropped in on Doctor Randall and his charming niece. There's one or two things they might help us to sort out.'

'No time like the present,' nodded Verity.

He regarded her with a slight frown.

'I guess you shouldn't get mixed up in this—just in case.'

'We'll go down immediately after dinner,' she announced.

'Yes, but Verity, I'm not too sure about this guy Randall . . .'

'All the more reason you should have a witness,' said Verity.

'I dare say, but I've a hunch this might be dangerous . . .'

'Are you trying to stand me up, Johnny?'

They looked at each other for a moment and laughed.

CHAPTER XVI

BEHIND THE PANEL

LEW PASKIN was not his real name, but he used it more than any of his other aliases, and was widely known by it from Hoxton to Wapping Stairs. At the moment, Lew was on to one of the cushiest berths he had come across for many a day. Nominally, he was in charge of the household at White Lodge, Caldicott Green, but he was not really expected to concern himself with domestic chores, unless he felt like polishing a few spoons to pass the time.

Two women came in every day from the village, and Lew's main job was to keep an eye on them to see they didn't come across or overhear anything that did not concern them. He also had to keep a sharp look-out for strangers. This was the pleasantest occupation Lew had struck since, by some fluke, he had found himself working in the prison library at Wandsworth. But this job at White Lodge was much better paid; he was getting a tenner a week with a promise of more to come if he was cut in on any of the jobs planned for the future.

Lew was a gaunt specimen, who looked like a seedy manservant who had seen better days. Now that his hair had grown again he no longer conformed to the popular conception of the appearance of a hardened criminal.

Johnny and Verity had rung the front door bell of White Lodge twice before they heard Lew slowly and ponderously drawing back the top and bottom bolts.

'It's a bit early in the evening for all this barricading,' Verity whispered, and he pressed her arm reassuringly. Presently, the door opened about a foot and the gaunt features of Lew Paskin surveyed them suspiciously.

'Good evening, sir,' he said quietly.

'Oh, good evening,' smiled Johnny. 'You remember me—er—'

'Paskin's the name, sir.'

'I rather wanted to see Doctor Randall,' continued Johnny pleasantly.

'I'm afraid he's out, sir. He went into Sevenoaks an hour ago.'

'Oh, I see.' Johnny considered this for a moment, then said, 'Well, perhaps Miss Hamilton—'

'She's with the doctor, sir,' interposed Paskin. He spoke in a non-committal tone, but something told Johnny that he was not speaking the truth.

'Was the doctor expecting you, sir?' continued Paskin.

Johnny shook his head.

'Not to my knowledge. But if he's only gone into Sevenoaks, maybe we could wait for him.'

Paskin did not seem to welcome this proposal, and made no attempt to open the door any wider.

'I'm not expecting the doctor back for some time,' he announced.

'That's too bad,' murmured Johnny. 'All the same, this matter's rather important—I think we'll wait if you don't mind.'

Lew Paskin hesitated. He knew Johnny was a near neighbour, and might be calling upon some purely local matter, and the doctor had been very emphatic that the suspicions of the village folk must not be in any way aroused. After an appreciable pause, Paskin slowly opened the front door to admit the visitors.

He led the way through the parquet-covered hall into the drawing-room, which was expensively furnished and seemed to be in frequent use. There was a small stack of magazines, including one or two of a highly technical scientific nature and of American origin. There were also several small-sized reproductions of classical statues.

Paskin waited for them to sit down, then lingered for quite an appreciable time before he moved to the door, as if he could not be certain as to whether he should leave them alone in the room. However at last the door closed quietly behind him, and Verity heaved a tiny sigh of relief.

'Thank goodness he's gone,' she said in a low voice. 'He certainly gives me the creeps—I don't know what you think of him.'

'I guess there are plenty worse types in Hollywood,' grinned Johnny.

'Strangely enough, that doesn't reassure me very much,' replied Verity. 'Anyhow, this is quite a swell place—just look at that lovely Persian rug. It must have cost a small fortune.'

Johnny who knew little about such things, nodded absently, for his thoughts were busy elsewhere. His roving eye took in the solid oak panels around the wall, the ornately figured ceiling, the wide bay window overlooking a similar view to that at the back of his own house. He got up and began to walk round slowly, eventually paused in front of the impressive Adam fireplace and looked into the empty grate.

Suddenly he stooped and picked up a cigarette-end which was still smouldering and regarded it thoughtfully.

'It doesn't look as if the guy who let us in was on the level when he said Miss Hamilton had gone with the doctor,' he mused.

Verity came over and looked at the cigarette-end.

'Of course it could have been the butler enjoying a quiet little smoke in the best room while the boss is away,' she hazarded. But Johnny waved aside the suggestion.

'I didn't notice he used orange lipstick, did you?' he murmured.

Verity had to agree that the owner of the cigarette had almost certainly been a woman. He flung the stub back into the grate and stood there for some minutes with his head leaning against the wide mantelpiece.

Meanwhile Verity was examining a statue of Apollo about eighteen inches high. She had exceptionally keen eye-sight and was intrigued by an almost invisible crack that seemed to divide the upper part of the torso from the lower.

'Johnny, come and look at this,' she exclaimed suddenly. He went over to the corner of the room in the same wall as the fireplace where she was standing. The statue was in a special alcove in the wall which might have been made specially for it. With her right hand, Verity gently twisted the top half of the statue and found it moved fairly easily.

'This top half is quite loose,' she told him and turned it through an angle of ninety degrees. As she did so, an adjacent section of the oak panelling of the wall nearby began to slide back with a soft grating noise. Johnny swung round and peered into the aperture. Then he glanced quickly towards the door and window to make sure they were not overlooked. Then he returned to the opening in the wall and tried to see what was on the other side.

'Shall I close it again?' whispered Verity, fearful that someone would come in.

'Not on your life,' he replied, feeling in his pocket and producing a pencil torch.

The narrow beam pierced the gloom beyond the opening but all he could see when he thrust his head through the narrow aperture was four bare walls, comprising a small room about six feet square.

Verity waited impatiently for him to withdraw his head and shoulders, meanwhile watching the door apprehensively.

'Can you see anything?' she whispered urgently.

Johnny turned and put out his torch.

'It's just a small empty room,' he told her. 'Rather like one of those old-fashioned clothes cupboards, only larger. All the same, there must be more to it than that, or there wouldn't be all this mysterious business with the statue. I'm going inside to look at it more closely.'

He managed to pull back the panel another inch or two and began to wriggle his way through it.

'I'm coming, too!' decided Verity who was still fearful that the gaunt manservant might return at any moment.

When he was inside, he held out his hand, and she put one foot cautiously through the aperture which was about eighteen inches above the floor level. She had to stoop a little, but she was through the panel much more quickly than her companion. He switched the torch on again, and they stood looking round somewhat uncertainly.

'Not very startling, eh?' he whispered.

She noticed that the walls were panelled with the same oak as the drawing-room, and there was a rubberoid linoleum on the floor. Set in the middle of the ceiling was a thick glass panel which betokened an electric light, but there was no switch visible. He guessed what she was thinking and said:

'Maybe if we close the door, that will operate the switch.'

Placing her palm against the sliding panel, she found that it closed quite easily, and almost at once a soft glow illuminated the little room. Even so, it seemed just as bare as ever, without any furniture or ornament.

Suddenly, they became conscious of a slight vibration and the distant hum of a dynamo. Feeling that something was amiss, Verity tried to force back the panel, only to discover that it would not budge.

'Here, let me try,' he said, moving over to her. But the panel would not yield, and it was not easy to get any sort of powerful grip upon the smooth woodwork.

'Johnny!' gasped Verity. 'This room is moving.'

He looked round anxiously trying to discover exactly what was happening. A few seconds later, it dawned on him.

'It's a lift of some sort!' he told her. 'For God's sake keep still . . .'

It was moving so slowly that it took a little time to make certain in which direction they were going. He knelt on the floor and placed his ear against the wall. The vibration seemed more intense than ever.

'We're going down . . . I'm sure we're going down!' cried Verity.

He gripped her arm.

'It's all right; we're only moving very slowly,' he assured her. They could distinctly feel a very slight sinking movement now. It went on for about a minute, but they would both have sworn it was at least half an hour, then there was a barely noticeable jerk and the vibration ceased.

'Here we are then, sound in wind and limb,' said Johnny, trying to sound as light-hearted as possible. Verity looked over his shoulder and clutched his arm. He turned his head sharply to see what had caught her eye.

'Johnny—look!'

Released by some hidden spring, the panel was slowly sliding open.

CHAPTER XVII

THE SECRET TUNNEL

JOHNNY WASHINGTON's fingers closed over the automatic in his coat pocket that he had been carrying around for the past week. But there was no sign or sound of any other person outside the lift. When the panel opened, the light had automatically switched off, so he produced his torch, and, holding it at arm's length, he shone it through the aperture.

They seemed to be in a passage which disappeared into the darkness ahead. The chalky walls reflected the light of his torch, and there was a dank, clammy smell that was chilling and depressing. Verity shivered as she followed him out of the lift.

The tunnel was about three feet wide and there was a single line of crude flagstones on the floor. Moisture ran down the shiny walls and dripped from the low roof.

'I've got to find out where it leads,' he told her in a subdued voice. 'Are you coming with me?'

'I'm certainly not staying here!' she replied emphatically, and motioned to him to lead the way. There was no room for them to walk abreast, even if they had wished to do so, and Johnny went on ahead, clicking down the safety catch of his automatic as he moved off.

The stone floor stretched ahead of them as far as he could see; at times they were a little uneven and a trifle slippery, but they moved along at a reasonable pace, though Johnny hesitated cautiously from time to time and flashed his torch a little farther ahead. But there was still no sign of any other person in the passage.

'This tunnel seems to be pretty old,' he murmured. 'I've

often heard rumours of such things—though they're usually between the monastery and convent!'

'You've been reading too many guide books,' she smiled.

'Anyhow, this would delight Mr Quince's heart if he knew about it. Excavations are right up his street.'

'Perhaps he does know,' she suggested lightly. The idea struck Johnny with some force.

'Yeah . . . that little guy's always nosing around . . . maybe he knows more than we think.'

'Maybe we'll find him down here, looking for fossils or something,' she could not resist adding.

When they had gone another twenty yards or so, Johnny suddenly stopped and began to fumble in his waistcoat pocket. He often carried a miniature compass around, and hoped it was in this particular suit. His luck was in. He produced the compass and showed it to Verity, then stood frowning for three or four minutes while he tried to get their bearings. At last he said:

'I make it that we're heading in a dead straight line towards the Kingfisher.'

'Then at least we'll get a drink at the end of our journey,' she laughed.

After a few more yards, he got the impression that the tunnel was rising slightly, and a little farther on this became even more pronounced. Looking ahead over his shoulders, Verity suddenly caught sight of a faint glimmer of light.

'Put the torch out!' she snapped, in a tense whisper, and he obeyed immediately.

'Can you see that light?'

He looked ahead and could just discern the dim glow of what seemed to be a small oil lamp.

'We must be getting near,' he whispered. 'The Kingfisher is just about a hundred yards from White Lodge in a direct line, and we've come about that far. I'm going to keep the torch switched off, just in case there's anyone about near that lamp.'

They had to move rather more cautiously now, for the flag-stones were occasionally uneven. Presently, moving very quickly indeed, they came up to the lamp which stood on a small ledge about four feet high and six inches wide. It was only a small hand lamp, and had been turned fairly low, with the result that there was a pungent smell of paraffin. The glass container was almost full, so it could not have been burning very long.

Verity stood beside him and silently indicated a flight of wooden steps about three feet away.

'We're right under the inn,' breathed Johnny, and they moved over to the foot of the steps. Almost immediately, they heard a distant murmur of voices. Johnny pulled Verity back flat against the wall, and they stood motionless for a couple of minutes. The voices went on. Once, they heard the sound of a woman talking rapidly; then the men droned on.

'I'm going up the stairs,' he whispered at length.

'Me, too,' she said, clasping the crude wooden handrail that ran up one side of the stairs. They went very cautiously, a step at a time, and the voices from above became more and more distinct. Once, she trod on a stair that creaked like a crack of a whip, and they both stopped and held their breath for some seconds. Still the voices went on.

Keeping well to the side nearest the rail, they presently reached the top and could discern the dim outline of a door. Johnny found they were looking through an opening at the back of the cupboard, which he remembered seeing in the club-room, and the door which they could see was that of the cupboard. So he had been right in his theory that the gang was using the club-room for their meetings.

At first, he had some difficulty in catching what the people in the room were saying, because there was a long robe partly draped in front of the open panel at the back of the cupboard, and he was afraid to move it aside. Presently, however, the voices became much clearer, and he could even recognize them as belonging to Harry Bache, the innkeeper, Doctor Randall and

Shelagh Hamilton. They had suddenly flared up in disagreement, and the voices were raised accordingly.

'What really happened to Slim—that's what I want to know?' demanded Harry Bache indignantly.

'Don't be a damned fool,' snapped Shelagh. 'You read the papers, the same as the rest of us.'

'Yes, I know. But they're hushing somethin' up. I got to know what really happened.'

'All right, Harry,' came the sardonic tones of Doctor Randall. 'If you really want it straight, Slim had to be—taken care of. He was liable to talk.'

There was a momentary pause while Harry Bache digested the information. Then he demanded hoarsely: 'You mean it was—it was Grey Moose?'

'He was killed, my dear Bache, by drinking from a flask, the contents of which were highly lethal. As to how the poison got inside the flask, the police can't quite decide. They might even ask you some questions about it.' Again, there was a pause. Then Harry Bache's voice, very subdued:

'I—I *did* fill his flask just before the Brighton job. But it was only Scotch whisky . . . I didn't put nothing else in . . .'

'We'll take your word for it,' came the suave tones of Randall. 'Let's hope the police will, too.'

'Now look 'ere,' began Bache angrily, 'why the 'ell should I want to poison Slim? 'E's always been a pal of mine.'

'I'm not disputing that,' replied Randall equably. 'I'm only warning you that the police might ask awkward questions, so mind what you tell them.'

'Never mind about that,' retorted the landlord. 'What I want to know is why Slim 'ad to be taken care of like that?'

'Because,' explained Randall patiently, 'the police had persuaded him to talk.'

'Who says so? How do we know?'

Johnny thought Harry Bache sounded as if he had been drinking. His voice was thicker than usual, and the note of defiance in it obviously owed something to an external source of stimulation.

'Never mind how I know,' snapped the doctor. 'You're quite aware that we never take any unnecessary chances of that sort.'

'That's all very well, but you told us the same tale about the driver at Preston and the watchman at Gloucester. They did the blooming dirty work and then they were just wiped out.'

'You know quite well the Preston man was a bungler who didn't even trouble to wear gloves on the job. We couldn't leave him in circulation with his fingerprints already in the files.'

'And the night watchman?'

'I'll admit that was my fault. I gave the poor devil too large a dose of chloroform.'

There was silence for a few moments. Johnny felt Verity's hand near his and gripped it tightly. At length, they heard Harry Bache say:

'Well, I dare say it sounds all right. But this Grey Moose cove is a sight too smart for my liking.'

'So you think Grey Moose is too smart?' It was a woman's voice speaking now, and Johnny immediately identified Shelagh Hamilton as its owner. 'It's a lucky thing for all of us he's as smart as he's been these last few months. Otherwise, we should all be several thousand pounds worse off.'

'That's very true, my friend,' confirmed the grim tones of Doctor Randall. 'Now, let's stop all this argument and get on with what we're here for.'

'Which is what?' inquired yet another voice, which Johnny did not recognize.

'If you'll give me a little time, I'll explain everything,' retorted Randall acidly. 'A few days ago, Grey Moose got the tip that the Brailsham Diamond was in the possession of Trevelyans, the Mayfair jewellers. Shelagh has been round there and taken a look at it, and it's the genuine article all right.'

'It's too soon to pull another job right away,' objected the strange voice. 'We've been takin' too many chances as it is.'

'If you will allow me to finish what I was saying,' continued the doctor bitingly, and the other man subsided.

'Soon after Shelagh had been to Trevelyans, the chief telephoned to say that the Brailsham Diamond was a trap, and if it hadn't been for him we should have stuck our necks right into it.'

'Strewth!' ejaculated the landlord, and there was an impressive silence for a few seconds. Then the strange voice asked:

'What about Shelagh? How do we know she wasn't spotted?'

'Don't worry,' said the girl. 'I wasn't the only one who inspected that stone. The man in the shop said there'd been twenty or thirty to see it.'

'All the same,' said Randall, 'you'd better lie low for a while. The chief insisted on it.'

'Yes, we don't want to run into trouble so soon after the Brighton job,' said Harry Bache. 'I wonder whose idea it was to plant that rock.'

'You can take it from me that it was Mr Johnny Washington's scheme,' rasped the doctor. 'And you may rest assured that Mr Washington's originality will be recognized—all in good time.'

''Ere, we don't want no fancy tricks, Doc,' said Bache, with a note of alarm in his voice. 'Like that time you used the air bubbles . . .'

'You leave it to me,' snapped Randall. 'I can handle these things.'

Johnny felt Verity give a tiny shudder, and he clasped her hand reassuringly.

'Well, I don't want any more murders round my place,' said Bache apprehensively.

'You can rest assured you won't be involved,' Randall grimly assured him. 'Now, the chief's got another idea up his sleeve, and it's going to be one of the biggest jobs we've tackled so far. He wants you all here on Saturday at ten sharp.'

'Is he coming down himself?' asked the landlord.

'He'll be here. And he'll have the proceeds of the Brighton job—the stuff fetched a high price, so I hope everybody will be satisfied.'

At this point, there were signs that the meeting was breaking up, so Johnny motioned to Verity to descend the stairs as quickly as possible. They made very little noise, and when they reached the bottom there was no sign of anyone following them down. They hurried back along the passage as fast as they could go. Once, Verity slipped on the slimy flagstones, and Johnny caught her arm just in time. He judged it safe to switch on his torch again now, as there was less chance of their being seen from behind. After what seemed an age, they came to the lift, which was just as they had left it. Verity hurried in first and Johnny followed. This time, he had little difficulty in closing the panel, and the light switched on immediately, as it had done before. Once again, they heard the hum of the electric motor, and after a few moments they felt the lift moving slowly upwards.

'It's working all right,' said Verity somewhat nervously.

'I hope the gent upstairs hasn't been in to see how we were getting on,' nodded Johnny. At length, the lift stopped and the panel slid open. He peered cautiously out into the room beyond, which was quite empty. It seemed that their absence had passed unnoticed. Wasting no time, Johnny helped Verity out of the lift, and twisted the statue to close the panel. With a sigh of relief, he watched it slide gently back into position.

'I guess that's a weight off my mind,' he murmured. 'Now, it might lead to a little unpleasantness if they found us here when they got back, so we'd better get going.'

He pressed the bell at the side of the fireplace, and presently they heard footsteps in the hall. When Lew Paskin reappeared, Johnny said with an air of an impatient caller:

'I'm afraid we can't wait for Doctor Randall any longer. Perhaps you'll let him know I called; maybe I can fix up to see him tomorrow.'

'I'll tell the doctor,' replied Paskin, holding the door open for them and ushered them out into the hall. He wished them good night, and they heard the front door close behind them, followed by a slamming of bolts. Johnny and Verity stood for a moment taking in deep breaths of the fresh night air. They found it hard to realize that they had crammed so much excitement into the past half-hour. Then they walked slowly over to the car.

'Well, things certainly went our way that time,' mused Johnny, as he pressed the self-starter. 'Though I guess it's about time we had a break.'

The engine roared into life, he slid into gear, and they moved off.

'Have you time for a bite of supper at my place?' he asked. She glanced at her wrist-watch and nodded.

'Good,' he said. 'Then we can have a little talk and I'll drive you back to Town afterwards.'

Winwood opened the door for them and seemed in no way perturbed by the unexpected guest. In less than ten minutes he produced a tray of sandwiches and Johnny's favourite coffee. Verity curled up on the rug in front of the blazing fire.

'Verity,' said Johnny presently, 'I'm getting worried about you.' She looked across at him.

'I was just about to say the same thing about you,' she confessed. 'I couldn't help hearing what Doctor Randall said about—"taking care of you" I think was the expression.'

'I've handled plenty tougher customers than Randall,' Johnny assured her. 'But I don't want you to be mixed up in this affair. It's too tough for a nice girl like you.'

She reached over and squeezed his elbow.

'I've tackled some ticklish assignments in my journalistic career,' she told him. 'I've written up everything from the smuggling racket in the South African diamond mines to night life in Marseilles, so I know a few things about human nature!'

But Johnny refused to be pacified.

'That's all very well, but these people stop at nothing; you've already seen that. You've got to be on the look-out every minute of the day, unless . . .'

'Unless what?'

He shifted uneasily in his chair.

'I was wondering if you couldn't take a little holiday; say a fortnight in Switzerland or the South of France. I reckon you could write your column just as easy from there.'

'I don't doubt that I could but I haven't the slightest intention of going away just yet.' Johnny drained his cup and reached for a cigarette.

'I can't for the life of me see why you want to be mixed up in this,' he said.

'Then I'll tell you,' she said firmly, locking her hands over her knees and looking him full in the eyes.

'I intend to be mixed up in it because it is my affair as much, or more than, anybody else's. Have you forgotten that Max Fulton killed my brother?'

'I know, honey, I know. But why throw yourself into danger as well?' There was a note of pleading in his tone.

'It goes much deeper than that,' she told him. 'Right from the start of those robberies in Cape Town, I had the feeling that sooner or later I should be face to face with Max Fulton. I can't keep running away from him.'

'And what happens if you do meet?' inquired Johnny. 'How do you think you'd handle him?'

She reached for her handbag, opened it, and took out a neat little .22 Redvers automatic.

'I haven't shown it you before,' she said, 'but I've been carrying it around with me since Gerald was killed.'

'Sure, that's all very well,' said Johnny. 'The point is, can you use it?'

'I've been a member of a shooting club ever since I landed here,' she told him. 'I know it's only a toy pistol, but I can use it lethally at any distance up to fifteen yards. So you see you can't get rid of me as easily as that.'

'I don't want to get rid of you,' Johnny fervently assured her. 'I simply want to keep you out of harm's way.'

'Well, it's very sweet of you, Johnny, but I'm afraid you've picked on a tough baby this time.'

Johnny could not repress a grin, but he was obviously still worried. Verity poured him some more coffee.

'At any rate, we know just how wise to us they really are,' she consoled him. 'What's more, we're certain now that Doctor Randall and his girl friend, not to mention that landlord, are in it up to the eyes. All we have to do now is close in on Grey Moose.'

'Yes, I'll see Sir Robert first thing in the morning,' he decided.

'And what will you suggest?'

'Isn't that obvious?' he said seriously. 'The Kingfisher will have to be raided on Saturday evening at all costs.'

CHAPTER XVIII

'THE BEST LAID PLANS . . .'

THE following morning, as he drove along the country lanes, Johnny speculated idly on how the Brailsham Diamond 'plant' had leaked out. As far as he knew, the only people in the secret were high officials at Scotland Yard, Eric Trevelyan, Verity and himself.

Where had the leak occurred? Could anyone have possibly overheard their conversation with Eric Trevelyan in that little pub off Bond Street? He had already telephoned Eric to ask if he had mentioned the matter to anyone else, only to receive a fervent assurance that he had not. Asked if his father might have let slip a careless word, Eric had insisted that the old man had been too scared about the whole affair to breathe a syllable to a soul. It seemed that Grey Moose had some mysterious source of information inside the enemy camp that always kept him at least one move ahead. Could they possibly keep the raid on the Kingfisher a secret?

Parking his car just off the Embankment, Johnny walked past the Receiver's Office and the administrative section until he came to the comparatively new C.I.D. building.

As he had previously telephoned to make an appointment, he was admitted to Sir Robert's room almost immediately, and he found the assistant commissioner looking just as worried as usual, with a varied assortment of files, letters and documents in front of him. He welcomed Johnny as if he were glad to get a few minutes' relief from the concentration of his desk work; Sir Robert also realized by now that if Johnny Washington made an appointment to see him, it would most certainly concern some new development that would call for his full attention.

Johnny lost no time in rapidly detailing his adventure of the previous evening. Sir Robert was plainly taken aback by the news that their carefully laid trap baited with the Brailsham Diamond had so soon been sprung. For over ten minutes they discussed how this could possibly have come about without arriving any nearer a solution.

'I don't know what to make of that secret passage,' said Sir Robert dubiously. 'You don't think it's been made recently, do you, Washington?'

'No, sir. It's been there for many a long year I guess. Some sort of smugglers' set-up between the old inn and the squire's house maybe. You know more about these fine old English traditions than I do.'

'Humph!' grunted the assistant commissioner. 'I wonder whether the fellow Quince knows anything about it. He's supposed to be an expert in such things.'

'Well, he's staying at the inn, and he had a good look round that club-room on the night of the murder,' said Johnny thoughtfully.

'Are you quite certain he wasn't there last night?'

'If he was, he didn't say a word,' replied Johnny. 'There was some guy there whose voice I didn't recognize, but it was not Mr Horatio Quince.'

'You don't think Quince could have got wise to anything about the Brailsham Diamond last time he was here? There's just a chance he might have overheard some remark as he came in or left this room. In that case—'

'Quince would be the man we're after,' Johnny agreed. 'But I'm afraid it isn't as simple as that, Sir Robert.'

Sir Robert stroked his moustache thoughtfully.

'No,' he said with some reluctance, 'I'm inclined to agree with you. All the same, there's something a bit peculiar about this fellow Quince.'

'He's certainly worth watching,' said Johnny. 'But I've a feeling that the man we're after is a bit nearer home than that.'

'Home?' queried the Assistant Commissioner, raising his eyebrows. 'You don't mean *here*?'

Johnny shrugged.

'It's up to you, Sir Robert. I'm only reminding you of the facts. That Brailsham Diamond business was known to Miss Glyn, the two Trevelyans, myself—and a bunch of high-ups here at the Yard. You can take your choice. Maybe you think I'm playing in with this gang; in that case I shall just have to try to handle this job on my own . . .'

'No, no,' interposed Hargreaves anxiously. 'You've been a tremendous help, Washington; we simply must continue to work together.'

'O.K.' nodded Johnny, lighting a cigarette. 'We've got to work fast, too.'

'You mean you've some idea as to who Grey Moose is?'

'By this time tomorrow night, I hope to have a pretty good idea.'

'You know where he'll be, then?' inquired Sir Robert, leaning forward eagerly in his chair, and bending his paper-knife with nervous fingers.

'He'll be in the club-room at the Kingfisher soon after ten. And I reckon we ought to look in on that meeting.'

'We'll certainly be there,' promised Sir Robert grimly. 'How did you know about this?'

'I overheard it through the panel last night. They're fixing up another big job; it's so important that Big Chief will be there in person.'

'You're absolutely certain about this—the time and place I mean?'

'Miss Glyn heard it as well. You can check with her at her office if you like.'

'No, no,' said Sir Robert quickly. 'That won't be necessary.' He picked up the telephone and asked to be put through to one of the Flying Squad inspectors.

'Maxwell? I shall want a couple of cars and—let me see—half

a dozen men for nine sharp tomorrow night. We may pick up one or two extras locally . . . yes, it's near Sevenoaks . . . come round to my office when you've a minute and I'll give you the details.' He slammed down the receiver and turned to Johnny.

'We've got to handle this carefully,' he meditated. 'This time he mustn't slip through our fingers . . .'

'You've got to keep your men out of sight,' said Johnny. 'They'll have to pick up anyone who leaves . . . and you must have a couple at least watching the White Lodge. At ten o'clock they must force an entrance and come right down the underground tunnel to the Kingfisher.'

'H'm, that seems pretty fool-proof. In the meantime, we close in on the pub and prevent anyone from leaving.'

'You'll have to draw a pretty tight net,' nodded Johnny. 'There may be still more ways out of that pub than we know of. Look at the way Slim Copley vanished that day when one of your men caught sight of him in there. The main thing is to take them completely by surprise before they have time to organize any escape.'

'They may have some escape plan already organized for just such an emergency,' said Hargreaves.

'In that case, we have to beat 'em to it. And if they get wind of this raid beforehand . . .' He hesitated.

'Eh? What's that?' said the assistant commissioner.

'If they get the low-down on our plans this time, Chief, well, I'll be the only man outside the Yard who's in the secret.'

'H'm . . .' murmured Hargreaves, 'I see what you mean.'

CHAPTER XIX

A CASE OF ABDUCTION?

As he had not seen Verity all day, Johnny telephoned her in the evening to make sure she had received no more unwelcome attentions from Grey Moose. But he said nothing about the raid on the Kingfisher, even when she tried to inquire about his future plans. She seemed quite cheerful, which she told him was largely due to an interesting day at the office and a particularly appetizing supper devised by Mrs Todd.

'By the way,' she said, 'I quite forgot to tell you that I had a letter this morning from your friend Mr Quince.'

'Quince? I didn't know you'd met him.'

'He wrote to me in my official capacity,' she said. 'He told me he was one of my regular readers and wondered if I could give him a little information.'

'What about?'

'He's very anxious to trace a book published about fifty years ago.'

'What sort of book?'

'It's called *Hideholes and Hidden Passages*, and he wanted me to print a request to readers to let him know of the whereabouts of a copy. Of course, I had to reply that it was against the policy of the feature. But it made me wonder if he's discovered that tunnel from the inn.'

'I wouldn't worry too much about that if I were you,' said Johnny. 'I've arranged for that passage to be watched pretty carefully.'

'In what way?' she asked quickly.

'Never mind that, honey,' he replied evasively. 'If old Quince is mixed up with that crowd, I guess we'll find out pretty soon.'

'Johnny, you're holding out on me,' she said reproachfully.

'Only for your own good,' he assured her. 'This is a full-sized man's job. Somebody's liable to get hurt.'

'Oh, dear! Johnny, you will be careful, won't you?' There was no mistaking the note of anxiety in her tone.

'I said *somebody's* liable to get hurt,' he repeated with a grin. 'I guess I'll be behind the door if there's any rough stuff.'

He paused for a moment, then went on in a much more serious tone. 'Verity, there's something else I want to tell you. I had a chat with Sir Robert about you today; I thought he should be told about that business of the gramophone record.'

'Well?'

'We agreed that someone should keep an eye on you.'

'What does that mean exactly?'

'He's going to put a plain-clothes man on to tailing you. Now, there's no need to get alarmed; it's just a precautionary measure. In fact, I was against telling you myself, but he thought you might get scared if you saw a strange man hanging around.'

'There's something in that,' she conceded. 'What am I expected to do about all this?'

'You just relax and pay no attention whatever. In fact, I doubt if you'll notice this guy unless you particularly look out for him.' Again there was a pause. Then she said:

'Well, thanks for telling me. I'll try not to panic.'

'Atta girl!' laughed Johnny. 'And I'll call you on Sunday morning if that's O.K?'

'Anything you say,' she murmured, burlesquing his intonation.

'Maybe I'll have some news then. And by the way, if you get any more parcels, don't open 'em.'

'I'll remember,' she promised.

After he had replaced the receiver, Johnny lay back in his arm-chair and speculated for some minutes as to whether he had done the right thing in telling Verity that she was to be kept under observation. He told himself that he hadn't really had very much experience of her type of woman; she was something special and you never knew quite how she was going to take things. For instance, she'd gone through that underground tunnel without hardly turning a hair, just as if it had merely been another newspaper assignment. He had come across one or two 'sob sisters' as they called them during his brief newspaper days, but none of them had remotely resembled Verity Glyn.

When the assistant commissioner and Inspector Kennard called for him the following evening, Johnny insisted on their having a double whisky while they ran through a brief outline of the plan for the raid on the Kingfisher. Kennard produced a rough plan of the inn and its surroundings and they discussed the disposition of their men.

'By the way,' said Johnny, 'I take it they'll be armed.'

'They are,' replied Sir Robert promptly. 'These men we're dealing with are dangerous, and we must leave nothing to chance. Don't you agree, Washington?'

'Sure, sure,' murmured Johnny, fingering his own automatic in his coat pocket, and hoping that the English police were not quite so ready to draw and not quite so erratic in their marksmanship as some Chicago cops of his acquaintance.

He turned to Kennard, who was due at White Lodge, and gave him precise instructions as to the whereabouts of the statue and how it worked. He was to take four men with him down the tunnel, leaving two behind to deal with any sudden emergency that might arise. Johnny could not help admiring the brisk, unemotional manner in which Kennard disposed of all the details and settled any minor problems.

'You have your search warrant, Kennard?' queried Hargreaves.

Kennard patted his breast pocket reassuringly.

'I've got the warrants for both places,' he replied.

'Good!' nodded Hargreaves. 'Well, take care in that passage—better move in single file, with a distance of two or three yards between you. And don't take any unnecessary chances. We've got enough men surrounding the inn to deal with a gang twice their size.'

'We don't really know their strength, Sir Robert,' Johnny reminded him.

'We've no reason to expect more than half a dozen at the outside,' replied Sir Robert. 'But it isn't very important if one or two of the lesser lights escape, as long as we get Grey Moose.'

'I quite understand, sir,' nodded Kennard, preparing to take his leave.

'He seems a very efficient type,' commented Johnny casually, after the chief inspector had gone.

'A bit reserved,' commented Sir Robert, 'but a wonderful organizer. He's only been at the Yard just over a year, but I don't mind admitting I should miss him.' He drained his glass and refused another drink.

'How much time have we got before we move off?' he inquired. Johnny glanced at his wrist-watch.

'Another ten minutes yet, Sir Robert. You said you'd have about nine or ten men surrounding the Kingfisher?'

'Yes, they should be there any minute now.'

'What about the cars?'

'One will stop a little way down the road; the other near at hand.'

Johnny was just lighting a cigarette when the telephone rang; he heard Winwood answering it in the hall outside. Presently, the butler came in and announced in dignified tones:

'There is a Scottish lady for you on the telephone, sir—a Mrs Todd. She says it is extremely urgent.'

'Mrs Todd?' repeated Johnny, with some misgiving. 'Put it through, will you, Winwood?'

He went over and picked up the receiver from the instrument on the bureau.

'Is that you, Mr Washington?' came the familiar voice of Verity's housekeeper.

'Sure it's me, Mrs Todd. Is anything wrong?'

'Yes, sir . . . it's about Miss Glyn.'

'Miss Glyn?'

Sir Robert, who had been standing with his back to the fire, looked up quickly as Johnny repeated the name.

'Yes, sir, she isn't with you, by any chance, is she?'

'No, Mrs Todd. I haven't seen her today. What time did she go out?'

'She had a phone call soon after ten this morning, while I was in the kitchen seeing about lunch. She seemed a wee bit flustered when she came in, and said they wanted her round at the office right away, but she'd be back in time for lunch. Since then, I hav'na' heard a word from her.'

'I wish you'd phoned before,' muttered Johnny.

'Och, I thought nothing of it at the time. She often misses a meal and sometimes forgets to phone and say she won't be in. I had to go out myself this afternoon to see my sister at Muswell Hill, and when I got back and there was no sign of Miss Verity, I got worried and phoned the newspaper office. They said she'd been there this morning and left before lunch. That's all they knew—there was no message or anything.'

'I see,' said Johnny, plainly taken aback.

'I'm sorry to trouble you, sir,' continued the agitated voice, 'but Miss Verity said I was to phone ye if I thought anything was wrong.'

'That's O.K., Mrs Todd. You did quite right. Leave this to me, and I'll call you back.'

He slammed down the telephone and said quickly: 'Verity Glyn has disappeared. What about the man who was tailing her?'

Sir Robert glanced at his watch. They still had over five minutes. He went across and picked up the telephone and asked to be connected to New Scotland Yard. When he had obtained the office he required, he said curtly: 'Any report from Jackson?'

There was a pause, then a brief reply from the other end.

'Humph! Well, tell Jackson right away she isn't inside that building. He'd better get busy.' Sir Robert put down the receiver and said:

'Jackson followed her to the office all right, but he hasn't seen her since she went in. Come on, Washington, we'd better get moving or we'll be late.'

CHAPTER XX

THEY collected their coats in the hall and went out through the front door, where there was a Flying Squad car waiting for them. Sir Robert issued a curt direction to the driver, and they set off in the direction of the inn, keeping well within the thirty m.p.h. limit, for they were anxious not to attract undue attention.

Inside the car, neither man spoke for a minute or so; they were obviously very busy weighing up this new complication that had arisen. At last Sir Robert muttered:

'D'you think they've got her, Washington?'

Johnny gazed moodily out of the window.

'I guess there's something mighty peculiar going on, Sir Robert,' he said at last.

'If they have kidnapped her, they might have brought her down here.'

'Not too easy in broad daylight, Sir Robert,' Johnny reminded him.

'These devils seem to get away with anything,' murmured Hargreaves gloomily.

'Maybe we should concentrate on the job in hand,' said Johnny with a certain reluctance. 'It may lead us to Verity in the end.'

'Yes, yes, of course,' nodded Hargreaves, though he did not sound particularly confident. At that moment, the car drove round the side of the inn and backed into position in the car park so that it could make an instant getaway. Almost at once, a figure loomed up from behind a nearby hawthorn hedge.

'Anything to report, Chambers?' asked Hargreaves.

'No, sir. It seems very quiet. Not a soul about, in fact. We haven't seen anybody go in the pub since we got here.'

'It's not a very popular pub,' explained Johnny. 'Shall we go in now, Sir Robert?'

'All right,' nodded the assistant commissioner. 'Stand by, Chambers. Bring the men as close in as possible.'

'They're moving in now, sir.'

The moon had drifted sullenly beyond a bank of heavy cloud and there was a slight breeze stirring the nearby trees as Sir Robert Hargreaves and Johnny Washington walked almost leisurely towards the front door of the inn. It was open, and Johnny led the way into the bar.

It was quite empty.

'What's that door on the opposite side of the passage?' whispered Sir Robert.

'It's the other bar. We'd better just look inside.'

That too was deserted: so was the back sitting-room.

'Looks like a wild goose-chase,' grunted Sir Robert.

'There's something sinister about it,' said Johnny. '*Somebody* should be on the premises.'

'What's that door?'

'It leads out to the back—a little courtyard and strip of garden. Nothing much there except pigeon-cotes.'

'It looks to me as if we were expected.'

They went back to the larger bar and Johnny indicated the door of the club-room.

'Is that the room?' whispered Sir Robert.

Johnny nodded.

Sir Robert walked up to it and tapped lightly.

'Anybody in there?' he called.

They stood in silence for ten seconds, waiting for an answer. Then Sir Robert nodded to Johnny to stand clear and turned the knob of the door. To their surprise, it opened quite readily. In the light reflected from the bar, they could see nothing but a couple of card tables and a few chairs. Johnny found the switch and in a moment the club-room was a blaze of light. But it was still as silent as the rest of the house.

'There's something damned mysterious about this,' mused Sir Robert, walking slowly round the room, very much on the alert and in a much nervier state than he would have been if he had encountered some signs of life.

'Whereabouts is this panel leading to the secret passage?' he asked, and Johnny indicated the long cupboard against the far wall. Sir Robert went over to it and was just about to open the door when there was a gentle rumbling sound as the panel slid back.

'That'll be Kennard,' said Johnny.

Sir Robert opened the cupboard door wide and called out in a low, distinct tone: 'That you, Kennard?'

'Yes, sir,' came the reply, somewhat muffled by the robes in the cupboard.

'He hasn't wasted much time,' commented Johnny.

But Sir Robert was still taking no chances, and he stood back and waited until Kennard stepped into the room.

'How does that panel work?' inquired Johnny curiously.

'It's quite simple,' replied Kennard. 'There's a little knob on the framework that releases a spring when you press it down.'

Kennard's men emerged from the panel cautiously, one by one, as if they expected a hostile reception.

'There doesn't seem to be anyone here, Kennard,' said the assistant commissioner. 'What about White Lodge? Any trouble there?'

'No, sir. The place was deserted. But I found this on the table in the hall.'

He handed his chief a plain gilt-edged postcard, on which was typed: 'Enter Scotland Yard—exit Verity Glyn.'

Sir Robert passed it over to Johnny, who read it without any comment and gave it back to him.

'We'd better search the place thoroughly while we're about

it,' decided Hargreaves. 'Take your men upstairs, Kennard, and report at once if you find anything.'

'Very good, sir.' The inspector was about to move off, when he suddenly stood quite still.

'I think I can hear somebody at the back, sir,' he whispered.

Johnny, who had also heard the footsteps, had already moved over to the door and was back in the bar just in time to see Inspector Dovey appear in the doorway.

'Good lord, Sir Robert!' exclaimed Dovey, seeing his chief come up behind Johnny. 'What's going on here?'

'Evening, Dovey,' said Sir Robert. 'What brings you down here?'

'I came to see Washington. His man said he was up at the Kingfisher and—' He broke off, as he saw more detectives. 'What is all this? A raid of some sort?'

'Never mind, now, Dovey. Did you want to see Washington urgently?'

'Yes, sir. I'm glad you're here . . . it's bad news.'

Sir Robert turned to Kennard.

'All right, take the men upstairs and let me know when you're through.'

After they had gone, Sir Robert closed both the doors.

'Is this news something to do with me, too?' he asked.

'It certainly is, Sir Robert. I came down to see Washington because it concerns his friend, Eric Trevelyan. He telephoned this evening just after you left to say that his shop had been burgled. The shop was closed this afternoon and . . . and—'

'Not the Brailsham Diamond?' queried Sir Robert quickly.

'No, sir. That went back to the safe deposit as soon as we knew the decoy plan had failed. But they got over twelve thousand pounds' worth of other stuff.'

'Twelve thousand . . .' The assistant commissioner whistled softly under his breath.

Johnny leaned his elbows on the bar and blew out a stream of cigarette smoke.

'That was certainly a masterstroke, Sir Robert,' he declared. 'Trevelyans was just about the last place in London we would expect them to choose. What time did it happen? Dovey?'

'About six o'clock. They used gelignite to blow the safe, but there was hardly a soul about to hear the explosion. All the shops were closed, and they made a getaway without any trouble at all. Young Trevelyan actually saw them drive away without realizing quite what had happened. He calls round about six every Saturday, just to make sure everything's safely locked up for the weekend.'

'What about the burglar alarms?' inquired Sir Robert.

'They're electric, and the gang took care of them simply by cutting off the current at the main. Taken all round, it was a very neat job.'

'Yes,' nodded Johnny, stubbing out his cigarette on a large china ash-tray, 'they must have got wind of this raid, switched their meeting to last night, and planned that little coup there and then. Grey Moose can certainly pull off a neat little job of organization in an emergency.'

'But how the devil could news of this raid have leaked out?' queried Hargreaves. 'Only the people immediately concerned were notified—I didn't even tell Dovey . . .'

'That's so,' said Dovey. 'Otherwise, I wouldn't have come barging in like this.'

'It beats me,' muttered Hargreaves, rubbing his chin.

They eyed each other a trifle dubiously, as if they all dreaded that one would produce a *coup d'etat* at any moment. They could hear heavy footsteps moving about overhead, but downstairs there was still no sign of life.

'I suppose I'd better tell Chambers the whole affair's a wash-out,' said Sir Robert gloomily.

'Wait a minute,' interrupted Johnny. 'I think I can hear someone coming downstairs.'

It was Kennard returning to report.

'There was the landlord's wife in her room, sir. She was fast asleep. She hasn't seen her husband all evening, and went to bed soon after closing time.'

'I see,' said Sir Robert. 'Who else was up there?'

'An old gentleman was sitting up reading in bed. When I told him you were here, he insisted on seeing you. He's coming down now.'

He turned to indicate the gentleman in question, clad in a most unsuitable dressing-gown of deep purple. Mr Horatio Quince came in smiling, holding out his hand.

'Sir Robert—Mr Washington,'—he beamed, 'how very nice to see you again.'

CHAPTER XXI

MR QUINCE HAD A CLUE

SIR ROBERT looked more bewildered than ever.

'Mr Quince!' he exclaimed. 'What the devil are you doing here?'

The little man smiled again, as imperturbable as ever.

'You remember, Sir Robert. I told you last Sunday that I am staying here for the time being, to investigate a Roman villa over at Chevening. I can assure you that the excavation has reached a most interesting stage. There's a fine mosaic—'

'Mr Quince,' interrupted the assistant commissioner in an irritable voice: 'I am not in the least interested in Roman villas at the moment.'

Johnny shot a warning glance at Sir Robert.

'Perhaps I could have a word with Mr Quince, sir,' he said quietly, and turned to the grotesque little figure in the dressing-gown.

'Mr Quince, I've a pretty good idea of the real reason why you are staying here,' he said softly. 'What's more I know who you are—and what you are.'

'Indeed?' replied Mr Quince with a certain dignity. 'I'm afraid I don't quite follow you, Mr Washington.'

'I guess we won't go into that now,' replied Johnny inscrutably. 'All I want is the answer to the question—where is Verity Glyn?'

'Verity Glyn?' repeated the little man in some surprise. 'The name is vaguely familiar. You mean the lady who writes in the *Daily Messenger*?'

'That's right,' nodded Johnny. 'Her real name is Locksley, and she's the sister of the superintendent who was murdered.'

Mr Quince was quite plainly taken aback.

'L—Locksley!' he stammered. 'Did Locksley really have a sister?'

'He certainly did,' replied Johnny briefly. 'And what's more, she has disappeared.'

There came an exclamation of surprise from Dovey, who was standing just behind Johnny.

'When did this happen?' queried Kennard, in a tone which seemed to imply a measure of doubt.

'Her housekeeper telephoned me half an hour ago,' Johnny informed him.

'Mr Quince,' interposed Sir Robert. 'Have you seen anyone come here tonight?'

'I'm afraid not, Sir Robert. I have been reading in my room for the greater part of the evening. In fact, I haven't been out of the house since tea time.'

Hargreaves was obviously becoming more and more irritated by the turn events had taken. He had wasted his time and that of a dozen men. It had been a wild-goose chase, and he was feeling tired and frustrated. And on top of it all, there was this news that the gang had pulled off another job right under their noses. This would mean more trouble; more awkward questions from politicians, sarcastic memoranda and talk of calling in 'new blood'. Maybe they were right; perhaps he was too old and ought to hand the job over to a more active mind . . .

'You'd better take your party back to White Lodge, Kennard,' he said wearily, 'and pick up your car there and go straight back to Town.'

'Yes, sir,' nodded Kennard, marshalling his men and returning to the club-room.

'And if there's anyone returned when you get back to White Lodge, question them closely about their movements this evening and make a full report.'

'I quite understand, sir.'

In a minute, the little party had disappeared. Realizing that

Johnny was anxious to see Mr Quince alone, Sir Robert turned to Dovey and said:

'Come along, Dovey; we'll have a word with Chambers. I'll be waiting in the car, Washington.'

'Thank you, Sir Robert,' said Johnny gratefully. When the door had closed behind them, Johnny motioned Mr Quince to a chair, then sat down himself.

Mr Quince watched the two Scotland Yard men rather quizzically as they went out, then turned to Johnny and asked:

'Who was that with Sir Robert?'

'Inspector Dovey. You've probably seen him around here. He was watching the place for a couple of days after the murder.'

'Ah, yes, I thought his face was familiar.'

Mr Quince leaned back in his chair and eyed Johnny thoughtfully.

'I'm rather intrigued by that remark you made some time ago, Mr Washington. In fact, I might say I am *most* intrigued. Perhaps you can tell me a little more about myself?'

There was a whimsical note in his voice.

'I know for one thing,' said Johnny, looking at him steadily, 'that you have been known to do a deal in diamonds every now and then.'

'How did you find that out?'

'Never mind that, Mr Quince. I've got a lot of contacts in unexpected places.'

Mr Quince folded his pudgy hands across his slightly protuberant stomach and said pleasantly:

'It's quite true that I have a small stock of diamonds, and sell one from time to time.'

'It's also true that you were never a schoolmaster, that for the past ten years, since you came from South Africa, you have made a living from buying and selling.'

'Always within the law, Mr Washington. Always within the law.'

'I am not disputing that,' said Johnny. 'But why go to all this trouble to pose as an ex-schoolmaster dabbling in Roman remains?'

The little man looked round the room, then said in a low voice that could not possibly have been heard more than three or four feet away:

'For precisely the same reason that Miss Verity Glyn adopted an alias. We are up against a very unscrupulous man, Mr Washington, who has a knack of penetrating into strange places. I have suffered from his diabolical methods in the past, and I have no intention of being caught again if I can help it.'

Johnny offered him a cigarette and lit one himself.

'You knew Max Fulton in South Africa?' he inquired casually.

Horatio Quince nodded his head slowly several times. There was a far-away look in his eyes.

'I think I was one of Mr Fulton's earliest victims,' he murmured, and there was a note of sadness in his voice. 'He robbed me of a small fortune nearly twenty years ago now. I'd staked everything I had to go prospecting for diamonds, and after two years' bad luck, I struck a nice little pocket. But Mr Fulton relieved me of most of them, and left me for dead with a knife wound in the back. I am very lucky indeed to be here to tell the tale.'

'What happened to the diamonds?'

'He sold them and lost the money gambling.'

'You think he'd know you again?'

The little man shook his head.

'I very much doubt it. My hair has turned white . . . and my beard is new to him . . . and I have become much stouter. In any case, he only saw me for a couple of minutes when he rifled my tent—he'd never remember.'

'And would you know him?'

'I'm afraid not,' was the wistful reply. 'You see Mr Washington, he attacked me in the dark . . .'

'Then how do you know it was Max Fulton?'

'That's rather a long story, I'm afraid. Let's say I made it my business to find out, just as I've made it my mission to help put an end to the career of this unscrupulous murderer. But he must not get a hint of my identity, Mr Washington. That's most important. And I trust no one; not even the police.'

'Not even me?' queried Johnny.

'Not altogether. I've had to tell you this because you've discovered a certain amount, and also because I think I may be able to help you to find Verity Glyn before it's too late.'

That ominous phrase sounded a jarring note on Johnny's ears. Even now, at this very minute, he realized it might be too late. Mr Quince said:

'I have no wish to be associated with the police, Mr Washington, in this affair, and I realize that it's more than possible that Sir Robert is planning to detain me on suspicion of being implicated in these gang robberies. If you can persuade him to hold his hand, then I think we stand an excellent chance of discovering the lady.'

Johnny surveyed him thoughtfully, from the tiny Arnold Bennett coif to the tips of his brown, pointed shoes. It was taking a chance; he suspected that Mr Quince had several other matters he wished to conceal from the police. But things were desperate now.

'O.K., Mr Quince,' he said deliberately. 'I guess that little thing can be arranged.'

With a little sigh of satisfaction, Mr Quince held out his pudgy hand.

'Well, that's all fine and dandy,' said Johnny, 'but where do we go from here?'

'We go,' declared Mr Quince precisely, 'to a place called Mincing Lane.'

'Where on earth—'

'It's in the heart of the City of London,' Mr Quince informed him. 'At least, it was . . .'

'Here, what goes on?' protested Johnny.

'There was a meeting held in the club-room here last night,' continued Mr Quince. 'I had taken the precaution of boring a hole in the floor, and as soon as I realized what was afoot, I did my best to overhear the conversation. Unfortunately, the hole was not in a very favourable position, and I could only catch an odd phrase. It wasn't until the end of the meeting that they moved in my direction, and I overheard them refer to a hide-out in some cellars opposite Plantation House in Mincing Lane. You may remember that this street was almost entirely blitzed during the air raids, but Plantation House is a concrete building, and withstood the attack. It seems that the entrance to the cellar is through an old courtyard and . . . Why, what's the matter?'

Johnny Washington was on his feet and impatiently urging Mr Quince to follow his example.

'Get dressed as quickly as you can, Mr Quince.'

The little man seemed a trifle surprised.

'You mean you'll take me with you?' he asked.

'Sure thing.'

'You think there might be a—er—rough house?' queried Mr Quince a little wistfully.

'Don't you worry about that. I'll take care of everything,' Johnny assured him.

'But I think I should come prepared . . .'

'I leave that to you,' shrugged Johnny.

The little man brightened perceptibly.

'That's splendid. I purchased an ancient knuckle-duster only last week. Quite a formidable weapon, Mr Washington.'

CHAPTER XXII

THE ENEMY CAMP

In a telephone box in Great Tower Street, Shelagh Hamilton stood talking in low, husky tones. From time to time, she looked round to see if there was anyone outside who might possibly overhear, but there were very few people about in the City on a Saturday evening.

'Is that you, Max? Yes, it's me . . . no, no trouble as far as we know. It all went off like clockwork. Not so much stuff as we thought . . . about eleven or twelve thousand . . . yes . . . the stuff will go at dawn tomorrow . . . Who? Oh, yes, we've got her safe enough in the cellars. All right, Max, leave it to me. 'Bye.'

A cool evening breeze was blowing up tiny whirls of dust as she came out of the telephone box and approached the vast emptiness that was once the busy thoroughfare of Mincing Lane: in the past tea and coffee brokers had surged over the pavements selling the contents of their bulging warehouses and cellars. Nowadays, Mincing Lane might almost have been a country thoroughfare, enclosed by fences one usually saw surrounding rural pastures. It was quite deserted now, and Shelagh walked on until she was almost level with Plantation House, scene of many a hectic auction. She looked round quickly and slipped behind a high board fence, to descend a flight of steps which led to the area of one of the former homes of a rich tea broker. The home was now reduced to a pile of rubble.

But the ancient builders had laid solid foundations, and the cellar she now entered was almost untouched by bomb damage. She went through the cellar, along a passage and turned sharply to the left, where two doors were immediately facing her. She chose the left-hand one, and went into a half-furnished room, where she switched on the light and flung herself on to the worn settee.

From time to time she glanced at the door as if she were expecting someone. She picked up a late edition of the evening paper and regarded it listlessly, re-reading the brief report of the jewel robbery in the stop press. She lighted a cigarette and stubbed it out before it was half smoked. Then she went to a small cupboard, took out a bottle of gin and poured herself a generous measure.

She had not agreed with the chief's decision that they should move into this hide-out, but he had seemed very emphatic about it, and he did not always tell her the full details behind his moves. But she had to admit that it was an unusual retreat which was very unlikely to attract attention, for few people were seen nowadays in this deserted part of the City, particularly after dark. The chief had been emphatic that they must not be seen either entering or leaving the cellars in broad daylight.

Shelagh was about to pour herself another drink when there was a sound of footsteps outside and the door opened. Doctor Randall came in and carefully closed the door behind him.

'Where the devil have you been?' she snapped. 'I told the chief the stuff was waiting to be sent off ages ago.'

Randall pushed his hat back from his forehead with a weary gesture and began to unbutton his coat.

'We had a hell of a job with my car—had to change the back tyre,' he replied, going to the cupboard and pouring himself a stiff whisky.

'Where's Cosh and the others?' she inquired.

'Lew went to stow my car away. Cosh and Bache are in the other car.'

'You got the stuff through all right?'

He nodded.

'Yes, that's all in order. By the way, what's happened about that girl?'

'Verity Glyn? She's here.'

'Here?' he echoed dubiously. 'That's taking a hell of a risk, isn't it?'

'It was the chief's orders,' she replied shortly. 'That's all I know.'

'Did she give any trouble?'

'She certainly did,' replied Shelagh grimly. 'Fought like hell before I could get that cloth over her face. I think I kept it there a bit too long; she was a devil of a time before she came round.'

Randall poured himself another liberal helping of whisky. He sat on the not very comfortable straight-backed chair opposite Shelagh, and sipped his drink in silence. Shelagh said:

'I want to have a talk with you, Doc, before the rest of the boys get here.'

'That suits me,' he agreed. 'In fact, I sent them to park the car so that I could have a word with you.'

'Well?' she said, with a note of challenge in her voice. Randall leaned back in his chair and thoughtfully regarded his glass.

'No doubt you can guess what I want to say.'

'I haven't the least idea,' she replied indifferently.

'Then I'll tell you,' he replied, though he seemed to find it a trifle difficult. 'You know as well as I do, of course, that six months ago I was an unpaid doctor on a fourth-rate tramp steamer from Argentina. Then one night in Scotland Road, Liverpool, I happened to come across the chief, whom I had met some years previously in Marseilles. He told me he had the very job for me and I was only too glad to give it a trial. Of course, I suspected right from the start that it wouldn't be strictly legal, but I had no idea then that it would be such a money-maker.'

'What's all this in aid of?' she demanded restlessly.

'I'm trying to tell you that whereas six months ago I should hardly have cared if my tramp steamer had hit a floating mine and gone to the bottom, I've rather changed my point of view since then. For the first time in some years, I am actually looking to the future!'

'What am I supposed to do about that?'

'Nothing at all, my dear Shelagh, as long as you don't do anything to upset my plans.' He hesitated a moment, then added significantly: 'The same applies to your friend Grey Moose.'

The trend of his remarks suddenly became obvious to her.

'Why do you think Grey Moose would want to interfere?' she said. Randall shrugged.

'We know what's happened to three members of our little set-up,' he murmured. 'All very neat, very timely and highly efficient . . . but very unfortunate for the individuals concerned.'

Shelagh took a sip at her glass.

'Why should you worry?' she said. 'It's paid a good dividend, hasn't it?'

'Yes,' he smiled grimly. 'It pays a good dividend to those who remain alive to draw it. And I have made certain that I shall be one of them.'

Shelagh looked a trifle puzzled.

'What are you getting at?'

'I am merely trying to tell you that I have taken certain precautions against anything happening to me.'

'Nothing will happen to you if you do as you're told,' she replied curtly.

'Nothing will happen to me in any case,' he asserted deliberately. 'If, by any chance, I should be the victim of an unfortunate accident, I have made all arrangements with a very reliable firm of family solicitors to deliver a letter direct to the Home Secretary. You won't need to be told that there is quite a lot of vital information in that letter.'

'You damned fool!' she exclaimed desperately. 'If you dare to—'

'It's not a question of my daring to do anything, my dear adopted niece. The initiative lies solely with your gentleman friend. That letter will neither be opened nor posted unless I die in circumstances necessitating an inquest.'

Her lips were narrowed into a cruel line, and there was a note of contempt in her tone as she said: 'Max has no intention of double-crossing you. You're much too valuable. He never gets rid of your sort . . . but the others . . .'

'What about the others?'

She hesitated a moment, then said slowly: 'The chief has decided they've got to go.'

'Why?'

'That was our last big job tonight, and the chief has been tipped off that there are warrants out for all of us except himself. Somebody overheard our meeting in the club-room on Thursday. So you see, if any of the others are picked up, they are almost certain to talk, and we can't take any chances on that.'

Randall said: 'Perhaps you're right, but frankly I don't like it, Shelagh.'

'It's the chief's orders,' she reminded him. 'As soon as we can get away he wants us to fly to Cannes. He'll join us there some time during next week. There'll be another four thousand each for us over there.'

Randall drank the rest of his whisky and considered the proposition.

'What about this girl, Verity Glyn?' he said presently.

'The chief will take care of her.'

'Why did he bring her here? I'm damned if I can see any point in it.'

Shelagh shrugged her elegant shoulders and said:

'She happens to be the sister of Superintendent Locksley.'

'Phew!' This was plainly news to Randall. 'You mean the man who was killed at the Kingfisher?'

'That's the man. He was right on our tail; he knew Max in South Africa, and he was dangerous. The girl knows too much. So does Mr Johnny Washington.'

'Is the chief dealing with him?'

'Don't worry; he can't do a thing while we've got the girl.'

'Have you heard from the chief?'

'Yes, I rang him up to tell him we were here and the Bond Street job was all O.K.'

'We haven't got the stuff out yet,' he reminded her. 'There may still be plain-clothes men hanging around the Kingfisher.'

'We'll deal with that all right,' she replied confidently. For a few minutes, neither spoke. He gazed unseeingly through half-closed eyes as he turned over the plans in his mind, visualizing himself living a pleasantly retired life at Cannes.

'All right, what's the scheme?' he said suddenly.

'Come this way.'

She led him out of the room and through the next door, which admitted them to a flight of steps leading down into the cellars where the old tea merchant had once stored his cases. She produced a small electric torch, and in a little alcove leading off the passage revealed a large wooden flap built into the floor. They drew back the bolts and lifted it a few inches. Almost at once, a rushing of waters was audible.

'It's a big culvert that runs into the Thames,' she told him. They let the flap fall and looked at each other for some seconds. Then he nodded.

'It seems pretty safe,' he decided. They straightened themselves and retraced their steps. As they came to the foot of the cellar steps, he asked her where the girl was.

'In the second room along there,' she replied, nodding towards the passage behind them. 'She's safe enough.'

'All right,' he nodded. 'I think I can handle this.'

She placed her hand on his arm for a moment, and said softly: 'You won't regret it.'

They went back upstairs and into the room she had first entered.

'What are you going to do?' she asked quickly, as he closed the door and went over to the cupboard. Opening it he took out the whisky bottle with three clean glasses, and placed them on a small, cheap table that stood against the wall and served as a sideboard. He held up the bottle to the light and saw that it was three-quarters full. Then, from an inside pocket he took out a dark green phial.

'What's that?' she inquired curiously.

'Just a little something to give an extra kick to the whisky,' he replied with a grim smile. 'I had been saving it for an occasion like this. Incidentally, it is very difficult to trace at a post-mortem—not that that need worry us unduly.'

Very deliberately he unscrewed the stopper and slowly emptied the colourless fluid into the whisky.

'And that's that,' he said, replacing the cork and slowly tilting the whisky bottle.

'Are you sure they all drink whisky?' she asked.

'They won't get anything else,' he assured her, 'and I have never known them refuse it before.'

He took her glass and his own and filled them up with gin and orange from the bottles in the cupboard.

'We must drink ourselves as if everything's quite normal,' he instructed her. 'Just watch me closely and appear as natural as possible.'

'There won't be any—struggle or—' she began apprehensively, but he shook his head.

'Practically instantaneous,' he replied.

There was a sound of footsteps descending the stone steps outside, and presently they heard a firm double knock on the door.

'Come in!' called Shelagh, picking up her glass.

CHAPTER XXIII

'Why, hallo, Cosh,' said Shelagh, with a smile. 'We wondered what had happened to you. We thought you were coming with Bache.'

Cosh scowled and pushed the door shut with his foot.

'This is a hell of a place,' he mumbled.

'Something upset you, Cosh?' hazarded Randall shrewdly. Cosh wiped his hand over his mouth with an expressive gesture.

'I'll say it has,' he muttered. 'I 'aven't 'ad a chance to tell either of you before, but when we made the getaway, it was all dead easy till a rozzer tried to stop us down Brixton Road. They must have put the alarm out by then, and 'e looked as if he meant business. Even then we'd have been all right if 'Arry hadn't lost his nerve and started shoutin'. Before you could say knife, the rozzer was jumpin' on the footboard and grabbin' for the brake. There was nothin' else to do—I 'ad to bash 'im. He fell right off in front of a lorry—my God, it was awful!'

'You damn fool!' exclaimed the doctor. 'This'll mean more trouble. They'll put out a description of that car and—'

'What the hell could I do?' snapped Cosh in a surly tone. 'We were in a jam. I changed the number plates as soon as we'd got clear.'

He slumped down on a chair and said thickly: 'I'm just about all in. What about a drink?'

Randall eyed him closely. 'You've had a few already,' he said.

'And what if I 'ave? I reckon I needed 'em.'

'All right,' said Randall. 'There's some whisky. Help yourself.' Cosh slouched over to the small table and poured himself three generous fingers of whisky.

'Harry was in a terrible state, and still is for that matter,' he said, as he recorked the bottle. 'He popped into that pub along the way for a quick one to steady him a bit.'

With the glass half-way to his lips, he said: 'Have you heard from the chief?'

'Yes,' replied Shelagh. 'He'll be in touch with us later.'

Cosh nodded, then seemed about to say something more, but Randall intervened and lifted his glass.

'Cheerio, Cosh! Here's to some more paying jobs like this!'

Cosh took a prolonged gulp at his whisky and drew in a deep breath.

'Yes,' he said, 'I don't mind telling you that was one of the neatest bits of work I—'

His features seemed to contract and he pressed both hands over his heart. His breath came in great gasps and he flopped heavily on to the worn settee. Randall and Shelagh stood looking at him without moving an inch. Neither made any attempt to help him at all.

For a minute or two he rocked from side to side, obviously in great pain. Perspiration had broken out on his forehead and streamed down his face.

Randall nodded to Shelagh.

'Open the door and give me a hand,' he said quietly. She did as he asked, and Randall took the inert body by the shoulders and started to drag it towards the door. Shelagh shone her torch down the cellar steps. The lifeless feet slithered and clattered down the stairs as Randall descended. Shelagh had the flap already open when he reached it. He paused for a moment, breathing hard.

'Help me to look through his pockets, just in case . . .'

They did so very quickly, but found nothing of any importance. Satisfied, Randall rolled the body towards the opening and gave it a final push. He closed the flap and dusted himself down.

'That's the last we'll see of him,' he murmured, half to himself.

They went back up the stairs, and into the sitting-room. Randall looked at Shelagh rather curiously. She did not seem in the least upset. As a doctor, he was accustomed to death and other disturbing sights, but he was mildly surprised that this girl seemed as indifferent as he was himself to the spectacle of Cosh's violent end.

In a matter-of-fact way, Shelagh straightened the ruffled carpet, then picked up Cosh's glass which had fallen to the floor. Randall took the glass, wiped it with his handkerchief, and put it back in the cupboard.

'The other two should be here any minute now,' he said casually.

She picked up the whisky bottle, looked at it and set it down again on the tray.

'What is that stuff?' she inquired again.

'I don't think you'd be much wiser if I gave you the chemical formula,' he replied, with the ghost of a smile. 'Why do you ask?'

She shrugged.

'In this game, one never knows when a quick way out might be useful . . .'

He was about to say something, when she held up her hand for silence and they heard the sound of approaching footsteps.

'That'll be Lew and Harry,' she said, picking up her glass. When the two newcomers arrived, Randall and Shelagh were sipping their drinks and apparently engaged in a casual conversation.

The little landlord was obviously still very much on edge.

'Hallo, Doc,' he said nervously, looking round the room and nodding to Shelagh. He took off his worn trilby and twisted it in his stubby fingers.

'Oh, there you are, Harry,' said the doctor. 'Where's Cosh?'

'Isn't 'e 'ere, yet?' asked the little man in some surprise. 'I thought 'e came on ahead of us.'

'That's right,' nodded Lew, speaking for the first time.

'Oh, well, perhaps he stopped somewhere for a drink after he'd put the car away,' suggested the doctor equably.

'Wasn't he supposed to be with you, Harry?' asked Shelagh.

'We 'ad a bit of trouble and did a quick change over,' said Harry somewhat shiftily, placing a small attaché case on the table.

'What have you got there?' asked Randall.

'It's the stuff—all of it . . .'

'But I distinctly told you it was to be left at the Kingfisher.'

'I'm trying to tell yer,' protested Harry hoarsely. 'There was plain-clothes men all over the place when we got there. Luckily Lew spotted one of their cars, so we turned back right away and come straight 'ere. Nothin' else we could do. I 'ad to bring the stuff with me.'

Randall looked questioningly at Shelagh, who gave him a barely perceptible nod and proceeded to open the little case.

The stuff was certainly there all right. There was a pair of diamond ear-rings worth over two thousand pounds and a necklace of small but exquisitely matched pearls. Shelagh picked up a platinum ring, examined it for a moment, then returned it to the pile.

'I suppose it will be safe enough here,' said Randall rather dubiously. 'Did Cosh give you the list?'

'There's no list here,' said Shelagh, searching inside the case.

'No, Cosh 'ad it. Where the devil's 'e got to?' said the landlord.

'I expect he's a bit nervy after that spot of bother you had, Harry,' said Randall.

Harry Bache looked up quickly. ''Ere, who told you about that? 'Ow did you know there'd been some bother?'

Randall stalled for a moment, but the girl came to his rescue.

'The chief told me on the phone,' she said. 'He'd picked up a police radio message.'

Harry Bache looked more scared than ever.

'A police message!' he repeated, in a hoarse undertone. 'Did 'e say if they'd got the car number?'

'They gave a description, but no number.'

'Ah,' said the innkeeper, relaxing a trifle. 'Well, I reckon we've earned a drink.'

He made a move towards the whisky, but before he could reach it, there was a piercing scream from somewhere in the cellars. It sounded particularly eerie as it echoed along the passage and faded into silence.

'What the 'ell's that?' exclaimed Harry Bache.

'It's all right,' said Randall reassuringly. 'Nothing to be alarmed about.' He took a large handkerchief from his pocket and passed it to Shelagh.

'Tie it tightly this time,' he ordered.

'Leave it to me,' she said, and went out quickly.

'Who've you got out there?' asked Lew Paskin.

'It's a girl named Verity Glyn.'

'What's she doin' 'ere? This is no time to 'ave women screamin' the place down. Somebody outside might 'ave 'eard . . .'

'There's nothing to worry about,' said Randall suavely. 'The chief had her brought here because she's dangerous—she knows too much.'

'What's he goin' to do with 'er?'

Randall shrugged.

'He just said hold her for the time being.'

'I don't like it,' said Paskin.

'It's really no business of ours,' replied Randall pointedly. 'What you two need is a nice stiff whisky. Go on, help yourselves.'

'Well, I wouldn't say no to a snifter,' admitted Bache. Paskin poured himself a drink and passed the bottle to Bache, who very nearly filled his glass. As they were about to drink, Shelagh re-entered the room.

'We won't be hearing from that young lady again just yet awhile,' she announced, in a satisfied tone.

'Good,' said Randall. 'Will you join us in a drink, Shelagh?'

'I've still got some gin left,' she smiled, holding up her glass. 'Why, what's the matter, Harry?'

Harry Bache had suddenly uttered an expressive exclamation.

'I've left those blasted numberplates in the back of the car. If it was searched . . .' He put down his glass and went towards the door. 'I reckon I'd better get rid of 'em right away.'

'Where are you going to put them?' she asked.

'Anywhere . . . plenty of heaps of rubble round 'ere . . . I'll stow 'em out of the way somewhere. Shan't be five minutes.'

Shelagh looked across at Randall as Harry departed and gave a tiny shrug.

'I should hide that stuff away somewhere,' said Paskin. indicating the attaché case. 'Well, cheerio!' He lifted his glass and drank more than half its contents. He was not such a sturdy man as Cosh, and the poison seemed to do its deadly work even more rapidly.

Once again they followed the same procedure, though rather more quickly, for Paskin was considerably lighter than Cosh.

As they replaced the trap door, Shelagh said:

'What are you going to tell Bache?'

He brushed the dust from the knees of his trousers. 'I'll tell him Lew is with the girl,' he decided, and they went back up the steps.

'Shall I refill Lew's glass?' she asked, when they were straightening the room. He shook his head.

'Harry Bache knows Lew would never leave an unemptied glass behind him. Leave it as it is.'

'I must say I never thought you had it in you, Doc,' she said quietly, as they waited for Harry Bache to return. His lips set in a tight, expressionless smile for a moment.

'If it comes to that, I'd no idea you could be quite so tough,' he murmured. At that moment, they heard Bache outside, and picked up their glasses.

'Did you get rid of them all right, Harry?' asked the doctor as Bache came in.

'Yes, I stowed 'em away under a heap of old scrap iron that looked as if it had been there for years.' He paused and looked round the room. ''Allo, what's 'appened to Lew?'

'Oh, he went downstairs to have a look at the girl. He wanted to see if she was the same one who called at White Lodge this week,' replied Randall easily.

'He'll never learn to keep his nose out of things that don't concern 'im,' declared Harry Bache.

The doctor leaned over and passed him a glass. 'Oh, well, he'll be back in a minute. Here's your drink.'

Bache took the glass and set it down on the table beside him.

'I can't 'elp feelin' a bit worried about that rozzer. 'E 'ad a good look at both of us. Did the radio message say 'e'd snuffed it?'

'The chief didn't say,' answered Shelagh.

The innkeeper shuffled his feet uncomfortably and looked from one to the other, a thoughtful frown creasing his none too clean features.

'What the devil is Lew doin'?' he demanded irritably. 'I can't hear any sound of talking . . .'

'For one thing, the lady is heavily gagged,' smiled Shelagh, 'and for another, they'd be too far away for you to hear anything less than a shout or scream.'

'Well, I wish 'e'd 'urry up and come back,' sniffed Bache, fumbling in his pocket and taking out a cigarette.

'You're pretty jumpy, Harry,' said Randall soothingly. 'Why don't you have a drink to steady your nerves?'

But Harry Bache made no effort to take the hint.

'What about the doings for the Brighton job?' he demanded in a dissatisfied tone. 'That was to 'ave come through in time for yesterday's meetin'.'

'The chief will be along with it tonight,' explained Shelagh.

'He told me on the phone your cut will be just on five thousand.'

'Five thousand!' Harry whistled. 'By God, I'll paint the ruddy town red! And after that, I'll get outer that stinkin' pub and get me a nice little place at Brighton—near the racecourse—see a bit o' life there.'

Randall smiled:

'That's fine!' he said, raising his glass. 'Here's luck to the new pub!' He took a sip at his drink, but Harry Bache did not join him.

'What's the matter with you?' demanded Randall curiously. 'Have you gone on the wagon?'

Harry Bache gave a mirthless little chuckle. 'Me on the wagon! That'd be a fine start to runnin' a new pub, that would!'

'Then drink up, Harry, and toast the new venture,' smiled Shelagh, raising her glass. But Harry Bache's whisky remained untouched. He and the doctor eyed each other.

'What's the matter?' asked Randall at last. 'Why aren't you drinking?'

For a moment the innkeeper did not reply. Then he rose slowly to his feet and with a sudden movement produced a revolver from an inside pocket.

'Because I'm no sucker!' he snapped.

Doctor Randall took an involuntary step backwards, and Bache construed it as a move to escape.

'You keep away from that door or I'll blow your blasted brains out!' he rasped. 'Don't think I 'aven't got a good idea what's in that glass.'

'Put down that gun, Harry, and don't be a damned fool,' advised the doctor. 'There's nothing wrong with that drink.'

'No?' said Bache sarcastically. 'All right then, *you* drink it.'

'I tell you it's harmless . . .'

'Of course it is,' said Shelagh.

'All right,' said Bache, swinging round on her. 'Then *you* drink it.'

'You know I never touch whisky.'

Harry Bache laughed sardonically.

'In that case, it's the doc who'll 'ave to oblige.' With his left hand he slid the glass along the table in the doctor's direction.

'But before you drink it, tell me what you've done with Lew and Cosh,' ordered Bache, waving his revolver threateningly.

'I told you we haven't seen Cosh,' said Randall somewhat shakily.

'Come on now—I want the truth,' rasped the innkeeper threateningly.

'Now listen to me, Harry,' began Randall in a persuasive tone.

'I'm not listenin' to yer—I'm tellin' yer. I don't want any of this soft soap business. What's 'appened to those two? You can tell me the truth or drink this whisky.'

Randall backed a step, but to his surprise Shelagh came forward and picked up the glass.

'You know I loathe whisky,' she said calmly, 'but just to satisfy you, Harry, I'll drink half of it.'

'Garn! You wouldn't dare,' retorted Bache disbelievingly.

'We've told you it was nothing but whisky. All right now, I'll prove it.'

Slowly, she raised the glass to her lips, but before it touched them she twisted her wrist and flung the contents full into Bache's face. For a moment, he was blinded, and in that instant Randall snatched up the whisky bottle and brought it down on Bache's head.

'Thanks, Shelagh,' gasped Randall. 'That was a near thing.' He seemed momentarily exhausted by his sudden effort, but presently stooped and examined the inert form.

'Listen!' said Shelagh suddenly. 'Isn't that a car?'

They awaited the slamming of the car doors, but heard nothing.

'Better move him out of sight, just in case,' decided Randall. 'Could you give me a hand?'

Together they lifted Harry Bache and pushed him behind the settee. But they were not quick enough.

'You really shouldn't go to all that trouble,' said a polite voice from the doorway, and they swung round to see Mr Quince standing there. For five seconds there was complete silence then Randall said quietly:

'Come in, Mr Quince. Come in and close the door.'

The little man did so without taking his eyes off them.

'Let me see, you will be Doctor Randall. I think we met on the night of—er—that deplorable affair at the Kingfisher.'

'That's so, Mr Quince.'

'And this, no doubt, is your charming niece I have heard so much about,' continued Mr Quince imperturbably.

'You seem to know quite a lot about us,' said Randall, with just a barely audible edge in his voice. 'But you haven't told us anything about yourself.'

'It's very charming of you to inquire,' smiled Mr Quince amiably. 'I'll be delighted to oblige. What exactly do you want to know about me?'

'Suppose you begin by telling us precisely who you are, and what you are doing here tonight.'

'But surely our old friend Bache told you who I am. I'm Horatio Quince, a retired schoolmaster, interested in antiques, and almost anything from a bygone age. As you know, I have been staying for some two weeks at the Kingfisher, exploring the local countryside, and I have come across the remains of a most interesting Roman villa at Chevening that—'

'Yes, yes,' interposed Randall, now slightly suspicious that for some reason Mr Quince was playing for time, 'but that doesn't explain why you are here.'

'But I should have thought that would be obvious, my dear Doctor. This place is teeming with ancient relics. Why, just along the way is the most remarkably preserved Roman bastion that is quite unbelievable. The aerial attacks on the City have revealed some really wonderful stretches of the ancient Roman wall—I assure you that they are well worth a visit. In fact, I am surprised you haven't seized the opportunity long before this to—'

'You don't look at ruins at this time of night,' interrupted Shelagh coldly, her eyes narrowing.

'I assure you those old walls look quite different by moonlight. There's a poem by Scott on the subject—'

'There is no moon tonight,' Shelagh interrupted him once more.

At that moment, Mr Quince noticed that Randall was covering him with the black revolver that had fallen from Harry Bache's hand.

'Really, Doctor Randall, is that necessary?' he said, in a mildly reproving tone.

The doctor made a threatening movement.

'We are still waiting for you to answer our questions, Mr Quince. What are you doing down here?'

'Please be careful with that revolver; it's a most dangerous weapon,' said Mr Quince apprehensively.

'I'm glad you appreciate that. Now, for the last time, will you answer my question?'

'Certainly—certainly. I came to look for a lady whom I understand is being detained here.'

'What's her name?'

Mr Quince hesitated, and the doctor repeated the question.

'I believe,' said Mr Quince, 'that her professional name is Miss Verity Glyn.'

Randall sat back on the edge of the table.

'I see,' he nodded. 'And may I ask how you knew she was here?'

'Really, Doctor, that's rather a long story.'

'Then you'd better tell it quickly. There's no time to lose.'

Mr Quince looked from one to the other with a remonstrating air. 'I must ask you to believe that Miss Glyn is really only an acquaintance—yes, indeed, the merest acquaintance,' he began mildly. 'I read something in her column about ancient buildings, and I wrote her a little note—'

'This is leading nowhere,' broke in Shelagh. 'He's just stalling for time.' She nodded to Randall, who motioned Mr Quince back towards the door.

'Come along, then, Mr Quince,' he said suavely. 'We'll take you to meet your friend Miss Glyn.'

Mr Quince looked round nervously.

'Open the door,' snapped Randall.

Slowly, Mr Quince turned the knob and pulled the door towards him. As it opened, he stood behind it, leaving a clear view of the doorway and the sight of Johnny Washington standing there holding an automatic.

'Drop that gun, Randall!'

With a metallic clank the doctor's revolver fell to the floor. Shelagh glanced across at him contemptuously.

'How the devil did you get here?' snapped Shelagh Hamilton.

'With Mr Quince,' replied Johnny curtly. 'And that's the last question from you, my friend. I'm getting a bit tired of monkeying around with your crowd, and I guess this affair's going to be cleared up right now. Come on in, Verity, and give us a hand.'

Verity came up behind him and into the room. She looked pale and there was a cut on her cheek and ominous red marks on her wrists. Her hair was untidy, but there was a triumphant gleam in her eye and she moved with a quiet intensity.

'Pick up that revolver, will you, Verity?' asked Johnny.

'I'm very much afraid there is a—er—body behind the settee,' interposed the gentle voice of Mr Quince. 'I just caught sight of a man's foot as I came into the room.'

'Move out the settee then, will you, Mr Quince?'

'Oh, dear,' murmured the little man. 'It's Mr Bache. He seems to have a very nasty head wound: I doubt if he'll recover consciousness for some time. He should have instant attention, Mr Washington.'

'He'll have to wait,' decided Johnny.

'What are we going to do with them?' asked Verity, indicating Randall and Shelagh.

'Take 'em downstairs and tie 'em up in the room where I found you,' decided Johnny. 'You go on ahead and I'll bring up in the rear. And don't hesitate to shoot if there's any nonsense.' He turned to the two captives.

'Miss Hamilton—Doctor Randall—you heard what I said.'

'Just a minute,' interposed Mr Quince. 'Are you forgetting this?' He indicated the attaché case on the table. Still keeping Randall and Shelagh covered, Johnny examined the pile of jewellery. He whistled softly.

'The Trevelyan job . . . Quite a nice little haul, eh, Doctor?' Randall made an involuntary movement, but Johnny's Colt waved him back.

'I think perhaps you'd better stay here, Mr Quince, and keep an eye on this stuff,' said Johnny. 'We'll be back in five minutes, then we'll prepare to receive a certain distinguished visitor.'

He looked across at Shelagh as he said this, but she avoided his eye.

'Certainly, I'll wait here,' agreed Mr Quince, settling himself as comfortably as possible and taking a much-used briar pipe from one pocket and a folded newspaper from the other. He was settling back to read it as Johnny and Verity shepherded their prisoners from the room and out into the passage.

Johnny produced his torch and they soon found their way down to the room where Verity had been tied to a chair. There were still several lengths of rope lying around, and Johnny tied up his captives very efficiently to a couple of chairs.

Verity was beginning to look rather tired now, and she was very glad when the unpleasant task had been completed. Johnny gagged both Randall and the girl, using his own handkerchief and the large one that he had untied from Verity's mouth when he released her.

As they closed the door behind them, she whispered:

'What are we going to do now?'

'Wait for Grey Moose,' he replied almost nonchalantly.

'What makes you so sure he'll come?'

'For one thing to see you; for another to pick up that stuff from Trevelyans. By the way, did you happen to overhear them say anything about that job?'

She shook her head.

'They didn't talk very much. . .though I did happen to catch one stray phrase that sounded queer.'

'What was it?'

'Something about "Release at dawn" . . .'

'Release at dawn,' he repeated thoughtfully. 'That seems to ring a bell.'

'What's it mean?'

'We'll sort it out, all in good time,' he assured her, as they quietly climbed the cellar steps and moved towards the room where they had left Mr Quince. 'As soon as we've dealt with our visitor, I'll phone the Yard and—'

He suddenly stood stockstill and gripped her wrist.

'That's my car!' he exclaimed, as they heard the unmistakable roar of an engine, and with flying leaps he went bounding up the basement steps. But he was only just in time to see a rapidly disappearing tail light turn into Great Tower Street and vanish.

'Johnny—who could it have been?' cried Verity, who had followed him up the steps, and was standing by his side, shivering in the night air.

Johnny stood lost in thought for a few moments.

'There's always a chance it might have been some car thief who saw it standing there with no one about,' he murmured. 'I'll phone the Yard and get 'em to put out a description. Come on, honey, let's see if our Mr Quince is ready.'

They retraced their footsteps and went back to the sitting-room.

Johnny went in first, and almost at once he turned and stretched out his arm to restrain Verity from following him; he realized that the man they had been waiting for had already left. Not only was there no sign of the attaché case containing the spoils of the robbery at Trevelyans, but slumped against the table, with a stiletto in his back, lay Horatio Quince.

CHAPTER XXIV

THE DESERTED CAR

By a stroke of good fortune they discovered a City policeman on duty at the corner of Great Tower Street and sent him back to the cellar to take charge of Randall and Shelagh Hamilton. Johnny went into the same telephone box which Shelagh had used a couple of hours previously and was immediately connected to New Scotland Yard; unfortunately Sir Robert Hargreaves had left an hour earlier. Johnny put in a call to Sir Robert's home address in Hampstead, and after a short delay, the assistant commissioner came to the telephone.

'Hallo, Washington,' said the familiar voice, 'we've been wondering what's happened to you.'

Johnny gave him a very rapid *résumé* of the events of the evening.

'H'm, you've certainly been busy,' commented the assistant commissioner grimly. 'Is Miss Glyn all right?'

'She's O.K.' said Johnny, 'and I guess we've pretty near broken up that gang.'

'But we still haven't got Grey Moose.'

'You said it. Maybe we will yet, though. I've still got a card or two up my sleeve.'

'Well for heaven's sake let's get busy,' said Hargreaves. 'Is there anything you want me to do?'

'Yes, first of all, have Randall and the girl taken in. I told the officer I saw not to budge till you sent someone along.'

'Right, I'll attend to that,' promised Sir Robert. 'We ought to get some useful information out of them. They know the identity of Grey Moose, of course.'

'They sure do. But whether we can make 'em talk is quite

another matter. That Randall guy's a tough customer, and
the girl wouldn't say a word if you tortured her with hot
irons.'

'What makes you say that?'

'I've been getting the dope on her. She's Max's special girl
friend—follows him round the world. I guess they've just been
planning a big getaway—that's if their past routine is anything
to go by.'

'Humph! Well, is there anything else you want me to do?'

'Yes, I'd like you to arrange with your Sevenoaks people to
let me have two or three men early tomorrow morning.'

'I'll get Dovey to fix that up right away.'

'I'd rather you didn't trouble Dovey or anyone at the Yard,'
said Johnny. 'Can't you get through direct to the inspector at
Sevenoaks?'

'Well, of course, if you say so,' said Sir Robert a trifle doubt-
fully. 'You're sure you wouldn't prefer a Squad car?'

'No, no, just a couple or three reliable men from the local
station. I shall want them down at my place fairly early—not
later than five.'

'What's going on?' inquired Sir Robert curiously.

'I'm afraid I can't answer that one just yet, Sir Robert. I'm
simply acting on a hunch.'

'It all sounds very mysterious,' said the assistant commissioner.

'Maybe,' replied Johnny. 'Anyway, I guess it's about my last
chance of getting my hands on the stuff from Trevelyans and
the man who organized the job. And I'd take it as a favour, Sir
Robert, if you didn't mention this to a soul except the inspector
at Sevenoaks—and tell him as little as possible.'

'Are you sure that three men will be enough?'

'Pretty sure,' replied Johnny. 'Harry Bache won't be fit for
much, and from what Verity tells me, Randall and the girl
bumped off Wilcox and Paskin before we got there tonight. I
guess we're coming mighty close to the final curtain.'

'All right, Washington, you shall have your men. They'll report to you at five sharp.'

'Thanks, Sir Robert,' said Johnny, then added as an after-thought: 'By the way, I almost forgot to mention that Grey Moose stole my car—it's a red saloon—a three and a half litre Columbia. I guess he's abandoned it by now, but I'd like to get it back as soon as possible.'

'I'll see to it,' promised Sir Robert. 'And Washington—'

'Yes, Sir Robert?'

'You'll be careful, won't you? This man is sure to be armed and desperate.'

'I can still hit the ace of hearts at ten yards,' chuckled Johnny. 'Good night, Sir Robert, I'll phone you first thing in the morning.'

'Good night, Washington—and good luck.'

Johnny came out of the telephone box, and Verity, who had been standing in the shadows, rejoined him. They looked round for a taxi, but the City on a Saturday night is as deserted as a country lane, and they set out to walk briskly in a westerly direction.

'Are you sure we oughtn't to go back to—that place, to make a statement to the police and see that everything is all right?' she asked.

'Sir Robert will look after all that. He'll send a Squad car to pick up Randall and the girl; there's already a warrant out for them. We'll make a full statement tomorrow.'

'Then what do we do now?'

'You go to bed and get a good night's sleep and try to forget everything,' he advised. 'I'm going to do the same, because I must be up long before the crack of dawn tomorrow.'

As the dome of St Paul's loomed towards them, they caught sight of an empty bus going towards Ludgate Hill, and managed to race it to the nearest stop. It happened to be a number eleven, which would take Verity almost to her door. They climbed the stairs and sat in the two seats at the back on the top deck, where they both lighted cigarettes. For some minutes they sat without speaking, drawing in and expelling long streams of tobacco smoke.

'Well, I guess this is one day of my life I wouldn't like to live over again,' said Johnny presently.

'Me, too,' she nodded. 'How ever did you manage to find me in that awful place, Johnny?'

'It was old Quince who put me on the track, or I wouldn't have had an idea,' he said.

'Poor old Quince. It's dreadful to think it cost him his life.'

'Yes,' said Johnny, 'that's one more good reason why I've got to level scores with Grey Moose.'

She sighed.

'He's always a move ahead of us, Johnny. It almost seems like thought-reading or some strange sort of trick.'

'It won't always come off,' he assured her. 'Even tonight he had a pretty near squeak. Maybe next time . . .'

She shivered slightly at the prospect. Presently, she asked: 'Why do you think he disappeared tonight, after he'd stabbed Mr Quince? He must have known Randall and Miss Hamilton were somewhere in the cellars.'

Johnny flicked the ash off his cigarette.

'I think Grey Moose made a pretty shrewd guess at what had happened,' he hazarded. 'The fact that Quince was guarding that stuff would have given him a tip that there was something unpleasant going on.'

'Yes, but surely he would have tried to help Randall and the girl.'

'Oh, no! Not Grey Moose!' said Johnny decisively. 'He must have backed out of more awkward situations and left more suckers to face the music than any man alive.'

'But I thought this girl was in love with him.'

'So what?' shrugged Johnny. 'I guess there isn't much room for that stuff in Max Fulton's life. But there was another thing to consider—he had to get that jewellery out of the country pronto. Just now, it's white hot and sizzling! His pals had fallen down on the job, so it was up to him.'

'It's tough on the girl,' said Verity.

Johnny stubbed out his cigarette.

'Anybody who associates with Max Fulton is asking for trouble, and she probably realizes it better than most people. From what I hear, she's had a pretty good run with him. They've been around together for over five years.'

The bus moved briskly along Fleet Street, where the traffic had dropped to a trickle. A few sub-editors were leaving their offices, with the last edition of their Sunday paper safely put to bed, and looking down they could see the lights in the basements of some of the large newspaper buildings. Verity imagined the throbbing of the presses sending a steady vibration through the entire structure. No doubt some of the stop press columns would contain a brief flash of that night's happenings in Mincing Lane.

'You seem to have found out quite a bit about Max Fulton,' she said presently.

'I have my spies,' he grinned. 'But it hasn't been any too easy. There's a lot of folk know *something* about Max, but they're scared to hell to open their mouths.'

'You never managed to get a photo of him?'

Johnny shook his head.

'Max Fulton is one of the few guys in this world who has never had his picture taken—not even on a bearskin rug.'

'I wonder how he gets from one country to another without a passport,' she speculated.

He half turned and grinned at her.

'Have you ever recognized anyone from their passport photograph?' he asked.

'But surely if he's as high up as you seem to suspect, he's had to have a photograph taken at some time or other.'

'If he has, then the photographer didn't know he was taking Max Fulton, and that name isn't attached to the picture.'

'Oh, dear,' sighed Verity. 'It sounds terribly involved.'

'Not a bit of it, when you take it a step at a time. A career like Max Fulton's isn't built in a day, you know.'

The bus rounded the corner of Trafalgar Square and sailed into Whitehall amidst the stragglers of the late theatre traffic. Under the passing glare of the overhead lights, Verity looked much paler than usual, and she had obviously by no means recovered from her experience. Suddenly she said:

'I wonder what Max Fulton was going to do with me.'

To take her mind off that aspect of the business, Johnny quickly interposed, 'I can't think how the Yard man lost you. He said you went into the office and he never saw you come out.'

She wrinkled her forehead for a moment, then said:

'I remember now . . . I went down to the comps to correct some stuff on the stone, and I came out by the printers' entrance on the Embankment, instead of the main hall. That's how he'd miss me.'

'What happened then?' inquired Johnny.

'I had just stepped out of the doorway when a man in a chauffeur's uniform came up and asked me if I was Verity Glyn. He said that you had sent him to fetch me on an urgent matter. Of course, I got in the car almost without thinking—and there was Randall pointing a revolver at me . . .'

'I see,' said Johnny slowly. 'They'd figured all that out quite nicely.'

'Maybe I should have taken a chance and screamed for help,' mused Verity.

'It would have been a pretty slim chance,' Johnny told her. 'I've no reason to doubt that Randall wouldn't have been as good as his word. He's a tough customer. Still, his chief had ordered 'em to bring you back alive, so maybe he'd only have hit you with the butt of the gun.'

Verity shuddered.

'I'm sorry,' said Johnny, 'you've had to put up with more than most girls could stand in one day. Let's forget it.'

'But I'm still curious about why he wanted me "brought back alive",' persisted Verity with a faint smile.

'I wouldn't worry about that now,' replied Johnny. 'Maybe, he simply wanted to use you as a trump card in case he needed one. Or he may have thought chasing after you would keep me from under his feet. Oh boy, he certainly made one mistake if he thought that!' added Johnny reflectively.

She smiled.

'I was never so glad to see anybody in my life as I was to see you walk into that horrid cellar,' she confessed.

'I certainly hope you'll go on being glad to see me,' he said quietly, as the bus jerked to a standstill outside of Victoria station. They peered down into a snack bar crowded with a strange assortment of humanity. Then the bus lurched on once more and rounded the corner past the Grosvenor Hotel.

'All the time I was in that car,' went on Verity with a slight shiver, 'I kept thinking: "Things like this don't happen to people in broad daylight." We passed several policemen, and once I caught my breath to cry out. But he guessed what was in my mind, and poked the gun right up against me . . .'

'You poor kid,' sympathized Johnny. 'I'm surprised you didn't pass right out.'

'I thought I was going to. But I dug my nails into my palms to stop myself. I thought there might be a chance of making a getaway when the car stopped. At least, I imagined I might scream and attract somebody's attention. But there was hardly a soul to be seen—it was Saturday lunch time, and that part of the world was practically deserted.'

'So they got you into the cellars without any trouble.'

'I did manage to work the gag from my mouth and scream when I had been tied up there for several hours,' she said, 'but that girl came in and replaced the gag.'

She rubbed her tender jawbone at the recollection of the incident. The bus swayed over Ebury Bridge and swung round to the right through the purlieus of Pimlico. A small group of revellers came out of a public house, singing discordantly.

'Well, I hand it to you,' said Johnny admiringly. 'You're pretty tough in that quiet way of yours. But I hope you won't have to face anything like that experience again.'

They were silent for a minute or two as the bus wound its way into Sloane Square, where a brilliantly lighted coffee stall was doing a brisk trade.

'Johnny,' said Verity at length, 'have you any idea who Grey Moose is?'

'I could make a near guess,' he said, 'but I won't. Tomorrow, I expect to know for certain.'

'Then you think you know his next move?'

'He has only two main interests at the moment,' explained Johnny. 'First, to get that stuff out of the country, and second to get out himself. He can't risk making it a combined operation, in case he should be searched, for Sir Robert is having all the ports carefully watched. So, as I see it, he'll try to get the stuff out by the same method as they've been using right from the start.'

Noticing the gleam in his eyes and the eager set of his mouth, she caught his elbow for a moment and murmured:

'Johnny, don't stick your chin out too far.'

He chuckled.

'Leave it to me, honey. By the way,' he added as a new thought struck him. 'I thought you told me you carried a neat little .22 around. Have you got it with you today?'

She shook her head, and looked down in her confusion.

'I—I changed my handbag, and I must have forgotten it.' she confessed. The bus lurched to a standstill outside Chelsea Town Hall, and they climbed down the stairs and dismounted.

'There's no need to come any farther. I'll be perfectly all right now,' she assured him, but he strode along beside her and insisted on accompanying her to her front door.

'But how on earth will you get back to Sevenoaks at this time of night?' she asked in a worried tone.

'Quite simple. I'll hire a car from a fellow I know who runs a hire service,' he told her.

'Will he be open at this time?'

'It's an all-night service, so there'll be no trouble.'

'I could give you a shakedown on the settee in the lounge,' she suggested, as they turned out of the King's Road into the street where she lived.

'No, thanks,' said Johnny. 'I must get back home tonight. It's very important.'

'I'm afraid you're not going to get much sleep,' she said.

'I guess an hour or two less beauty sleep can't make much difference to my ugly mug,' he grinned. At that moment they turned the corner as the road twisted at a fairly sharp angle, and Johnny suddenly stopped dead. Less than twenty yards away was a large American saloon car drawn up to the kerb. The tail lamp was still on and he could see the rear number plate quite clearly. It was undoubtedly his Columbia.

'Well, what d'you know about that?' he whistled.

'Is—is it—?' began Verity.

'I'll say it is! And it's right outside your flat.'

For a few moments they did not move.

'What are you going to do?' she whispered.

'You stay here,' he said. 'I'll go and take a look.' His hand closed over the Colt in his jacket pocket, as he moved softly towards the car. Suddenly, he crossed the road and approached it cautiously on the opposite side. When he came level with it he could see no one inside, so he turned and slowly walked back. Then he re-crossed and came up to the car so that he could look inside. A gas lamp a few yards away lit the interior sufficiently for him to see that it was quite obviously empty. He beckoned to Verity, who joined him.

'What on earth's going on?' she asked, in a low tone.

'That's what I want to find out.'

'D'you think there's someone inside the flat?'

'Have you got your key?'

She shook her head.

'I'm afraid I left that in my other handbag, too.'

'In that case, we'll have to ring. You stay down here—I'll do it.'

He mounted the four steps from the pavement and rang the bell of Verity's flat. There was a long silence, and he rang again. Presently, a light appeared in the hall, and he could hear someone descending the stairs. He motioned to Verity to keep out of line with the door as the person inside fumbled with the catch. A moment later, the door was carefully opened, and Mrs Todd stood there, wearing a heavy woollen dressing-gown over a long nightdress. She recognized him almost at once.

'Mr Washington! Is anything the matter?'

'Sorry to drag you out of bed, Mrs Todd. I've brought Miss Glyn back.'

'Thank God she's safe! But where is she?' cried the housekeeper.

'Just a minute, Mrs Todd,' said Johnny quietly. 'Have you had any visitors this evening?'

'Not a soul, sir.'

'You didn't see this car out here arrive?'

'No, sir. I've been in my kitchen at the back all the evening.'

Johnny signalled to Verity who came up the steps. They went inside and shut the door.

'Stay here while I go up and take a look round,' he said to the two women, who were talking rapidly in loud whispers. He left Verity explaining the events of the day to an open-mouthed Mrs Todd, and went cautiously into the lounge, quickly switching on the light as soon as he was through the door. The room was empty and just as he had seen it on his previous visit. Methodically, he went through the other rooms, but they were all quite deserted, and he called to the women below to join him. When Mrs Todd suggested getting them a cup of coffee, he found himself agreeing, though he rarely drank coffee except under his own roof. But he was feeling a sudden reaction to the events of the day, and decided that a hot drink would lift his spirits for the journey home.

He and Verity went into the lounge and switched on the electric fire. It was just after midnight by the electric clock on the mantelpiece.

While they waited for the coffee, Johnny paced restlessly up and down.

'I can't think why he should dump my car outside your door, of all places,' he said, with a worried frown.

'It does seem strange,' she had to admit. 'Johnny, you don't think he's somewhere around here now?'

'I'm fairly certain he isn't,' he reassured her. 'I've got reasons for saying so that we won't go into now—it's so darn late . . .' He stifled a yawn.

When Mrs Todd came in with the coffee, he drained his cup almost at a gulp and announced that he must be going. He promised to telephone Verity in the morning as soon as he had any news, and made his way out to the car.

But he was still vaguely worried. He walked round the car and examined it carefully. It seemed exactly as he had left it in Mincing Lane. Finally, he opened the door somewhat gingerly, climbed in and switched on the dashboard light. As he looked at the instruments, he suddenly recalled that he had not checked his oil lately, and wondered if he would be all right for the return journey. Maybe Max Fulton had driven the car quite a way, and in that case the oil would be low. He got out and lifted the bonnet and searched for the dipstick. The gas lamp was only a few yards away, so he could see fairly well. He found the dipstick and was unscrewing the cap of the oil tank when he noticed an unfamiliar length of thin rubber-covered wire. Johnny pulled out his pocket torch and warily traced the wire to the back of the dashboard. It was connected to the self-starter button. The other end went to the car battery, then disappeared somewhere beneath the floorboards. For a

minute or two, Johnny ferreted around, and presently discovered a neat little oblong canister, with what was obviously a
tiny detonator wired in series with the starter and battery.

One push of that starter button and the car and passengers
would have been blown to fragments.

CHAPTER XXV

JOHNNY carefully disconnected the bomb and placed it on the rear seat of the car. So that was why Max Fulton had brought back the car to Verity's flat. He had guessed that Johnny would take her home after her trying ordeal, and naturally he would use his car to return to Caldicott Manor. It was rather an obvious trick, but it might easily have worked when one was tired and off guard. Fulton would have taken that into account; he didn't miss much.

Johnny was so immersed in disconnecting the bomb that he did not notice the front door open. Verity was calling down to him.

'Johnny—what's wrong?'

He straightened himself and pulled down the bonnet of the car.

'Oh, just a little trouble getting her started,' he replied casually.

'Has it been tampered with at all?' she inquired anxiously.

'No, no, I guess it'll be all right.'

To add credibility to this he extricated the starting handle from under the seat and inserted it under the bonnet. As he did so, he consoled himself that if there were any more booby traps in the car, at least he wouldn't be caught inside. He found himself standing over a foot away from the end of the handle as he lifted it somewhat tentatively. But it was all right. The engine sprang into life immediately.

He withdrew the handle and waved to Verity.

'Go to bed, honey,' he called. 'See you soon.'

He climbed into the car, waved to her once more, and engaged first gear.

He sped along the deserted roads, passing only a very occasional all-night tram, and was soon into the outer suburbs. It took him thirty-five minutes to get home. He locked the car in the garage and went upstairs, where he set his alarm clock for four-thirty, calculating he would get a good three hours' sleep. But it seemed not more than three minutes later that the persistent buzzing of the alarm woke him. Johnny tiptoed downstairs carrying his shoes and went into the kitchen where he set his favourite coffee-pot on the stove. It was still quite dark outside.

Johnny noted that a tray was already set for his morning coffee, and he went to the cupboard and fetched three more cups.

At ten minutes to five, there was a smart rap on the side-door, and he went to open it. Three men were standing there. He noted approvingly that they were all in plain clothes.

'Morning, sir,' said a gruff voice. 'I'm Sergeant Huish—we had orders from the Yard to report here.'

'Come in, Sergeant,' said Johnny. 'There's just time for a cup of coffee before we start.'

'Very nice of you, sir. A hot drink would be a help if we've got to wait around. It's nippy this morning.'

'I hope there won't be much waiting,' said Johnny, leading them into the kitchen and pouring out the cups of coffee.

'We didn't get any instructions from the Yard, except that we were to come armed,' said the sergeant.

'I'm glad they suggested that,' nodded Johnny. 'This guy we're after is a pretty desperate type. He's sure to be armed and he'll use his gun if he gets half a chance.'

The sergeant looked thoughtful.

'In that case, sir, we don't want to take any more risks than we can help. The thing is to catch him by surprise.'

'That's exactly what I'm hoping to do,' nodded Johnny, stirring his coffee. 'I'm pretty certain he won't be expecting us, and he is almost certain to be on his own.'

'I see, sir. Shall we take the car?'

Johnny considered this for a moment, then decided against it.

'Too risky,' he murmured. 'He might hear the car in the distance, even if we didn't drive right up, and I don't want this bird scared off if we can possibly avoid it.'

The sergeant stroked his moustache with his forefinger.

'Are you sure he won't hear us walkin' along the road, sir?' he speculated.

Johnny's gaze travelled down to the large size boots worn by his visitors.

'We'll have to hope for the best, that's all,' he sighed. 'But we've got to be careful. Everything's dead quiet at this time of morning.'

'You haven't told us yet where we are going, sir,' the sergeant reminded him.

'Sorry,' said Johnny. 'We're going just down the road—to the Kingfisher.'

'You mean the place where the Yard man was murdered?' queried the sergeant.

'That's the place,' nodded Johnny.

'We've had that pub under observation on and off for quite a while,' said the sergeant thoughtfully. 'I hadn't heard there was likely to be trouble there today—and at this time of morning, too.'

'I'm not so sure about it myself,' said Johnny candidly. 'But I've a hunch you won't have had a wasted journey.'

The sergeant drank what remained of his coffee and set down his cup on the kitchen table.

'Well, sir, we're ready when you are,' he said.

'Right,' murmured Johnny, feeling in his coat pocket for his automatic. He went into the hall and slipped on a light overcoat, for the morning was chilly.

A watery moon was gliding through masses of cloud as they came out into the drive and moved off towards the front gates.

'Keep in the shadows as far as possible,' instructed Johnny, and they split up into two pairs. Johnny and the sergeant walking ahead at an even pace with no outward sign of hurry.

'How are we going to get in the place at this time of morning? And have you got a warrant?' the sergeant wanted to know.

'We're not going inside the pub itself—at least, not as far as I know,' Johnny told him. 'So I guess we can ignore any little technicalities if we corner our bird.'

'D'you know who he is?'

'I can make a pretty good guess, but maybe we'd better wait and see if I'm right.'

On the eastern horizon there was a faint pink smudge, heralding the dawn. Just as the Kingfisher loomed up before them, the sergeant caught Johnny's arm.

'There's a car drawn up there,' he said, indicating a car standing on the far side of the inn. Cautiously, they approached it from the other side of the road, with their two colleagues a few yards in the rear. There was no sound to be heard except the snort of a distant horse in a meadow and the sleepy chirrup of a blackbird in the hedgerow. The sergeant made signs to his men, and when he and Johnny were just past the car, they approached it simultaneously from all sides. The figure of a solitary occupant was almost immediately visible.

He was sitting in the driving seat with the window down, and seemed to be listening intently. When he saw the figures approaching out of the dusk, he suddenly switched on a powerful torch.

'Good lord, Johnny! What the devil are you doing here at this time of morning?' came the familiar voice of Inspector Dovey.

'You practically took the words right out of my mouth,' replied Johnny quietly. Discovering Dovey like this was a complete surprise to him. There was a grim set to the inspector's usually pleasant features, as if he were equally suspicious. He was just about to make a further remark when a sound overhead suddenly attracted their attention. All five men looked up instinctively.

'The first of the pigeons!' said Johhny softly.

'Pigeons!' echoed Dovey.

'Come on,' said Johnny, 'you'd better join us, Dovey—and there's no time to be lost. And for God's sake don't slam that car door.'

Dovey got out of the car as noiselessly as possible. Johnny led the way towards the pigeon cotes, which were in a corner of the bowling green that adjoined the small car park at the back of the inn. They bent almost double and moved carefully under the cover of the hedge, for it was much lighter now. When they were about ten yards away, there was another violent flutter of wings as a pigeon shot upwards, circled two or three times, then headed unhesitantly in a north-easterly direction. A chilly dawn breeze stirred the leaves of the privet hedge. One of the men trod upon a twig which snapped loudly, and they all paused for some seconds before moving forward again. They were approaching the cotes from the blind side, and Johnny was trying to get right up to them without being discovered.

As he came within arm's reach, there was a sound of fluttering wings, and, after making a swift signal to his followers, Johnny poked his head round the corner of the cotes.

The man he saw standing there was attaching a small cylinder to the leg of a flustered pigeon, and was much too preoccupied to pay attention to anything else. As the bird shot into the air almost vertically, Johnny edged round the corner of the cote and said quietly:

'Those are a fine lot of birds you've got there, Kennard.'

Kennard dropped the cylinder he had just taken from his pocket and made a sudden movement towards his hip.

'Don't do that!' snapped Johnny quickly, displaying his Colt automatic for the first time. Kennard dropped his hand with a helpless shrug.

'My God! It's Kennard!' exclaimed Dovey, coming into view at that moment. Kennard looked at the little group of men that had fanned out to cut off his retreat, but still he did not speak.

Johnny strolled over and picked up the cylinder that had fallen to the ground. It had a screw-top that unfastened quite easily. Johnny tilted some highly polished rubies into his palm.

'Where's the rest of the stuff?' he asked.

Kennard motioned with his head towards the inside of the pigeon cotes.

'Get it!' ordered Johnny.

Kennard looked round the little group once more, hesitated a moment, then turned to obey. Johnny beckoned to the sergeant and Dovey to move in a little, and changed his position so that he could keep Kennard under observation. However, he had reckoned without the fact that although it was rapidly getting lighter, the inside of the cote was still very obscure from the point of view of anyone standing outside.

'I want all the stuff, mind,' he called, and he could hear Kennard moving around, presumably collecting it together.

'This is going to cause a damned scandal,' whispered Dovey to Johnny, as they waited for Kennard to re-emerge. 'A Yard man as the head of a gang of crooks—it's never been heard of before.'

'Max Fulton never lets little things like that worry him,' said Johnny grimly.

'How the devil has he managed to get away with it?' demanded the bewildered Dovey.

'I guess he won't get away with it much longer,' shrugged Johnny.

'But I can't think how he *got* inside the Yard to start with. It took me years . . .' Dovey was almost talking to himself now, as Johnny moved a pace nearer the doorway.

A few seconds later they exchanged a glance and without speaking a word made for the door of the pigeon cote. Dovey snapped on his torch and flashed it round the gloomy interior, where half a dozen startled birds blinked at them and rustled their wings. The small attaché case and a number of cylinders lay on the floor just inside, but there was no sign of Inspector

Kennard. The beam of the torch swept quickly round the wooden structure, which was surprisingly spacious, and finally settled on some decayed brickwork in a distant corner.

Johnny hastened over to it at once.

'It's an old well,' he whispered. As Dovey came up with the torch, they noticed that a rope ladder was fastened to a hook just below the rim of the brickwork.

'So that's how he comes and goes,' said Johnny, preparing to descend the ladder. 'It must lead to some underground passage—this district seems to be honeycombed with 'em.'

'Wait,' said Dovey. 'He's sure to be armed.'

'Of course he's armed—but he's mainly interested in making his getaway; not stopping to fight it out,' said Johnny, swinging a leg over and placing his foot on the top rung of the ladder.

'Where will the passage lead?' asked Dovey.

Johnny paused.

'It may come out in the pub somewhere—or it may link up with White Lodge. Better send a couple of men to each place as quickly as possible. Those going to White Lodge had better use your car.'

Dovey turned and rapped out the orders without wasting any time, but Johnny was almost down to the foot of the rope ladder when he was ready to follow. Dovey realized that the ladder would probably not take the weight of two at the same time, so he waited until Johnny had reached the bottom of the well before he stepped on to the top rung.

'All right, Dovey,' called Johnny. 'Make it snappy!'

Dovey came clambering down two rungs at a time. It was only about a twelve-foot ladder, which ended about two feet above the well bottom. 'Any sign of him?' asked Dovey, as he stepped off the ladder, breathing rather quickly.

'Not yet,' said Johnny. 'Keep that torch down and hold it away from you.'

The tunnel they were in led in one direction only—towards the inn. It was narrower and lower than the one between the

inn and White Lodge, and at times Dovey stooped considerably
as he led the way, all too slowly for Johnny's liking. But Dovey
was still obviously expecting an ambush of some sort, and had
decided to take as few risks as possible. He knew from his Yard
experience that Kennard could be a very awkward customer in
a tight corner. He recalled taking part with him in a Soho raid
when Kennard had dealt with a couple of young Greeks in a
manner which Dovey had considered a trifle unnecessarily
tough.

But there was still no sign of Max Fulton alias Inspector
Kennard. When they had progressed about forty yards, there
was a sudden bend in the tunnel, and as they came up to it
Dovey hesitated once again.

'Any idea where we are?' he whispered to Johnny, who was
almost treading on his heels.

'Haven't a clue,' replied Johnny, somewhat impatient at the
delay. 'Wait a minute, though. Shine the torch along to the right
. . . further . . .'

They edged round the corner, following the beam of light.
A second later they saw the foot of a flight of stairs which
Johnny recognized as those leading up to the inn and emerging
behind the club-room wall. He remembered that when he had
climbed those steps with Verity he had noticed that the tunnel
continued beyond them, but they had not had the opportunity
to explore further.

'What now?' asked Dovey.

Johnny sized up the situation rapidly. If Kennard had gone
up the stairs and out by way of the club room, the men up there
would most likely have picked him up. He would probably
foresee this and prefer to take a long chance of getting through
to White Lodge before his retreat could be cut off there.

'This way,' said Johnny, ignoring the stairs and moving off
quickly along the tunnel towards White Lodge. 'Put your torch
out; I'll use mine.' He produced his pencil torch which gave
less light, but quite sufficient for their purpose, and they hurried

along the tunnel that led to the shaft beneath White Lodge. Johnny led the way down the incline at a brisk pace, which did not slacken very much until he judged they were within twenty yards of their objective.

A distant sound like a persistent hammering made Johnny stop for a moment.

He turned to Dovey and said quietly:

'Sounds to me as if the door of the lift has jammed.'

Even as he spoke, the hammering noise stopped and they heard Kennard's rasping command:

'Get back or I shall shoot!'

Johnny switched off the torch at once.

'My God! We've got him,' breathed Dovey, clicking the safety catch of his revolver. Johnny's fingers caressed his Colt automatic, and every nerve tensed.

'Flat against the wall,' he whispered to Dovey. But even as they took up position, a blinding beam of light from a powerful torch dazzled them.

'Back—back to the end of the tunnel!' snapped Kennard.

'Take it easy, Kennard,' said Johnny. 'There are men waiting there, even if you got past us. You'll never get away.'

'Shut up, damn you!'

A loud report echoed through the tunnel and a bullet whistled past Johnny's head. He realized that Kennard was not particular whether they retreated or were disposed of by some other alternative—in fact, he would probably prefer them dead so that there would be less chance of their hampering his escape from the country. He was snapping the torch on and off, and during the split second of its dazzling light was firing at anything he saw. Dovey had taken cover against the opposite wall of the tunnel a little farther back, and the next time the light flicked on Johnny aimed just above it and fired twice in return, but the light came on again a few seconds later and was followed by more shots.

The next time the light jerked on, Johnny and Dovey fired

simultaneously and also saw the flash of Kennard's revolver. The explosions reverberated through the tunnel and the echoes had not died before they were submerged by an ominous rumble from above their heads.

'Get back!' cried Dovey, grabbing Johnny's arm. 'The roof . . . the roof's caving in . . .'

What caused the collapse of the roof they never discovered. It might have been the displacement of a stone by one of the bullets that started the landslide; a landslide that seemed to grow in proportion every second. Johnny and Dovey took to their heels and ran blindly back the way they had come. Twice they slipped on the slimy flagstones; recovered and stumbled on. The roar of falling stones echoed behind them as they reached the steps of the stairs that led into the club-room, and it was only when they reached the top that they paused for breath.

'Looks as if the whole tunnel has caved in,' gasped Dovey.

'There's one thing about it,' panted Johnny. 'He'll never get out this way. Come on, Dovey, let's get down to White Lodge as quickly as we can make it.'

CHAPTER XXVI

THE END OF GREY MOOSE?

JOHNNY selected a particularly attractive mayfly, attached it to his line and skimmed it expertly across the still waters of the pond. Verity tried to wriggle into a more comfortable position on her camp stool without much success and rubbed a tingling gnat-bite on her ankle. She glanced at her wrist-watch for the twelfth time.

'How much longer do we have to stay here, Johnny?' she inquired, trying not to sound too bored.

'Why, all day, of course,' replied Johnny. 'The fish'll be biting any minute now . . .'

'And then am I supposed to cook them over a wood fire?'

Johnny laughed. 'Heck, no! There's a whole basketful of food and drink in the back of the car.'

This information cheered her slightly, but a few minutes later she found herself looking at her watch again. It was just a quarter to eleven. They had already been sitting beside this deserted pond for nearly two hours without a fish as much as raising its nose above the surface.

'Gee, can't you feel this sun soaking into the pores?' enthused Johnny. 'I guess this is just what the doctor ordered.'

'Don't you find it a bit dull—I mean when the fish aren't biting?' said Verity.

'Not a dull moment,' he assured her, cheerfully.

'But you've got such an active brain, Johnny.'

'Even the most active brain needs to relax some time,' he informed her. 'Besides, I'm a lazy guy at heart. Just sitting around, that's the life for me, I guess.'

'Oh no it isn't,' she contradicted. 'You're just in that sort of mood. It's a reaction from all the excitement you've been through lately.'

Johnny looked up at her and grinned.

'Certainly was exciting,' he agreed.

They sat watching his float for a few moments without speaking, each busy with their thoughts of the events of the past few weeks.

'That was pretty smart of you to find out about those pigeons being used to get the stuff out of the country,' she murmured.

'Yes,' he nodded. 'I'd often seen 'em circling round the Kingfisher, and I asked the landlord about them once or twice. He told me about the races you hold over here—it was all new to me, so I was kinda interested. Maybe that's why it stuck in my mind, and when you'd overheard 'em say: "Release at dawn", something went click. By the way, I forgot to tell you, I heard from Sir Robert this morning that Fabian was at the receiving end. The police were on the watch in all the cities where he has his undercover business. The two pigeons that got away came down in Brussels, and Fabian's agent was caught redhanded taking off the cylinders.'

'But of course they didn't get Fabian,' she said.

'Well, it means his Brussels place closes down from now on, and he daren't show his face in Belgium anyhow,' said Johnny cheerfully. 'It's only a matter of time before these guys make a slip.'

'Maybe you'll make one yourself one of these days, Johnny,' she observed softly. Johnny laughed.

'Maybe I will. But why worry about that on a lovely morning?'

A large pike came to the surface in the centre of the pond and promptly went to sleep in the morning sunlight.

'There—why don't you catch that one?' cried Verity excitedly. Johnny shook his head.

'I guess he's had more than enough food for the next few hours. Besides, I never was partial to pike.'

'Weren't you a bit suspicious of Inspector Dovey when he turned up that morning?' she asked presently.

'It did give me a start for a moment,' he admitted. 'Simply because I couldn't altogether leave Dovey out of my list of suspects: and Dovey was in the room that morning Slim Copley took the poison—he actually had access to that flask. What was more, he knew you were Locksley's sister. All the same, I'd known Dovey for quite a while, and he didn't seem right for the part of Grey Moose. He'd told me stories of his days with the county constabularies, and they seemed genuine enough. When I heard that pigeon go up from the back of the pub, I was pretty sure Dovey wasn't our man.'

'It could have been released by an associate,' she suggested.

'Except that, as far as we know, Grey Moose's organization had been reduced to one man—Grey Moose himself.'

'He could have roped in someone to do the dirty work,' she pointed out. 'He's been rather good at that in the past.'

'You think of everything,' grinned Johnny, drawing in his line and casting it in a new direction. 'Anyhow, Kennard didn't bother to deny anything when we caught him with the stuff.'

'You're very lucky to have got out of that tunnel alive,' said Verity, with a slight shudder. She hesitated a moment, then asked: 'Have they found anything down there yet?'

'Nothing except a piece of an old Roman drinking vessel that would have delighted the heart of poor Mr Quince,' replied Johnny.

'Poor old Quince,' she murmured. 'It's a shame he didn't live to see the end of Max Fulton.'

Johnny laid down his rod for a moment to light a cigarette. 'I'm not so sure we've seen the end of Max Fulton,' he said quietly.

'But I thought you said that tunnel had caved in for over thirty yards . . .'

'The fact remains that they haven't yet found Max's body.'

'But how could he have possibly got out?'

Johnny shrugged.

'He might have got the lift to work somehow, even climbed

the lift shaft. He might even have escaped by another tunnel beyond the lift and sealed it up after him. One thing's certain, anyway—if he did get away, he's out of the country by this time, and we shan't see any more of him for quite a while.'

'Well, it's a relief to know that,' said Verity, looking at her watch again and wondering how soon she dare suggest they should begin lunch. 'I expect Sir Robert's pleased. I'm surprised he didn't offer to put you on the permanent strength at the Yard.'

'He knew better than that.'

Verity scratched another gnat-bite on her right ankle.

'It was certainly an amazing achievement on Fulton's part to get into Scotland Yard. Have they found out exactly how he managed it?' she inquired.

'Actually, it was comparatively straightforward,' Johnny told her. 'Max simply murdered the real Kennard, who was being sent by the South African police to London to clear up a diamond smuggling case, and assumed his identity. After that, he got special permission to stay on and study Scotland Yard methods.'

'But surely there was a body?' queried Verity.

'Oh, yes, a body went overboard all right. But it was supposed to be that of a Mr Marcus Soden, which was Max's name on the ship's passenger register. As it happened on the first night out, hardly anybody knew anyone else, and it was comparatively easy for Max to slip into the dead man's shoes.'

Verity made a futile dab at a threatening fly and changed her position on the camp stool.

'How did you get to hear all this?' she asked.

'We eventually persuaded Doctor Randall to talk.'

'And the girl?'

'She wouldn't say a word.'

'She's still in love with him, of course.'

'Love's a wonderful thing when it makes a woman hold her tongue,' said Johnny thoughtfully.

'Are you hinting that our chatter is frightening away the fish?' she suggested.

'Well, they're certainly not biting,' he smiled.

'We've not scared the old pike—he's still fast asleep,' she reminded him, indicating that ancient placidly floating on the surface of the pond.

'Why not let me have a go?' she suggested.

Johnny looked surprised.

'But—but you don't want to fish, do you?' he stammered.

'At least it's better than doing nothing,' she replied gravely. 'Besides, it'll be something to write about in my column.'

'Well,' he said, somewhat grudgingly handing over the rod, 'I guess it can't do much harm if you hold it for a few minutes.'

'Thank you, Johnny,' she smiled sweetly. 'I'll take great care of it.'

'Keep your hand steady,' he advised, watching her closely.

'Wouldn't it seem more natural if the fly at the end of the line moved around a bit?' she suggested. 'Otherwise, it's pretty dull for everybody.'

'No, no, it won't do at all,' he said so anxiously, that she sat perfectly still and obeyed his instructions. Presently, she said quietly:

'When are you going back to America, Johnny?'

'Did I say anything about going back?' he demanded in some surprise.

'Well, no, but it's your home, isn't it?'

'I guess so, but I like it here, too. I can relax here.' He blew out a leisurely stream of smoke from his cigarette.

'There's more money to be made over there, of course,' she ventured.

'Who cares about money? I get by all right!'

'I'm afraid you won't make much out of the fish you catch. And the States must be much more exciting . . .'

Johnny eased himself on his haunches and looked at her with a puzzled frown.

'Say, are you trying to tell me I've outstayed my welcome?' he demanded.

She laughed.

'Of course not, Johnny. I just thought that perhaps some nice American girl was patiently waiting for you.'

'You don't know much about our girls if you think they wait patiently. No, there's nothing like that. As a matter of fact, I've been seriously thinking of settling down here. I like this part of the world—it suits me. The fishing's O.K. and a guy can take time off to think.'

'That's true,' she nodded. 'You've a lovely old house and a perfect butler. What more could a man want?'

Johnny shifted his feet awkwardly, plucked a blade of grass, and looked frankly worried.

'I guess there is something else,' he said at last.

'Oh?' murmured Verity absently, her eyes on the float. 'What's that?'

'It's a woman,' he blurted out. 'I thought maybe you and me, Verity. I thought . . .'

'Yes?' said Verity, rubbing yet another gnat-bite just below her knee.

'Well,' continued Johnny desperately, 'you've often said how you like the old manor, and you're crazy about Winwood, and I thought maybe in time you could get around to letting me keep an eye on you, just in case Max Fulton came back and—'

'Johnny!' she cried with sudden fervour.

'Yes?' he responded, eagerly stumbling to his feet.

'Johnny! Look! I believe I've got a bite!'

THE END

POSTSCRIPT

In addition to adapting his radio plays into novels, Francis Durbridge was often asked to write short stories featuring the popular duo of Paul and Steve Temple. Although he only rarely took up the invitation, stories did occasionally appear in publications such as *Radio Times* and the *Daily Mail Annual for Boys and Girls*. One of the earliest examples, 'A Present for Paul', appeared in the Christmas Eve edition of the *Yorkshire Evening Post* on Tuesday 24 December 1946, and is reprinted here for the first time.

A PRESENT FOR PAUL

A Paul Temple Christmas Short Story written for 'The Yorkshire Evening Post' by the BBC's No. 1 Thriller Writer, Francis Durbridge.

It was exactly six days before Christmas when Steve saw the clock. It was in a jeweller's on the corner of Regent Street, and it was marked £74 10s.

It was a very small clock for such a large sum of money, but the moment Steve saw it she knew it was just what she had been looking for. The clock was made of onyx and silver and was shaped like a miniature bookcase. It was the ideal Christmas present for a popular novelist.

Steve stood for a moment staring in at the shop window and admiring the clock, then, with a dirty look at the price ticket, she pushed open the door. The assistant was a tall man with a bald head and a curious habit of flicking the end of his nose. His name was O'Hara, and Steve took an instant dislike to him.

O'Hara's salary was £5 15s, but he dismissed the £74 10s with a gesture of contempt. It was hardly to be considered. A trifle. A mere bagatelle. 'It's an infinitesimal sum for such a lovely time-piece', he said.

While the assistant was making the clock into a neat little parcel, Steve scribbled a cheque for the mere bagatelle. She resisted the temptation to add 'chicken-feed' as she pushed it across the counter.

When the parcel was ready O'Hara said: 'There's no official guarantee with the clock, madam, but if it does give you any trouble I hope you'll let us know.'

'You can depend on it,' said Steve and carried the parcel out to the waiting car.

*

When she arrived at the flat she rang the bell for Charlie instead of using her key. She didn't want Temple to catch even a glimpse of his Christmas present.

Charlie smiled when he saw her standing on the steps trying to conceal the parcel.

'The coast's clear, Mrs T.,' he said, 'Mr Temple left for Scotland Yard just over 'alf an hour ago.' Steve said, very quietly: 'Scotland Yard, Charlie?'

Charlie nodded.

'Sir Graham Forbes telephoned. He said it was urgent.'

Sir Graham Forbes was perturbed. Temple noticed this as soon as he entered the Commissioner's office at New Scotland Yard. Forbes was frowning and nervously tapping the corner of the blotting-pad with a paper-knife. Temple said: 'What's on your mind, Sir Graham?'

'Royston's escaped, Temple. I don't have to tell you what that means.'

Paul Temple took out his cigarette case, extracted a cigarette, and flicked his lighter. 'Royston? he said. His tone was polite and non-committal.

The Commissioner looked up. He was still frowning, and there was a note of irritation in his voice.

'Don't tell me you don't remember Royston,' he said. 'He called himself Caesar Antonio, and he was the trumpet player with Ted Wayne.'

Temple laughed and replaced his cigarette case. He remembered Royston alias Caesar Antonio only too well. He remembered the tall, lithe figure in the grey suit; the way Royston walked across the dance floor at the Palais de Danse; the way he held his hands dangling down by the side of his pockets.

He remembered Royston's eyes, too. Dark brown eyes with flecks of cold light in them.

Temple said: 'Why are you telling me about Royston?'

'Because Royston's a pretty unpleasant customer, and he hasn't forgotten the part you played in the Gregory affair. It's my bet he'll pay you an unexpected visit.'

Temple said: 'If he does he'll get an unexpected welcome.'

'Watch your step,' warned Forbes, 'Royston isn't a fool, not by any stretch of imagination.'

The Commissioner hesitated and put down the paper knife. He looked very serious. He said: 'He's a very dangerous man, Temple.'

Paul Temple nodded. He knew that Sir Graham was speaking the truth. Royston was a man to be reckoned with.

In the taxi, on the way back to the flat, Paul Temple thought a great deal about Mr Royston, alias Caesar Antonio. He remembered the night that Royston had carefully placed the bomb in the cloakroom at the Belgravia Hotel. That was what Sir Graham had meant, of course. Carefully placed time-bombs were a speciality of Mr Royston's. Temple was still thinking of the notorious Mr Royston when he arrived at the flat.

Steve had prepared tea, the sort of tea Temple liked. Hot scones and strawberry jam.

They sat in front of the open fire place.

After she had poured him his cup of tea Steve said: 'What did Sir Graham want?'

Temple evaded the question. He had no intention of telling Steve that Royston was at large. He said: 'We'll have Christmas on top of us before we know where we are.' Then with a smile: 'I saw an awfully nice cigarette case today!' Temple described the gold cigarette case in great detail and at great length.

Steve laughed. She was thinking of the clock. 'You'll get half a dozen handkerchiefs,' she said, 'and like it.'

After ten, Temple retired to the study. He was writing a 10,000-word story for a popular magazine and he still had a thousand words to write.

It was a quarter to eight when he laid down his pen, stretched his legs and sat staring across the room at the photo of Steve and Sir Graham Forbes. It had been taken in Scotland in 1940 when Temple had investigated the Z4 mystery. He was still staring at the photo when he became conscious of a ticking noise. He realised now that he'd been conscious of it for some little time. He got up from the desk and crossed to the cupboard. The cupboard was full of old books and discarded manuscripts. As soon as he opened the cupboard door and turned over the manuscripts, Temple saw the parcel.

It had been put there deliberately. There was no doubt about it. The small, neat brown-paper parcel had been concealed beneath the mass of odds and ends.

Temple hesitated for a moment, then lifted the parcel off the ledge. He held it close to his ear. He could hear it ticking.

What was it Sir Graham had said? 'Watch your step, Royston isn't a fool . . .'

Temple remembered the warning and for the second time that day he found himself thinking of the cloakroom at the Belgravia Hotel.

Quickly he carried the parcel out of the study, through the hall, down the stairs and into the street.

Steve's car was still outside the flat. Temple climbed into the driver's seat and rather gingerly put the parcel down on the seat beside him.

The thing was still ticking. Even when the car was running he imagined he could still hear the tick tock, tick tack, tick tock.

It took him just over 12 minutes to reach the river. Slowly, almost tenderly, he lifted the parcel out of the car and crossed to the parapet. There was no explosion when the parcel hit the water. Fifteen minutes later Paul Temple was back in the flat.

One morning at breakfast several days later Steve said: 'I see they've caught Royston.'

Temple was surprised. 'How did you know about Royston?' he asked.

'It was in last night's paper. They said he escaped from gaol several days ago.'

Temple nodded. Then, after a momentary hesitation, he told Steve about the mysterious parcel.

Steve didn't know whether to laugh or cry. She had the peculiar sensation of feeling both relieved and horrified.

'It's a good job you had your wits about you,' she said, 'or we'd have all been blown to pieces.' Temple laughed and helped himself to another piece of toast. Now that it was all over he felt that he could treat the matter with a certain degree of unconcern. His manner was quite nonchalant, almost gay in fact.

Steve said: 'You've been such a darling you can have your Christmas present today – now – this very minute in fact.'

'I hope it's a surprise,' said Temple.

There was a twinkle in Steve's eyes as she left the room.

'Don't worry, you'll be surprised all right.' Temple waited.

He waited nearly five minutes.

Suddenly the door opened and Steve returned. Steve was still smiling and carrying a neat little brown-paper parcel. 'I certainly didn't intend you to find it,' she said. 'I hid it behind the wardrobe in the spare bedroom.'

'But what is it?' said Temple.

Steve untied the string, unwrapped the parcel and proudly revealed the clock.

Temple stared. He'd never seen anything like it in his life before.

'Well?' beamed Steve. 'Are you surprised?'

'Surprised?' gasped her husband. As a matter of fact he was dumbfounded. He'd expected the gold cigarette case.

THE END